TO THE

# TO THE MOON

### Jang Ryujin

Translated from the Korean
by Sean Lin Halbert

BLOOMSBURY PUBLISHING
LONDON · OXFORD · NEW YORK · NEW DELHI · SYDNEY

BLOOMSBURY PUBLISHING
Bloomsbury Publishing Plc
50 Bedford Square, London, WC1B 3DP, UK
Bloomsbury Publishing Ireland Limited,
29 Earlsfort Terrace, Dublin 2, D02 AY28, Ireland

BLOOMSBURY, BLOOMSBURY PUBLISHING and the Diana logo
are trademarks of Bloomsbury Publishing Plc

First published in 2021 in Korean as 달까지 가자 by Changbi Publishers
First published in Great Britain in 2025

A catalogue record for this book is available from the British Library

ISBN: PB: 978-1-5266-8201-7; EBOOK: 978-1-5266-8572-8;
EPDF: 978-1-5266-8571-1; ANZ-ONLY EXPORT: 978-1-5266-9098-2

2 4 6 8 10 9 7 5 3 1

Typeset by Integra Software Services Pvt. Ltd.
Printed and bound in Great Britain by CPI Group (UK) Ltd, Croydon CR0 4YY

To find out more about our authors and books visit www.bloomsbury.com
and sign up for our newsletters
For product safety related questions contact productsafety@bloomsbury.com

# CONTENTS

# A NOTE ON THE TRANSLATION

In this translation, all references to specific amounts of money have been kept in Korean won (KRW). Between 2017 and 2018, the value of the Korean won fluctuated between 0.00083 to 0.00094 US dollars. For quick conversions, 1,000 won is roughly equal to 1 US dollar.

Towards the end of the book, the concept of *jeonse* is referred to. Jeonse is a unique form of housing payment in which tenants make a lump-sum deposit on a rental space, sometimes tens or hundreds of millions of won, which is then returned at the end of the tenancy. In return, the tenant pays no monthly rent. Barring potential scams, this is the preferred method of renting living spaces in Korea.

# DISCLAIMER

The financial and investment scenarios depicted in this book are completely fictional and for entertainment purposes only. This book is not intended as financial or investment advice.

# Part One

# Thank Goodness

*17 January 2017*

If there was one misalignment of circumstances that made office life unbearable for me, it was working outside the office with my team leader, Mr Koh. Work outside the office, like everything else, came in both good and bad varieties. And Team Leader Koh wasn't always awful. But when I had to work outside the office with Team Leader Koh, just the two of us together, trouble of all varieties was an inevitability.

I hadn't expected we would be late as we hailed the taxi in front of our office building. In fact, we'd left the office early for once. But five minutes into our journey to the headquarters of J Mart, an important client of our company, Mr Koh decided to open his mouth:

'Dahae. Have you heard about that new cafe next to J Mart HQ? The pour-over coffee place? It's all the rage in Gangnam. It's their second store, but I heard it's better than the first. There's always a line.'

He paused as if he was waiting for me. But I didn't respond, so he continued on his own.

'I skipped my morning coffee today so I could go there before the meeting, remember?'

Team Leader Koh worshipped coffee. In fact, he arrived at work every day with a different takeaway cup in his hand and wouldn't leave work until he'd had at least three more. But today, just so he could take his first sip of the day at that new cafe near J Mart HQ, he'd deliberately abstained from caffeine in the morning – a truly impressive feat of determination for someone like him. At the time, I had no objections. In fact, hearing him rave about the place, despite not being much of a coffee connoisseur myself, I figured I might as well see what all the fuss was about while we were there.

When we got out of the taxi, however, I was confronted with a cafe much smaller than expected and a line that stretched out the front door despite it being well past morning rush hour. Looking in shock at the line dividers that had been set up outside the cafe like it was some ride at an amusement park, I turned to him.

'You know, that's a lot of people.'

'You're right. That is a lot of people.'

Technically, he'd agreed with me. But really, he hadn't.

'This many people must mean the coffee is amazing. I can't wait to try it.'

He took his place at the back of the line. The meeting was still thirty minutes from now and just one building over, but lines were impossible to predict. Even if we did manage to place our order, we would still need to wait for them to pour the coffee and call our number. I waited impatiently, glancing over at Team Leader Koh in the hope that he would come to his senses. After several minutes of barely progressing, I decided I had to be the one to speak up.

'Don't you think it would be better to come here after the meeting? We're going to be late at this rate.'

'It's fine. We're almost there. We won't be late. Stop worrying.'

He waved his hand in a dismissive manner. Then, out of nowhere, he started scolding me. He seemed angry that despite my working in the food industry I couldn't understand his reasoning for coming to this cafe.

'Dahae, you know what a complementary good is, right?'

This was an insulting question to ask someone in our industry, but I held my tongue. Confectionaries and coffee, he continued to explain to me, were basically the same business, and their continued success boiled down to the same few key elements: development, sales, quality control. He then claimed this escapade was a form of 'benchmarking' and 'market research' – a claim I doubted he was making in good faith. Was now really the time? I glanced at my phone. 10:45 a.m.

'We only have fifteen minutes. Do you really need to drink coffee right now?'

'I do. And we've come so far. It'll just be a few more minutes.'

I wanted to let it go, but I knew we were going to be late. And I knew if we were late, I would end up taking the blame for it. 'If we're late because of this, I'm not taking responsibility.'

Team Leader Koh, who had been half-listening to me as he looked up at the menu above the counter, turned around and glared at me. He pulled back the left sleeve of his coat and pointed to his watch.

'Dahae, it's almost 11 a.m. and I still haven't had any caffeine. Coffee is precious to me, you know that. I need it. If I start my presentation and can't speak properly because I haven't had my morning coffee, you'd better well take responsibility.'

Mr Koh was our team leader; taking responsibility was literally the first line in his job description. And yet he never, under any circumstances, took the blame for anything – even and especially when it mattered most. I couldn't see how an eight-ounce cup of brown liquid could be more important than being on time for a meeting. And if what he said about needing coffee to speak properly was true, perhaps what he really needed was less caffeine, not more.

By 10:52, we were leaving the cafe with our coffees. Team Leader Koh told me to run. As we jogged to the next building, the lid of the takeaway cup in my hand flew off, spilling hot cafe latte all over me. The sleeve of my cream-coloured woollen coat, the centre of my beige woollen sweater, the toe of my suede boots, the entirety of my laptop bag – all of them were now splashed with coffee. Team Leader Koh took out a dingy handkerchief from the inner pocket of his jacket and started to frantically wipe down the laptop bag. I was almost as stunned by his misplaced concern – 'The laptop will be OK, right?' – as I was by his scolding me – 'Dahae! We don't have the time for your shenanigans!' At 10:56, we were exchanging our IDs for visitor badges at the information desk at J Mart HQ. By 10:59, we'd got out of the elevators on the fourteenth floor. I was parched and desperate for something to drink, but there wasn't a single drop of coffee left in my paper cup. And finally, 11:00. Team Leader Koh burst into the meeting room and immediately began bellowing like a Broadway actor greeting his audience as he made his entrance: 'Good morning! Tae-young Koh, team leader of snacks at Maron Confectionaries.'

And thus, there we were. Me, a sulking employee smelling of steamed milk and espresso with a large light-brown stain in the middle of my sweater, and Team Leader Koh, ignoring his troubled colleague as he blithely introduced himself to everyone in the room. Had Management – who'd come in a separate car – not been in attendance, I would have had no witnesses to ease the embarrassment. The presentation, a promotional pitch to target Valentine's Day next month, ended without any mishaps. Perhaps Team Leader Koh was right: he *did* present better after an expensive cup of coffee. I was ready to forget the whole incident when, during the taxi ride back to the office, he decided to open his mouth again.

'About the coffee from earlier—'

He paused to noisily savour the taste in his mouth.

'—it was good, wasn't it? It really brightened my mood.'

Three years and eleven months ago, I would have just said, 'Yes, sir', and moved on. But I'd come to the realisation that, after years of biting one's tongue, a person started to become unstable, like a pressure cooker filled with hot gas screaming to be let out. People needed to vent, but the hole didn't need to be large. All they needed was a slight crack to relieve whatever scalding gas was building up inside. I couldn't let myself explode; I couldn't let this cooker break. So, when I finally responded, I did so while remembering to release some of the pressure.

'Well, thank goodness you're in a good mood.'

He didn't even blink: 'Thank goodness, indeed. I was in a bad mood all morning because of your sulking. But that coffee really lifted my spirits.'

I should have known that Team Leader Koh, being the peculiar man he was, wouldn't let it go. I squinted my eyes as I showed him a fake smile.

'Thank goodness, indeed.'

I turned away from him without saying anything else and looked out the window. I relaxed the muscles in my cheeks, letting the corners of my mouth, which I had been holding up with great effort, return to their rightful position with the help of gravity.

It was the middle of winter, but the weather was quite mild. Not a cloud in the sky, and the afternoon sun was falling obliquely across the cityscape. Everything passing in front of my eyes seemed to shimmer: silhouettes of tall, jagged buildings, between which I could glimpse a baby-blue afternoon sky; thin, frozen branches of barren trees that the occasional gust of wind sent swaying; faces of people dressed in warm clothes, walking along the sun-bathed concrete. As I followed pedestrians with my eyes, I wondered to myself where all these people could be headed. For some reason, they all looked like they were headed home. I wished *I* could go home. If only this taxi were headed there, instead of back to the office.


'We're here.'

I open my eyes to find the taxi stopped in front of not my office but the redbrick apartment building that I call home. Did Mr Koh get out at the office and send me home out of the kindness of his heart while I was asleep? I get out and use the iron handrails to propel myself up a flight of stairs to my studio apartment. I open the front door, take off my coffee-stained coat and damp knitted sweater, toss them on the floor, and jump in the shower. I turn on the hot water, squeeze honey-scented body wash on my loofah, wet it slightly, and lather the ball until it is full of bubbles. I then apply the suds to every inch of my body. Once I'm done, I close my eyes and surrender myself to the hot stream of water pouring out from the showerhead – waiting for the fatigue in my shoulders to thaw, for my wrists and ankles to become red and supple.

By the time I come to my senses, the floor of my bathroom is flooded with soapy water. The water has even spread beyond the top-loading washing machine – which takes up more than half of the floor space in the bathroom – and is now flowing out of the bathroom door. Shit. Somehow, I've forgotten that my bathroom is the poorly designed kind: no separation between the shower, the toilet or the sink, and large gaps at the top and bottom of the door to the bathroom, which were intended to compensate for the lack of a fan but which only make it look like a public restroom. Worse yet, there isn't a lip separating the bathroom and the bedroom. The edge of the tile transitions seamlessly to linoleum without any change in elevation. To prevent water from seeping into my bedroom, I've put down several layers of transparent packaging tape, but even then, it only takes a few careless seconds before the water and soap bubbles push themselves over this makeshift threshold. Under no circumstances can I let myself get distracted.

I frantically turn off the shower and wrap myself in a towel before opening the bathroom door to assess the damage. It's worse than I expected. The entirety of my cramped room is flooded. The soap bubbles that began in the bathroom have made their way to the single-sized bed-frame at the edge of the room. The white cardboard storage boxes beneath my bed have turned a dark brown colour, and the clothes on the floor are now like islands in the Pacific. Hoping this is just a bad dream, I squeeze my eyelids, then open them again.


Sure enough, the taxi was parked in front of our office building and not my apartment. I'd hoped that imagining myself going home would brighten my mood. Why couldn't I have a peaceful, uninterrupted dream for once? At some point in time, my dreams had been infiltrated by the worries and happenings of my waking reality. They were also embarrassingly transparent, lacking any symbolism or metaphor. The truth was that all I could think about recently was my apartment. The two-year lease to my small studio apartment, which I'd already renewed twice, was coming to an end this summer. I'd told myself that I couldn't live here any more and was determined to move somewhere nicer. This was the reason for my nightmare. My subconscious was so unimaginative it mortified me. As I paid the taxi fare with the company card, I vowed to visit a real estate agency that weekend.

Before I knew it, Team Leader Koh was already past the front entrance and inside the lobby. I wanted to chase after him, but my legs felt too heavy. It was 1 p.m., which meant there were still five hours left in the day. I desperately wanted to go home and change out of these clothes, which were soaked through to the skin. Perhaps I could ask for a half day? But I knew Team Leader Koh wouldn't give me permission, as there was a lot of work to be done before tomorrow. Perhaps I could ask to go home just to change my clothes? But even I knew that was basically throwing away the day. Perhaps I could buy a new sweater from a nearby clothing store? But payday was still a week away and my bank account had already started its countdown to zero; a new outfit just wasn't an expense I could afford right now. Maybe if it were summer, but not in winter when clothes were more expensive.

I tried to think of something, *anything*, positive about going back to the office. There had to be at least one, but for some reason, I couldn't think of any. As I racked my brain trying to squeeze something out of it, a dark yellow box popped into my consciousness. It was the box of banana bread that the team leader of

Pies, the team next door to us, had given me earlier that morning, purchased on an international business trip. In fact, I'd been gifted the same box of bread last year by someone else who'd gone abroad on business. The box contained palm-sized pieces of individually packaged bread, a picture of a banana with a blue ribbon tied to its stem on each wrapper. Inside each wrapper was bread in the shape of a banana, the exact same size as the one on the wrapper. They were filled with sweet, sticky cream that was the flavour and texture of mashed banana. He'd bought one for everyone in the office, and my box would still be waiting for me, if someone else hadn't got to it first.

'In which case I'll leave early,' I muttered this to myself, even though I knew I didn't have the courage to go through with it. And it was this thought – the thought that someone else might be sinking their teeth into my sweet, cream-filled banana bread – that drew me back into the office.

# Mid

There was one day of the year that seemed, on the surface, no different from any other, but on which the air in the office seemed somewhat off. A day when people stared at their monitors with darting eyes, when there was a palpable sense of tension with each click of the mouse and every clop of shoes on the linoleum floor. A day when people could hear a loud rattling coming from within, despite it being as quiet – if not quieter – than usual. A day of psychological restlessness.

As soon as I arrived at the office, I realised the day had come once again. As I waited for my computer to boot up, I focused on taking slow, deep breaths. I went to my inbox, opened the email from HR, and followed the link they'd sent me.

My first reaction was a sigh. With my elbows on the desk, I rested the heels of both hands on my temples. I felt the energy being sapped from my body as my eyelids shut. After a few moments, I opened them again and stared at the dust accumulating on my desk for a while before rubbing my lifeless face. I opened the company messenger and sent a message to the group chat titled NOR(3):

**Dahae**
I got M.
**Eun-sang**
M.
**Jisong**
Me too.

It was March: the month for performance evaluations. Time, in other words, to receive our yearly report cards. There were a total of five letter grades, starting with the highest, E, and working down through A, M and B, until you got down to the lowest grade, N. Because performances were graded on a curve – aside from the highest and lowest grades, which were reserved for exceptional cases – there was always at least one A, one M and one B.

The letter grades stood for the following evaluations: E for Extraordinary, A for Above expectations, M for Meets expectations, B for Below expectations, and N for Needs supervision. But we had modified the company's nomenclature to something more informative: Extra, Acceptable, Mid, Bad and Needs to leave the company.

This year was the fourth year in a row since entering the company that Eun-sang Kang, Jisong Kim and I had received 'Mid'. The first year, we assumed it was normal for new employees to get low marks, but with each subsequent Mid we started to feel worse and worse about ourselves. Now, having received the same grade for the fourth year in a row, we couldn't help but feel defeated – especially because we thought we'd put in the necessary extra effort for at least an A. What was the point of trying if it still meant being labelled a 'Mid'? Adding insult to injury was the fact that I'd just been voted 'Overtime Employee of the Month' at the year-end party and given a cheap bottle of wine as a consolation prize. Verbally they'd praised me: 'Good job', 'Great work', 'What would we do without you?' And yet my actual performance evaluation, the thing that really mattered, was a middling Mid. I didn't want to believe it. By now, I was beginning to wonder who, if anyone, was receiving 'Above expectations'. There was an unverified rumour going round that only people who had received 'Above expectations' at least once would be considered for a promotion to assistant manager, even if they'd been with the company long enough to be guaranteed such a promotion.

But what bothered me more than not being considered for a promotion, and what was by far the most important to me, was not getting the raise that such a promotion would be accompanied by.


I remember the day, four years ago, when I finally received the news that I'd been hired after many months of job hunting. Despite knowing that the industry wasn't particularly known for its high salaries, and despite my determination to be OK with that, I was stunned by the number written on the employment contract placed atop the meeting room table. The salary was far below my lowest expectations. As I gazed down at those digits that looked like they'd been printed one point size too small, I wondered how this could be possible for a company like Maron.

There wasn't anyone in Korea who didn't know Maron Confectionaries, whose products were sold in every convenience store in the country. They owned Choco Chestnuts and its ice cream variant – all-time bestsellers – and had a significant slice of the chocolate candy bar and ice cream bar market. And even though the company's popularity as a career destination didn't quite match its consumer popularity, Maron still boasted a small but modern office building in the middle of Seoul, as well as large factories on the outskirts of the city and Gyeonggi Province. Naturally, I'd expected a respectable pay check. When I found out how wrong I was, I couldn't help but wonder how much lesser companies paid their employees.

Of course, I couldn't *not* sign the contract. A job was a job, after all.


My phone was buzzing and flashing the day I received my first yearly performance evaluations, roughly a year after being hired. Eun-sang had just sent two texts in rapid succession:

**Eun-sang**
Mids only get a 2% raise. Can you believe that?
**Eun-sang**
They already pay us pennies, and they're only giving us 2%?

Eun-sang worked in Procurement and was good with numbers because she'd graduated from college with a degree in business management:

**Eun-sang**
CPI increased by 1.9% this year, and they only give us 2%?
**Dahae**
It's basically a wage freeze.
**Eun-sang**
Basically? It IS a wage freeze.
**Eun-sang**
But perceived price is usually higher. The Bank of Korea says perceived inflation is 2.6%. And perceived is what really matters.
**Dahae**
So, it's a pay cut.
**Eun-sang**
There's no other way to look at it.

Jisong, who had been quiet until now, finally replied:

**Jisong**
That kills my motivation. I don't think I can work late tonight. I just wanna go home…
**Jisong**
I heard a rumour that they don't give people Acceptable unless they were recruited.

Now that I thought about it, this must have been why Eun-sang changed the name of our group chat from 'Eun-sang Kang, Jisong Kim, Dahae Jeong (3)' to 'NOR(3)'. NOR was short for Non-Open Recruits. Our company was unique in the sense that every year, they had open recruitment for college graduates with the goal of hiring upwards of six new employees; this open recruitment started in the fall and went on until the end of the year. But because the company wasn't overwhelmingly big and didn't have a high staff turnover, it was common for people to create friendship groups with their *donggi*, the people they entered with. I had no way of knowing for sure, but it seemed like donggi even had their own group chats and exclusive hangouts. In such an environment, the small minority of employees who'd been hired by less established routes had no choice but to be treated – whether it was known to them or not – as people without any basis for existing in the company.

Eun-sang, who was a few years older than me, had originally worked in procurement at a car parts company. But then she'd made the somewhat uncommon decision to transfer to Maron in just her second year after entering the workforce. This made her too experienced to be grouped with the new recruits, and too inexperienced to be grouped with the veterans of the company.

Then there was Jisong, who was a year younger than me. She was hired out of necessity after a mass exodus from Accounting four years ago. This made her yet another outsider.

As for me, after graduating I started working in Ice Cream on a three-month stint as a part-time office assistant. But my team leader at the time liked me enough to promote me to a regular intern, allowing me to work a full year. Things like that just didn't happen at our company. I'd been hired as a part-time worker, so normally I would either have had to stay like that or leave the company. My team leader said he was giving me special treatment, so I made a 'special' effort to act grateful, but secretly I was submitting job applications because working at a company that made potato chips and cookies for the rest of my life just wasn't the career I'd envisioned for myself. Maron Confectionaries was a stepping stone, something to help me fill out a few lines on my CV.

I used their name to apply to any and every company that looked like a better place to work than Maron. But of all the companies I applied to, not one replied to me. Before applying, I had been worried about what excuse I would give if I got an interview and had to leave the office. I even went through the pain of calculating how many sick days I was willing to use. But in the end, my worries turned out to be woefully premature. And when my last choice – a publicity agency I had applied to as a backup, fully knowing I might be better off sticking with Maron – rejected my CV, doubt began to creep in. Perhaps I was nothing but a pity hire. Perhaps Maron was the best I could do.

Around that time, HR suggested that I go through the process of transitioning from intern to permanent employee. I had just one month before the end of my internship, after which I would be jobless once again and without any affiliations. I would need to start that depressing, repetitive struggle of typing up personal statement after personal statement with arbitrary word limits. All I could think about was how I didn't want to go back to that life. Maron Confectionaries was the only thing I had. My last hope. My last chance. So I submitted branding and marketing samples, gave a presentation for a working interview, took another interview with HR, as well as a panel interview with the board members. And finally, after all of that, I just barely managed to become a permanent employee.

The problem was what came next. The team leader of Ice Cream, my boss and the one who had initially vouched for me, was headhunted for a high-ranking position at another large food company. He left before I could start my new position, leaving me without my basis for existing in the company. I worried that the company would retract their offer, but thankfully HR was able to find a place for me in Snacks, which had an opening. But the team leader of Snacks must not have liked the fact that someone he didn't personally hire was taking a spot on *his* team. I knew this because from the very first day, he was always giving me a contemptuous look. At our first encounter, he said:

'You're the kid the ex-team leader from Ice Cream snuck in, right? Hey, I'm just kidding! It's just a joke. You're not mad, are you?'

I realised I had entered the company through an unconventional route – which wasn't something to be proud of – and because of this, I would often hear things like:

'Dahae, did you enter with Ji-yeong? No? Then who did you enter with? Oh… Is that so? I guess your last manager was a real guardian angel. It's not easy getting a job these days, you know. What about your friends, Dahae? Have they all found work? I bet they envy you.'


Eun-sang in Procurement, Jisong in Accounting – both of which were located in the Management Support office – and me in Snacks, located in the Branding office. Each of us worked on different teams and had entered the company under different circumstances, but HR had made us all start on the same day because we'd all been hired close to one another. We even received a one-hour orientation together in the same meeting room. From then on, the three of us, despite our slight differences in age and work experience, thought of each other as donggi.

During the year I'd worked as an intern, being around my co-workers always made me somewhat uncomfortable. And that was because they always did one of three things: give me more work, make work harder for me, or evaluate how well I was doing my work. It wasn't until I met Eun-sang and Jisong that I discovered the joy of having friends at the office. And because we were on different teams, we never crossed paths or had the opportunity to make each other's lives difficult.

In fact, I felt closer to Eun-sang and Jisong than I did my own childhood friends. I had much more to talk about with them and, in some respects, we understood each other better – a fact that never failed to surprise me when I sat down to think about it. But looking back at it now, it shouldn't have been a surprise. I only came home to sleep and spent the rest of my waking hours at the office. Everything that happened to me – the good, the bad, the funny, the infuriating, the joyous, the unbelievable – was directly or indirectly related to work. And because Eun-sang and Jisong already knew all the main characters and background stories, there was no need for me to give long explanations.

Their friendship was indispensable for coping with office life. Every day, we gave each other real time updates on the latest team drama via the NOR(3) group chat. If we didn't have each other, we would be out of the loop when it came to company gossip, unspoken rules and office connections – information that only regular recruits normally had access to.

As usual, Eun-sang came to us with some company gossip on performance evaluation day.

**Eun-sang**
I heard Professor Ham's bonus last year was 500,000,000 won. I can't imagine how much he's going to get this year.
**Dahae**
500,000,000? Are you sure?
**Eun-sang**
Have I ever said something I wasn't sure about?
**Jisong**
No way. Eun-sang, how do you learn these things?
**Eun-sang**
It's publicly disclosed information.

Professor Ham was the only person in the company who was referred to not by job rank or title but by his academic qualifications. Early last year, he entered the company as a 'big data analyst', a position that had, until then, not existed in the company. Subsequently, a branch with the name 'Big Data Task Force' suddenly appeared in the R&D organisational chart, and prominently displayed below this were the names of Professor Ham and his secretary. Apparently, the professor and the CEO were cousins; they'd even gone to the same university. Perhaps that was why he was allowed to come to and leave the office when he wanted. I typed noisily as my fingers flew across the keyboard:

**Dahae**
That guy does nothing! What did he do last year aside from counting the boxes of Choco Chestnuts and chewing gum?

**Jisong**
He also made some report. It said our sales would increase if we reduced the weight of Choco Chestnuts by 20% and changed the packaging.

**Eun-sang**
I could tell you that. Where's my PhD?

But Eun-sang, who hated the company and its nepotism as much as anyone, wasn't willing to get fired over it, and suggested that we delete the entire chat history. We were, after all, using the company's internal messaging system.

**Jisong**
You can delete chat history?

**Eun-sang**

Do you see the menu button at the top right?

**Jisong**

Yeah.

**Eun-sang**

Click on settings and then 'delete chat history'.

**Jisong**

You mean 'share chat history'?

I was reading this with my mouth agape.

**Eun-sang**

Are you crazy! We'll all be fired if you share.

I clenched my jaw and tried to hold back the laughter.

**Eun-sang**

How about we do this in person? Are The Three Mids free for lunch? At the usual place.

It was then that I realised the name of our group chat had been updated from 'NOR(3)' to 'NOR(3)_Mids'.

# A Not-So-Obvious
# Suggestion

*13 March 2017*

There was a more or less accepted theory at our company: colleagues go to Starbucks after lunch, and office romances go to Coffee Bean.

Here's why such a theory might be useful. Let's say you think you're somewhat close with someone at work. You've only exchanged messages about work until, one day, you're talking about personal things, non-work-related topics. The two of you have eaten lunch together outside the office a few times but have yet to go out for dinner. You don't know if the relationship has potential or if it's just your imagination. Ask yourself, after lunch do you go for coffee at Starbucks or Coffee Bean? If it's the former, you should just move on to protect your mental health. If it's the latter, you can make the move by suggesting dinner next time.

The theory works on other people, too. Suppose there's a new recruit and a veteran employee in the team next to yours. It feels like there's a bit of spicy tension between the two. Everyone in the office thinks there's something going on between them, especially because they're always working late together. They're the only ones who don't seem to know they're exuding the heat of a smoking office romance. If you want to know what's really going on, just look at the coffee in their hands when they come back to the office after lunch. If the straw is Coffee Bean-purple and not Starbucks-green, then you can assume that something is going on between them – although it's impossible to be a hundred per cent sure until they announce it.

Coffee Bean didn't have any special significance, per se. There were two Starbucks in the area, one across the street and another just two blocks down – convenient walking distances. Coffee Bean, however, was in a somewhat remote location and required extra effort: one more block and a street crossing, to be exact. Going all that way for a comparable cup of coffee would be counterproductive if you didn't want to spend time alone with the person, if you didn't have something to hide from people at the office. It was a difference of only five minutes, but five minutes of an hour-long lunch break was 8.33 per cent. And unlike the local Starbucks, Coffee Bean had four private booths, perfect for private conversations. We likened them to train cabins and gave each a number: Cabin 1, Cabin 2, Cabin 3 and Cabin 4, with 1 being closest to the entrance.

NOR(3) always met at Coffee Bean, never Starbucks. Were the three of us in a ménage à trois? I hope not. But we did have something to hide. Most of our conversations involved complaining about the company, and the tables at Starbucks – which were always crawling with employees from Maron – were too small and close to each other for proper corporate bad-mouthing. Five extra minutes was a small price to pay for freedom of speech.

That day, after making lunch plans with Eun-sang and Jisong, I was anxiously checking the clock at one-minute intervals. 11:55. 56. 57. 58. 58. Why was the time passing so slowly? 59. 59. 59. 59… Finally, the hands hit 12:00. But everyone including Team Leader Koh remained glued to their seats. 12:01. No one was even budging. 12:02. Still, nothing. Once the clock turned to 12:03, I rolled my office chair back and said in a barely audible voice as I stood up:

'Sorry, everyone. I've got lunch plans today. Have a nice lunch.'

I took my coat from the coat rack, draped it over my arm, and snuck out into the hallway. When the elevator door opened, I was met by a large crowd of people on their way downstairs. In the middle of the crowd were Jisong and Eun-sang. I couldn't help but crack a smile when we made eye contact.

We'd decided on Jeonju-style bean sprout soup for lunch, something that wasn't too spicy, so we could continue our conversation from earlier. Bean sprout soup was good, but more importantly it was easy to finish quickly. In fact, we finished the soup in ten minutes and immediately headed to Coffee Bean. Thankfully, Cabin 4 was still vacant. Eun-sang took off her long coat, pulled out her wallet, and offered to pay.

'That's unlike you,' I said.

Eun-sang responded with a bright smile. 'I just wanted to do something nice.'

Her unusually high-pitched answer made me a bit suspicious; the Eun-sang I knew never talked with such excitement. Her response was short and simple, but it exuded a subtle yet unmistakable air of happiness.

'What do you want to drink?'

There it was again. The bright, light-hearted tone. Jisong said caramel latte, and I asked for an iced Americano. Eun-sang headed towards the counter before turning around as if remembering something.

'How about some cake?'

'Not a bad idea.'

'Let's do it. Bean sprout soup isn't very filling. I'm always hungry again by two,' Eun-sang said.

'Nuh-uh,' Jisong said. 'That's way too early to be hungry again.'

'I was being conservative. It's more like 1:30. Anyway, I'll pay for the cake too. One piece each. I want cheesecake. What about you two?'

Once Eun-sang left to place our order, Jisong glanced sideways at me, covering her mouth slightly with the back of her hand.

'Is it just me, or does something seem unusual about Eun-sang today?'

I knew I wasn't the only one who thought so.

'Right? She looks almost *too* happy.'

'It's weird.'

I looked in Eun-sang's direction. It *was* weird. Very weird. There was this unusual look in her eyes, caring and overflowing with joy in a way I'd never seen before. She was even engaging in small talk with the cashier, tilting her head back and laughing aloud. And as she waited for the coffee, she bounced her shoulders up and down with both hands stuck deep in the pockets of her thermal gilet. With each bounce, the faint smile of her lips spread to the rest of her face. What was up with her? This was so unlike Eun-sang.

She didn't smile often. She was the calmest of the three of us, the most logical, the most down-to-earth, and experienced the fewest emotional ups and downs. It wasn't just that; she was by far the most restrained person I knew. Whatever this was, it had to be something so overwhelming that even she couldn't control her excitement.

I watched as she snatched her phone out of her gilet pocket, like someone who'd just remembered something. Her eyes opened wide as she gazed into the phone's screen. She then brought her hand to her mouth. Her eyebrows raised like tall arches, and she blinked her eyes several times before slowly lowering her hand from her mouth and placing the phone back in her gilet pocket. She concealed her lips by rolling them inside her mouth and locking her jaw. Her lips weren't visible, but the corners of her mouth couldn't lie.

When Eun-sang returned to the table, she was carrying a plastic tray with three cups of coffee and three pieces of cake. She put down the tray as she said in a voice bursting with excitement:

'Ladies, cake is served.'

'Eun-sang! What is up with you today?' Jisong asked as she made a slightly confused laugh.

'What?'

'I thought you were in a bad mood,' I said. 'Earlier you were in a complete fit about your performance evaluation.'

'But now you're in such good spirits. It's weird.'

'Who? Me?'

She wasn't a good liar.

'It's weird,' I said. 'Don't tell me you got an A and are trying to hide it.'

'I would never! What kind of friend do you think I am? That hurts.'

'If you got an A then we should be celebrating. You don't need to hide it because of us.'

'That's not it,' Jisong said with a suspicious look. 'I know what this is. She's met someone.'

Hearing this, I thought that must be it. Now that I thought about it, she hadn't had a boyfriend since her last one two years ago. Eun-sang grinned and said no, waving her hands in the air dismissively. But Jisong was onto something. I'd always known Eun-sang to be pessimistic and slightly depressed. This was the only way to explain the uncontrollable, strangely optimistic vibe that was emanating from her every movement. But when? How did she have the time to date? We had each other's schedules memorised, and Eun-sang spent all her time either at home or in the office. Perhaps Jisong, who got into surfing last year and went to the beach on weekends, might have time to date, but not Eun-sang. Maybe she was just lucky enough to find a flower in the desert. Hopefully it wasn't someone in the company. If it was, we would need to stage an intervention because there were no good men at Maron. As I thought about all this, Eun-sang looked at her phone again, quickly checked something, and put the phone back on the table.

'It *is* a guy,' I said, having made up my mind. 'Look at what you just did. You have a boyfriend.'

'Really, Eun-sang? Have you started dating someone? Who is it? Who are you texting?'

Jisong quickly grabbed the top of Eun-sang's white phone, which was lying on the table across from her. Eun-sang snatched it back with a little shriek.

'Hey, you guys! I said that's not it.'

Only after pestering her for several more minutes did Eun-sang finally seem to give in. She took out her phone, wiped the screen on her thigh, then leaned over the table as she rested her chin on her hand with a carefree smile. Her movements were slow and elegant, as though she were living life in slow motion. With her head slightly tilted, she made eye contact once with Jisong and then once with me.

'If I tell you, will you join me?'

The words 'join me' made Jisong and I look at each other. Our eyes met for a second before turning back to Eun-sang.

'Join what?' Jisong asked hesitantly.

Eun-sang took a noisy sip of her Americano, locked her fingers together, then placed her round chin atop them as she whispered:

'Have you two heard of Bitcoin?'

Silence fell between the three of us. I was caught off guard by this word, the feeling of which was so different from what I had expected. It was like I'd taken a bite of smooth, moist cheesecake only to realise I'd actually got a mouthful of crunchy bean sprout. I nodded my head in silence.

'That's like, cyber money, right?' Jisong asked.

'It's not called cyber money,' I corrected Jisong. 'I think the correct term is virtual currency.'

'Cyber, virtual. Money, currency. Tomayto tomahto.'

'Well, kind of,' Eun-sang began. 'Bitcoin is a form of cryptocurrency.'

To understand cryptocurrency, Eun-sang explained to us, we first needed to understand what a 'blockchain' was. Participating in a blockchain system meant using your own cell phone or computer as a 'public ledger'. Once every ten minutes, the digital ledger of everyone participating in these transactions was logged. That bundle of transaction history created a block, and a series of blocks made a chain... Or at least that's what I think she said. Eun-sang hadn't even got to explaining Bitcoin, and I was already confused. Glancing over, I realised it wasn't just me; Jisong was also equally confused. Her nostrils were flaring as she tried to stifle a large yawn. Picking up on our confusion, Eun-sang tried one more time to explain.

'OK, focus. This is a lot simpler than you think. Jisong, imagine you want to take out 10,000 won from your bank account. You'd go to the bank and say, Give me my 10,000 won. Right? But will the bank just give you the money? No. They first need to check their records to see if you've deposited 10,000 won in the bank before. And for that, they'll open their ledgers, which should have a record of such a transaction. They'll see that you actually put 100,000 won in the bank at some point in time, and only then will they give you your 10,000 won. After that, they'll write in their ledger, "Jisong Kim withdrew 10,000 won. Her new balance is 90,000 won." They do the same thing when you deposit money. That's the only way that you can withdraw money from the bank. It's all about bookkeeping.'

We both nodded.

'But a system like this needs a central authority, and that costs money. You need a physical bank and bankers to make it work. Even online banking has associated fees. They need to prevent people and hackers from tampering with the ledgers. Otherwise, anyone could change the digits on their bank account or steal other people's money. Right? That's why they need two, sometimes three, levels of security to protect the ledgers. All that manifests as fees that the customer pays. Another problem is that, so long as they have that ledger, anyone can have complete access to individual transaction histories and who took how much.'

The blockchain, according to Eun-sang, was developed to overcome these limitations. Because the ledger was copied as many times as there were participants in the blockchain, essentially everyone got a copy. Instead of being managed by a single centralised entity, the ledger was managed publicly by everyone participating in the system. 'Because the ledger is distributed to computers all around the world, there are practically no maintenance fees, thus no transaction fees, and no threat of someone monitoring you.' It didn't matter if someone destroyed the ledger or altered it because there were always other copies. And, of course, every transaction was regularly encrypted and automatically updated.

'What you mean to say is, everyone's assets become safer, even though everyone only participates for their own self-interest?' I asked. 'I feel like I've heard this before.'

'The invisible hand?' Eun-sang said as she brought the palm of her hand down noisily on the table. 'Isn't it fascinating?'

The act of participating in a blockchain was called 'mining'. Encryption, algorithms, blah blah blah… Try as I might, I couldn't see where she was going with this. That was until she explained that people were rewarded for mining with 'coins' – the most famous example being Bitcoin, something both Jisong and I had heard of. Seeing the doubtful looks on our faces, Eun-sang was about to explain it again for us, but I cut her off because I didn't want to hear it any more.

'Eun-sang. What are you trying to say? You want us to buy Bitcoin?'

'Dahae,' Eun-sang said as she leaned across the table. 'You think I'd suggest something so obvious?'

# Wind Advisory

Eun-sang suggested instead that we buy Ethereum.

The moment she said this, the door to the cafe started rattling loudly. Everyone in the cafe turned towards the commotion as the large glass door burst open, sending a cold gust of wind in through the entrance. The people seated near the door let out a small shriek as the wind knocked over their coffees. Although we were seated deep inside the cafe and safely away from the worst of it, we could still feel the chill lapping at our legs. The employee at the counter ran over and tried to close the door, but the wind was too strong. Eventually, the other barista ran over to help. Only then were they able to slam the door shut and bring an end to the incident. Eun-sang half-heartedly looked over at the commotion with a disinterested look on her face as if to say: 'Huh, must be windy today.' She then began her explanation of Ethereum, and specifically, how it was different to Bitcoin.

I was at least somewhat familiar with Bitcoin, although I didn't completely understand the concept. I'd heard stories of computer geeks in America who got in on Bitcoin before it was famous. One article talked about someone who forgot about their Bitcoin for a decade and came back to discover they'd become a millionaire. Of course, I'd also heard stories of the opposite happening – people who once traded in their bitcoin for a pizza, not realising that if they hadn't, they would have been rich today.

But I never imagined that someone I knew would be into Bitcoin. I simply didn't belong to that world. I also assumed, for some reason, that the rush was already over. If there were Bitcoin millionaires, that meant the price of Bitcoin had already exploded. The doors were already closed. The now coveted bitcoin – just one of them – was worth more than 1,000,000 won. But Ethereum? This was the first time I had heard of it. Its name was bizarre, too close to 'ethereal', and it didn't even have 'coin' in it. How could you confidently buy something that didn't physically exist, something that could turn to thin air in the morning? How could anyone be stupid enough to buy something virtual?

Eun-sang wrinkled the bridge of her nose as she spoke.

'That's exactly what I'm trying to get at. Everything you just said means *now* is the time to buy, dummy!'

Ethereum, according to Eun-sang, was a second-generation blockchain developed two years ago by genius Russian-Canadian programmer Vitalik Buterin. In simple terms, Ethereum was a system that guaranteed credit of not just cryptocurrency transactions like bitcoin, but also real-world transactions. The currency or coin used in Ethereum was called 'ether'. Comparing it to real estate, Eun-sang said that it would be like taking a rental contract and automatically copying, renewing and sending it to all parties. Because everything in the real world uses contracts, Ethereum was a much more versatile, safer and innovative technology. And therefore, Eun-sang claimed, Ethereum was the next big thing.

'Hmmm,' Jisong said ambiguously as she put a large piece of chiffon cake in her mouth.

But despite our lukewarm reaction, Eun-sang continued her lecture on Ethereum without any sign of stopping. She told us that, while not many people in Korea knew of Ethereum, it was becoming popular in North America and Europe. The price of one ether was 13,950 won. She then reminded us that the current cost of one bitcoin was 1,500,000 won. It was at this moment that it happened. I could clearly detect something flash across Eun-sang's dark, well-defined pupils. She told us to imagine ether reaching prices of 1,000,000 or even 2,000,000 won, just like bitcoin.

'You understand, right? We're at the left ankle of it.'

Eun-sang had started off explaining to us how a blockchain was an improved alternative to traditional banking, but now she was just telling us to buy a new type of stock. To summarise the rest of what Eun-sang said, you had to buy at the ankles (not the knees, as the saying usually went) and sell at the shoulders to make a great profit. And right now was what she presumed to be the ankles.

'And here I was thinking she'd finally found a boyfriend,' Jisong said as she leaned one shoulder into the back cushion of Cabin 4. 'But again with the business ideas. I guess I shouldn't have expected anything less from Eun-sang Kang.'

'I don't need a boyfriend. Love doesn't put food on the table.'

'Then does that thing, ether or whatever it is, put food on the table?'

To answer Jisong's question, Eun-sang lifted the phone on her lap and brought it in front of Jisong's nose.

'It'll put a lot more than just food on the table. Wanna see?'

Jisong shuddered with disgust as she pushed Eun-sang's phone away with her palm.

'So, you're telling us you've been investing in virtual currency, is that it? I knew you were a troublemaker.'

Eun-sang was quick to respond.

'I'm not a troublemaker; I'm a money-maker.' Eun-sang then narrowed her eyes as she added, 'You're the one who wastes money flying to Taiwan to meet that boy. You should use your money to buy ether instead.'

Last year during her summer holiday, Jisong went to Bali on her first surfing trip. There she met a guy from Taipei seven years her junior, with whom she was now in a long-distance relationship. But whether you could call it an actual relationship or not was up for debate. His name was Wei Lin, and since meeting him, Jisong had flown to Taipei four times to see him, averaging about one visit every other month. Eun-sang thought such a relationship wasn't really a proper relationship but a waste of time and would frequently bring it up as a way of attacking Jisong. I was half-listening to the two of them bickering back and forth about what Jisong should be spending her money on, when I realised I had been intently staring at Eun-sang's phone.

In all honesty, *I* wanted to see. *I* was curious about what could possibly make the great Eun-sang Kang grin from ear to ear like this. But because Jisong had reacted so negatively, I couldn't bring myself to ask any more questions. Eun-sang was looking sideways at Jisong with a scowl.

'If you don't want to know, then you shouldn't have asked.'

*Me! Me! I want to know.* But at the same time, I didn't. I couldn't be sure why. Perhaps it was because I was afraid of feeling envious if by some chance Eun-sang was a millionaire, like that lucky teen from America; afraid of feeling envious if Eun-sang no longer had to care about whether she got A or M like I did, whether her raise was 2 per cent or 3 per cent.

'Oh my god, it's already 12:49!'

Startled by Eun-sang's exclamation, I looked at the time.

'No way.'

'Already? We just sat down,' Jisong said with a look of disbelief.

Even though this happened to us every time, we were *always* surprised. Whenever we were in this train cabin racing away from our company, time seemed to run twice as fast. We hurriedly gobbled down the remaining bites of cake, left the cafe, and started speed-walking to the office.

Our company was unreasonably strict about how long a lunch break we took. At other companies, I had heard, people would get up for lunch around 11:50. That way, they could arrive at the restaurant or cafeteria by 12:00 before the rush. I was absolutely floored when I heard from a friend that they left for lunch at 11:40 when they had personal engagements. Some laid-back companies even allowed their employees to come back from lunch as late as 1:30. But not Maron. Never. It didn't matter which team you worked for, everyone in the company could only be away from their post from 12:00 to 1:00. My team leader loved giving us looks when we were late. Because of this, most people in Snacks returned to their desks by 12:55. And yet, the same didn't apply for the start of our lunch break; it was frowned upon to stand up from your desk at twelve o'clock sharp if the team leader hadn't stood up first. But I always got up at 12:03, even if it didn't seem like anyone else was going to get up with me. When the other people in my team saw me do this, they probably thought to themselves that I was just another maladjusted millennial, the type that always got up first and didn't care what others thought. They weren't totally wrong. Although their glares drove me crazy, after three minutes of waiting, I eventually had no choice but to get up; the hunger was just too much to bear. How nice would it be, I wondered, if everyone could eat according to their own biological clock? It was 2017, after all; it wasn't the 1980s any more. Korea was a modern nation. I never imagined such draconian companies would still exist here, let alone that I would be working at one of them. And yet here I was. The five main confectionary companies in Korea were all packed into this neighbourhood, and yet, the only people hustling back to their offices at 12:50 were the ones with bright yellow company badges hanging from their necks.

But today I couldn't run. The wind was blowing too hard. Eun-sang told us there was a wind advisory, and indeed, a strong wind was blowing in the opposite direction from where we wanted to go, making our bodies feel twice as heavy as we walked. With her scarf up to the tip of her nose, Jisong's wavy hair was whipping about in the wind.

'It's so cold!'

We locked arms, both to fight against the wind and to keep each other warm. Eun-sang in the middle, me on the left, and Jisong on the right, stuck to each other like glue. Another gust of wind came, so strong it made it hard to walk. Flying through the air were the grit, cigarette butts and other unknown debris that had piled up in the gutter. We turned around to avoid the flying garbage as we shrieked, our arms still locked as though we were in a four-legged race. We trudged left and right, screaming as we avoided the ghost-like debris floating in the wind. Before we knew it, our shrieks had turned to laughter.

Of course, we were only laughing because of how ridiculously futile we felt. Perhaps screaming and laughter came together. As another gust of wind hit us, the plastic cases of Jisong's company badge and mine slapped against each other, making a clattering sound. We burst out into another volley of screams and laughter. Eun-sang was hunched over and starting to get frustrated.

'Let us pass!' she yelled out. 'Why is it so hard to just walk?'

'It's just like a video game,' Jisong said with a frown as she held down her bangs. 'Like when you get hit with a debuff spell and are slowed. No matter how hard you press the forward key, it's like bags of sand are tied to your feet preventing you from going any faster.'

'Wow. That sounds like life, no?' I asked.

'Ugh, don't be so depressing. We'll get out of this somehow,' Eun-sang said.

'How?' I asked.

Eun-sang squeezed my arm tighter. 'You have to use your dispel skill.'

The wind blew again, and we screamed and laughed.


It was 12:56 when we arrived at the company lobby on the first floor.

Unsurprisingly, there was a long line for the elevators. After lunch they were always like a packed subway train during rush hour. In a mad struggle not to be late at all costs, people pushed their way into the elevator until the alarm went off. The three of us were the last ones in. I was so close to the door as it closed that I feared my nose might get pinched, but I was relieved that we managed to board the elevator at all. My relief was short-lived. In my carelessness, I had forgotten to push the button for my floor. The elevator was now rising straight past the third floor towards Management Support, which was on the seventh. Eun-sang and Jisong were snickering.

After everyone got off, I pressed the button for the third floor. The door closed. Finally alone, I couldn't help myself from pulling out my phone and looking up Ethereum. There weren't many results. I scrolled down a bit before tapping the power button. The time on my lock screen showed 1:03. Shit.

I entered the office, pulled out my chair, and quietly sat down. As expected, Team Leader Koh was glancing in my direction.

'Please, be early.'

I left at 12:03 and returned at 1:03. So technically, I had observed the one-hour lunch break outlined in my contract.

'Yes, sir!' I said loudly, avoiding looking in his direction.

Inside, I was thinking about how talentless people always obsessed over punctuality because they couldn't do anything else.

He turned to me and added:

'It's always the one who leaves first.'

I should've known. If I had just answered him in a dispirited manner, instead of giving him a sassy 'Yes, sir!', he wouldn't have needed to have the last word. It didn't really matter to him that I had an extra three minutes of lunch. He just hated the fact that a subordinate wasn't submitting to him. He couldn't stand that I wasn't paying respect to his seniority, his experience and the authority they afforded him.

It was an open secret in our company that Dae-young Koh – Team Leader Koh, that is – was royally incompetent. Because he'd entered the company in 1996, his rank (determined by one's time with the company) was 'department manager of branding'. But he probably didn't even know how to spell branding; he was that stupid. Thankfully, our team was able to survive on the hard work of its other employees. Then again, Snacks wasn't really responsible for any of the company's main products. Sidelined by Chocolates and Ice Cream, the real bread and butter of our company, so to speak, Snacks was the smallest team, and hadn't released any new products in several years. No one expected much from us. Nor did they expect much from our team leader, who also happened to be department manager of branding. It was something of a paradox that someone as highly ranked as him would be given the menial job of managing the Snacks team. Traditionally, if your rank was department manager, your job title would be the more important 'office head' and not 'team leader'. But because his rank was fixed by how long he had been in the company, and because they couldn't fire him, the company had settled on giving him the job of managing the smallest team of workers. Of course, this last part was just my conjecture.

Other people – general managers (one rank below department manager) and assistant managers (one rank below that) – would raise the white flag in front of him. They did this despite knowing he was incompetent, despite knowing that he was just a puppet with a title, despite talking badly about him behind his back every day. They treated him like their boss. They avoided directly disagreeing with him, would only pretend to listen to his strange instructions, and would always end up doing things their own way. This was the only way that anything got done in Snacks. People who'd worked at the company far longer than me were pros at ignoring him while showing respect. But I just couldn't do it. I knew it would be easier just to say, 'Yes, sir,' in a dispirited manner, to not show any rebelliousness. Perhaps this was the reason I'd never receive an A, why I wasn't moving up in the company. But being sarcastic and making snide remarks was in my blood. Someone had to mock him, someone had to let him know he was an imbecile. And if not that, I at least wanted to get on his nerves. Was I being mean? Hardly. But I decided to not make a second remark today and let him have the last word.

It was time for me to go and brush my teeth, but because it seemed like he was going to say something more if I did that, I decided to sacrifice proper dental hygiene today and popped two pieces of tropical fruit gum into my mouth. I woke up my laptop, opened the internet browser, and searched for Ethereum. First in Korean, then in English once I worked out the spelling. Compared to just a few seconds ago, there was a much larger number of results. It seemed that people had a lot to say about it. The only problem was, because it was all in English, it was hard to get a quick grasp of what I was reading.

As I scrolled down and scanned the article titles, I sensed Team Leader Koh get up from his seat and walk towards me. I pressed Ctrl + W. He passed by the back of my chair and left. I quickly pressed Ctrl + Shift + T. In the distance, I could see Professor Ham through the glass, picking his teeth as he sauntered into the office.

# 1.2-Room Apartment

*27 April 2017*

There were three criteria I'd decided on when looking for a new apartment.

First, it couldn't be smaller than my current apartment. And because I'd saved up enough money over the last four years to afford a more expensive security deposit, which usually meant cheaper rent and more square footage. Speaking of which, criteria number two: the rent couldn't be any more expensive. Lastly, and this was the most important, it needed to have an area at the front entrance to take off your shoes and a lip between the bathroom and the main living area.

The reason I'd finally decided to move out of my current place was because of those last two things, or rather, the lack of them. An area at the front entrance to take off your shoes and a threshold in front of the bathroom. No-brainers in Korea, but no-shows in my current apartment for some reason. The linoleum floor began as soon as you entered the apartment, and because of this the dirt on my shoes found little resistance in infiltrating the rest of the apartment. Carefully taking off my shoes didn't help either. The bathroom had a similar problem. Although it had its own tile, there was no ledge between the tile and the linoleum. No barrier, no change in elevation. And because there was no tub or shower cubicle, just a shower head in the corner of the tiled bathroom, one minute of carelessness was enough for the dingy water to make its way to where I ate and slept.

I hadn't known these things when I first signed the contract. I only thought that this apartment was good for the price. I never imagined not having those two things would bring me such discomfort. It might sound trivial, but once you've experienced it, you know how much of a deal breaker it is. It only took two days of living there to realise this. I knew that studio apartments were a single room by definition, but did there have to be such little separation between the sections of the room?

I found my own ways to cope. I put a mat in front of the door, and I took showers as quickly as I could. I brought out the broom to sweep every day and regularly used a drain cleaner for the shower. This didn't completely solve the problem, but I was able to make do. Now, however, I wanted things to be different. I promised myself I would visit the real estate agency on my way home, the same one I'd visited last weekend.

The real estate agent had shown me three places. The first, despite being much smaller than my current apartment (something I realised as soon as I stepped into the cramped room), was clean and relatively new. Sigh. I probably should have gone with that place. The second was too far away from the bus stop, and even farther away from the subway station. And the last place was out of my budget, both in terms of the rent and the security deposit. After seeing the last apartment, I told the agent I wanted to go with the first, but in that short space of time someone had already put money down on it. After that, I realised I needed to stop sitting on the fence and go with the next place I liked. It was at this time that the real estate agency called me about another place. 'There's an apartment that's going to be available soon. You should wait for it if you're not in a rush. It's really nice.'

At six o'clock on the dot, I left work and hurried over to the meeting place, a small apartment building located at the end of a street filled with restaurants. On the first floor was a pizza delivery shop and a nail salon; thirteen studio apartments filled the remaining floors of the quaint, five-storey building. I met the real estate agent at the front entrance to the building. She said she was going to show me Unit 301. We didn't need to walk up the stairs because there was an elevator.

'This place is nice and doesn't come on the market very often. The last tenant lived here for six years. She lived alone, so it's clean and in good condition.'

The agent also explained to me that the landlord had decided to take this opportunity to fix the old kitchen and plumbing; that's why the apartment was left vacant for a while.

'You've got great timing,' she said. 'The kitchen at this place used to be a drawback. But the landlord is replacing all the countertops.'

She then lowered her voice as if she was telling me some big secret.

'And the last tenant is leaving because of good fortune. She got married to an attorney. It's really lucky.'

Things weren't looking good. The more I listened to the real estate agent's high praise, the more anxious I became. To her, this apartment was perfect. And this meant I needed to find the defects on my own, because perfect apartments just didn't exist. I could feel a headache coming on. I'd been sweet-talked by a realtor for my current apartment, too – it was large for the price, it had a wall-mounted, ductless air conditioning unit, there was a mini fridge. I hadn't thought much of those non-existent few centimetres of elevation that should have been separating the entrance and bathroom from the main room. But now I was so tired of mysterious bits of grit that continued to find their way to the edge of my bed no matter how well I wiped my shoes on the door mat, tired of the wine-coloured tiles in the bathroom that were clearly visible even when the door was closed, of needing a rubber squeegee to push back the water seeping through the large gap beneath the door, of lightning-fast showers, of bubbling wallpaper and linoleum flooring.

We arrived at the third floor. Unit 301 was the first door on the left. Because no one was living there, the realtor didn't bother knocking and simply entered the passcode into the padlock. My heart was pounding.

When the front door opened, my first thought was 'not bad'. Straight ahead was a large window, to the left a bathroom door, and to the right a low shoe rack.

Just beyond the shoe rack was a wide space carved out for the sink. Admittedly, the wallpaper and linoleum weren't particularly clean and the kitchen had mould everywhere, but I reminded myself that the landlord was going to fix up the kitchen. The real estate agent had mentioned this apartment was 200 square feet, the same as the apartment I was living in now, but it looked larger, perhaps because there was no furniture. There were inoffensive grey tiles at the front entrance, as well as a threshold separating the tile from the elevated linoleum flooring. Check, check.

The realtor told me I could keep my shoes on. I carefully stepped up onto the linoleum floor and started inspecting every inch of the room in earnest. The bathroom was a normal bathroom – the type I'd so missed. I was a bit troubled by the jade-coloured door, but at least it didn't have large gaps at the top and bottom. Check. Perhaps I could think of it as mint green instead of jade. There was also a fan in the bathroom and, upon opening the door, I discovered yet another threshold. Check. I turned on the water in the sink and flushed the toilet. Both worked well. Check.

I liked the apartment so far, and I had yet to find a deal-breaker. Somehow, this made me more anxious. The fact that I hadn't seen or heard of any defects so far meant that the defect would be all the more fatal. And if that weren't the case, it probably meant that this place was going to be really expensive. The real estate agent hadn't told me the rent; because I couldn't move in immediately anyway, she had only suggested we 'take a look'.

Using my incredulity to protect me from what I might find, I slowly walked towards the window and stood in the centre of the room. From behind me, I could hear the self-assured voice of the real estate agent:

'Try opening it. It's a double window.'

I did as she said and opened the window. A waft of pizza rose from the delivery shop downstairs. A karaoke shop sign was fixed to the top of the building diagonally opposite. Although I didn't think it was close enough to be noisy, I was afraid of the blaring light from the neon sign and the drunkards it would attract. Thinking that these things might bother me, I decided to defer judgement on this place for now, as I turned my head back into the apartment.

What I saw made me gasp in surprise. And indeed, I was so surprised it felt like I forgot how to breathe for a moment.

Through the wall on the right was a hidden room.

This apartment room, which until then I had thought to be a rectangle, turned out *not* to be a rectangle. Well, not quite. Perhaps a rectangle with a bit of a tail was the best way to describe it. And in this cozy tail was just enough room for a single bed. A vaulted ceiling; two small halogen lamps mounted on one side of the wall. It was gorgeous!

I couldn't believe it. I also couldn't believe I had been so helplessly won over by such a silly thing. The real estate agent was looking at me with a self-satisfied expression on her face, but what she said next was rather reserved.

'It is nice, isn't it?'

I was unable to say anything and just nodded my head over and over. This unexpected sight had flung me into a thought simulation. I redid the furniture layout I'd been drawing in my head since entering the room. Originally, I planned on putting the bed in the left corner of the room, diagonally opposite the kitchen. But once I discovered this little space, I mentally lifted my bed and inserted it there. I then imagined myself going out into the hallway so I could come in through the front door again. When I entered, I couldn't see my bed. Nor would I see my bed while I was eating. And with this newfound floor space, I now had enough room for a sofa. The main room would be where I ate and watched TV. And when I was done for the day, I could take one step to the left and retire to my little bedroom.

'This is a bonus space,' the real estate agent said. 'I bet you have a lot of clothes. If you put a clothes rack in there, it'd be perfect as a walk-in closet.'

I could do that, or I could use it for my bed. Besides, I didn't have as many clothes as she might have thought. More important to me was not seeing my bed as soon as I came in through the front door, nor the kitchen from where I slept, nor the bathroom tiles while I ate. No one wanted to eat, sleep and poop in the same area. Spatial separation between different parts of your life should be a human right. As I thought this, I had another idea. If I installed blinds that were just the right width, I could raise and close them like a door, completely separating my makeshift bedroom from the main living area.

I spread my palm as wide as I could and then carefully measured how wide the space was. From one wall to the other. Over and over, I closed and opened my hand as I moved it through the empty air, imitating a crawling caterpillar.

One... two... three... four... five... six... and a half.

I had made my decision. This was the place. Only now did I voice my opinion, something I had been consciously avoiding.

'This place is nice.'

'I knew you'd like it,' the real estate agent said as she clicked on and off the halogen light. The image of my bedroom was appearing and disappearing before my eyes. *Blink, blink.*

I ran the entire way home.

I was so excited that, as soon as I opened the front door, I walked guilt-free all the way to my bed with my shoes on. It was unexpectedly liberating. After all, what was the point of taking off your shoes in an apartment like this? Perhaps I should live like this until I move out. After all, this wasn't really my home. Not for long. I crouched in front of my bed, the impression of where I'd jumped out of it that morning still visible. I then opened my hand and measured the width of my bed-frame.

One... two... three... four... five... six.

Perfect. That meant my bed would fit perfectly in my new bedroom.

I'd always hoped to live in a one-bedroom apartment, or at least a studio apartment with dividers. Sometimes I would imagine myself working hard until one day I had enough money to live in such a place. Other times,

I was less optimistic. With my current salary, I thought, I'd have to work until I was thirty, maybe even forty, before I could afford such a place. I had no idea this day would come so soon.

Of course, the apartment was still technically a studio apartment, a one-room apartment, minus the bed. But it wasn't like other studio apartments. Nor was it big enough to qualify as a 1.5-room apartment, a ridiculous term which real estate agencies like to use... Perhaps I could call it a 1.2-room apartment.

1.2.

I wanted that extra 20 per cent.

I *needed* that extra 20 per cent.

It was clear that I was bewitched by that narrow yet deep, cozy two tenths of a room.

I heated up some instant rice in the microwave, transferred some side dishes from Tupperware onto saucers, and prepared a pan with cooking oil to fry an egg. The smell and heat of cooking food quickly filled my small apartment.

As I put another egg into the pan, I thought hard about my financial situation. If I managed to sign the contract for that place, I would need to pay 20,000,000 won more for the security deposit and 150,000 won more in rent. Including the payments I would have to make on a new loan, I would be paying 350,000 won more every month.

After finishing my food and doing the dishes, I took out a small cup of ice cream from the freezer. This was a new flavour: milky vanilla with bits of caramel syrup and chocolate chunks scattered throughout. It was still too hard for me to sink my spoon into. As I waited for the surface of the ice cream to thaw, I messaged Eun-sang — not through the NOR(3) group chat but through our personal chat.

**Dahae**
Eun-sang, are you asleep?

There was no reply. I scrolled through Instagram for a while before putting my phone down and slowly spooning some ice cream into my mouth. The ice cream melted, coating my tastebuds with the taste of sweet milk. The texture of sticky caramel syrup and crunchy chocolate chunks. Eun-sang still hadn't messaged me back. I tossed my phone on my bed and went into the bathroom to take a shower. When I came out, I discovered a bit of soapy water had seeped onto the linoleum again. With the window squeegee I had leaning up against the wall, I pushed the water back into the bathroom. The pieces of transparent tape dividing the tile and linoleum flooring were fraying. I dried my body with a towel, wiped the remaining moisture off the floor, and threw the towel into the washing machine.

I pumped some toner onto a cotton pad and, more thoroughly than usual, wiped off my make-up. I continued to glance at my phone as I applied lotion to my face. Still nothing from Eun-sang. With nothing else to do, I turned off the lights and got into bed, but I couldn't fall asleep. I had wanted to ask Eun-sang a question even before going to the real estate agency. Although, I was still undecided whether I really wanted to ask it. To ask, or not to ask. That was the... Just then, my phone lit up. Eun-sang had finally replied.

**Eun-sang**
Not yet. Why?

I could see her reply on my lock screen, but I didn't open it. I wanted to sleep on it and text her in the morning. It was too late to start such an important conversation.
But then again.
I knew I couldn't fall asleep if I went to bed like this, without asking Eun-sang my question. I unlocked my phone, lay sideways, shoved my face into that square of light, and sent Eun-sang a message.

**Dahae**
That thing you talked about last time... how do you do it?
**Eun-sang**
Do what?
**Dahae**
Cryptocurrency.
**Eun-sang**
No way.

Eun-sang then sent another message:

**Eun-sang**
I thought you said you weren't interested.

# Eun-sang Kang's Mini Mart

*4 May 2017*

Of all my friends, Eun-sang was the biggest money lover. But perhaps calling her a 'money lover' was a bit mean-spirited. It wasn't that she was obsessed with it. Perhaps there was a better word. Eun-sang was economical? No. She had a golden thumb? Not that either. She was always thinking about how to make a quick buck? She always wanted to choose the most profitable option in every circumstance? *Eun-sang liked money*. As simple as it might sound, she had an almost childlike fondness for the stuff. Just like Team Leader Koh liked coffee and Jisong liked surfing, Eun-sang liked money.

The first time I sensed this was one autumn day during my first year at the company. I was walking with Eun-sang to work after bumping into her on the subway. The station seemed oddly busy, but it wasn't until we left the station that I discovered why. The scene above ground was so chaotic that I thought we had got off at the wrong place. Inching slowly in the direction of the local university was a long line of people. Even the traffic headed in that direction was gridlocked.

'What's going on?'

As Eun-sang and I marvelled at the commotion, a voice came from inside the crowd: 'Entrance exam!'

This was all it took for us to understand. These were students and their parents, and today was the local private university's entrance exam.

'Yuck, they're like ants,' I said.

Eun-sang shook her head.

'The college must be making a fortune in application fees.'

'I wonder if the parents wait outside during the entire exam.'

'Good question. It's so cold.'

I sympathised with the students, thinking back to when I was in high school. Meanwhile, Eun-sang craned her neck as she scanned the crowd.

'I bet you could make good money selling hand-warmers and blankets to these people,' Eun-sang said abruptly.

I'd personally never associated the pain of taking college entrance exams with making money. Nor had I seen someone make the connection so shamelessly, or with such enthusiasm. Eun-sang hurriedly took off her gloves, put them in her pocket, and took out her phone to look up the wholesale price of microfibre blankets.

'You can buy five hundred... for about 2,500 won per blanket...'

Eun-sang held up her fingers as she did the maths in her head.

'Even if I sold them for 5,000 won a piece, I would net 1,250,000 won for five hundred blankets. If I bought and sold one thousand blankets, that would be

2,500,000... No, wait. The unit price would be less if I bought that many at once... It would be... Yes, I would earn at least 2,600,000 won. Hey, that's more than our monthly pay check.'

We were walking towards the office and getting farther from the crowd, but every other moment, Eun-sang would turn around to look back at the crowd of people as she continued to crunch the numbers.

'What if I sold the blankets for 6,000 won each or even 7,000 won?'

She looked up the unit price of handwarmers and in the few minutes it took to arrive at the office, she was able to conclude that blankets were more lucrative than handwarmers.

'Dahae, do you think I should use a sick day next year to come here and sell blankets?'

At the time, I thought she was joking. But once we became close friends, I started to suspect that she might have been serious. So, every autumn on the day of the local university's entrance exam, I spent a few extra moments outside the subway looking for Eun-sang and her blankets. Thankfully, I had yet to see her there.

She also liked to talk about business ideas while having lunch together. One day, while waiting for our food, she asked us a question:

'Which restaurant in the neighbourhood do you two think is the most successful?'

Obviously it had to be the popular sushi restaurant, which always had a line and whose lunch special was a good deal. Jisong's guess was the simple budae-jjigae chain restaurant because of its ubiquity.

'You think?' Eun-sang said, as if she was somewhat puzzled by our answers.

She lightly tapped on the table with her two fingers as she told us that, in her opinion, it was this restaurant, the one we were currently sitting in. As she said this, our food came out: Jeonju-style bean sprout soup with a poached egg in a stainless steel bowl. Jisong and I licked our lips while we spooned hot broth into the bowl with the poached egg and whisked it. Eun-sang continued.

'Just look at this. The food comes out so quickly. And because rice soup like this is by nature a quick meal, bean sprout soup restaurants are second to none when it comes to getting customers in and out the door. I bet they can serve four parties at the same table over the lunch break, maybe five if they're good. And the ingredients are really basic. Poached egg is probably the most expensive thing here. I can't imagine bean sprouts costing much. And, from the looks of it, they only have one cook in the kitchen, so the cost of labour must be low. This isn't a franchise chain either, so the owner shouldn't be paying any royalties. Most importantly, it's cheap and delicious. The surrounding companies love this bean sprout soup restaurant. It's good for hangovers, and it's so popular there's often a line. Even *we* come here about three times a month. Right?'

Eun-sang then started looking up production prices, labour costs, and average time spent at the restaurant to check her estimates. She even looked up how much it would cost to rent a commercial space like this and eventually estimated the net profit of a bean sprout restaurant in this exact neighbourhood.

I always had to pull out my phone for calculations that required the multiplication of anything bigger than two digits. And because I never even tried mental calculations beyond the boundaries of the multiplication table, anytime Eun-sang talked maths, it just went in one ear and out the other. Jisong didn't look like she was particularly enthralled by business talk either. But Eun-sang, who had stopped caring some time ago about whether we were listening, continued to talk in a manner that was almost like the mumblings of a lunatic. You could say we were used to it by now, Eun-sang's blabbering on about money while Jisong and I ate our food, because it happened so often. And every time she got like this, Jisong and I would just exchange the 'she's at it again' look and secretly make fun of her.

There's one more story I'd be remiss not to mention. Almost everyone at our company knew Eun-sang because two years ago she opened and ran a small shop called Eun-sang Kang's Mini Mart. It started one day when she came back from Suwon with a whole box of toothpaste from the small supermarket her parents ran in the suburbs. Instead of giving toothpaste out to colleagues who needed a squeeze, she started selling it.

Toothpaste in the office was a surprisingly bothersome item to buy and keep. When you were running low, you would make a mental note to buy some the next time you were at the convenience store. And then you would forget about it, until you reached the point where it seemed like you still had toothpaste left but no matter how hard you squeezed it wouldn't come out, and you would need to ask to use some of your neighbour's. There was a convenience store just across the street from the office, but who had the time to wait for the elevator, ride it all the way down to the ground floor, and cross the street just for a tube of toothpaste? And what if the weather was foul? Heat waves, cold snaps, blizzards, torrential rains – there was always something. No one wanted to brave the elements just for a measly tube of minty paste.

People who bought toothpaste from Eun-sang – which she conveniently sold inside the office – quickly spread the word for her. Out of toothpaste? Look for Eun-sang Kang from Procurement on the seventh floor. And within a few days, the box of toothpaste she was selling was empty. If it were me, I would have stopped at that point. Eun-sang, however, continued to refill the box with new toothpaste, and even made her own ledger.

It wasn't long before she started siphoning off other products from her parents' supermarket. Baking soda and dish sponges for cleaning coffee mugs and tumblers, tan stockings for when yours had holes, Febreze, which came in handy when you had a meeting right after eating fermented soybean stew or Korean barbecue. She even sold things like Band-Aids, Fucidin, Roihi Tsuboko and Tylenol. I wasn't sure how she obtained these items because most supermarkets didn't have a licence to stock pharmaceuticals. Her bestseller by far was cup ramen: kimchi ramen, jjajang ramen, bibim ramen, you name it. She even had pho-flavoured ramen. These sold like hot cakes, so to speak, in the late afternoons and evenings. Every weekend she went to her parents with a suitcase to fill with merchandise, but ramen sold so well that eventually she needed to find her own supplier in Seoul.

At one point, her inventory became so large that it was impossible not to recognise it as a serious business. And once that happened, Eun-sang decided to print and laminate a sign with the words 'Eun-sang Kang's Mini Mart' to hang on the outside wall of her cubicle. Even back when all she was selling was toothpaste, Eun-sang had the foresight to set up an honour system to avoid being pulled away from work too often. Her desk was in the far corner of the office. To the right of her was the walkway, and in front of her cubicle was a wall. There was an empty space between her cubicle and the wall where people placed unused boxes, basically a storage closet. But once Eun-sang opened her business, she decided to claim this area for herself. She cleared out all the boxes and placed a plastic cart there to display her products. To one side of the cart was a golden piggy bank for people to put their money into, and taped to the outside wall of Eun-sang's cubicle, just beneath the sign 'Eun-sang Kang's Mini Mart', was a product price list, a piece of paper with a bank account number written on it for wire transfers, and an instant-pay QR code. Of course, she also had a system of credit. People would write their name on a notepad with the pen Eun-sang had conveniently hung from the wall, and every day she would organise this list and send out a payment reminder email.

One night after finishing work late, I visited Eun-sang at her desk, who unsurprisingly was also working late. It was almost midnight, so there was barely anyone on the floor. Most of the lights were out, but way in the corner was Eun-sang's lamp, hanging over her hunched shoulders like a spotlight shining on a dark stage. The outline of her figure from behind looked so focused and determined. I walked up behind her chair and looked down to see what she was doing.

On her desk was the piggy bank, belly open and upside down. She was sifting through the pile of coins with her finger to find 500-won coins. She would transfer two at a time to her hand as she rhythmically counted in a barely audible voice, 'One thousand, two thousand, three thousand, four thousand...' Once she had ten 500-won coins, she would stack them into a neat tower and write down five tally marks. Eun-sang continued to do this over and over, methodically and without resting. For a reason that I couldn't understand, I was getting goosebumps on my upper arms listening to the cold clinking of coins. Uniform towers of 100-won and 500-won coins were slowly being amassed into neat rows and columns. The tally marks on her notepad were propagating as they filled the paper. She was focusing so intently on her counting that she was unable to sense me for quite some time. Only when I finally let out an exclamation in admiration did she notice me and turn around.

'Oh, Dahae. I thought you said you were going home. What are you doing here?'

'Nothing really,' I said as I grabbed her hunched shoulders and pulled them back to fix her posture. Her muscles were tight and stiff. 'Ouch, ouch,' she said before asking me to rub her shoulders a bit.

'Eun-sang,' I said as I pressed my fingertips into the knots in her neck and shoulders. 'Why do you take that business of yours so seriously? It doesn't seem worth the trouble.'

Eun-sang took both of her hands and squared off the towers of coins she had been stacking. She turned around, looked up at me, and showed me a faint but discernible smile.

'Actually, it's a lot more profitable than you think.'

As she said the word 'profitable', she wrinkled her nose in a cute way, as though the thought was exciting her.

'How much do you make?'

Eun-sang hesitated for a moment before covering her mouth with the back of her hand, as if she were letting me in on a secret.

'Nine.'

'90,000 won?'

'Yep.'

'A month?'

'Yep.'

I was stunned. 90,000 won would not be worth it for me. It occurred to me that Eun-sang must really be serious about money. The rows of coin towers sparkled brilliantly in the light of the lamp.

Not long after that night at the office, the curtain fell on the era of Eun-sang Kang's Mini Mart. Nearly a year and six months of rave reviews, but someone had tipped off HR about Eun-sang's commercial activities inside the company. She was even summoned in front of a disciplinary committee. Thankfully there was no punishment, but because her employment contract prohibited her from having a side job, she was forced to suspend operations. Many people were disappointed. Even the employee from HR who came to Eun-sang with an agreement for her to sign, which made her promise she wasn't going to sell any more items inside the company, was a regular at Eun-sang Kang's Mini Mart. As she handed Eun-sang the document to sign, she said:

'It's too bad. If I were in charge, I would have invested. Really.'


Come to think of it, that was probably a better way to describe it. Eun-sang didn't just want to make money, per se, but rather invest. She was always thinking about leverage. That is, she wasn't just satisfied with having money in her pockets. No, she was always trying to figure out how she could use money to make even more money. She wanted to know which option would result in her netting the most profit, and at the same time, which option would lead to the fewest losses.

But just because she wanted to create leverage did not mean she always succeeded. Far from it. When her mini mart had to suddenly close, she was left with a lot of merchandise, and from what I heard the entire venture was a net loss for her. Another time, she lost half of her severance package because she dumped all of it into stocks. It was uncomfortable listening to her talk about that painful memory. In fact, after hearing the story, I intentionally avoided ever mentioning the words 'stocks' or 'severance package'. But one time while we were having dinner at a restaurant near our office, the company she had invested in came on TV. 'Those dumb fucks. Only they could go bankrupt during a bull market like this.' I didn't know Eun-sang could swear like that.

She'd also bought a nice studio apartment near Hongdae Station with her friends and rented it out on Airbnb. They had split the earnings according to how much each person contributed; Eun-sang, who'd contributed the least (because she had the smallest savings) earned 150,000 won a month from the Airbnb. But even that venture went up in flames after about a year because Eun-sang got into a huge fight with her friends and withdrew all her investments, effectively ending their relationship. Eun-sang's complaint was about cleaning duties. She just couldn't understand why she had to clean as often as everyone else when she owned the smallest share. It was a lot of pressure hearing that Jisong and I were her last remaining friends. We also didn't know how to react when she confessed to us that it was technically illegal to rent out a studio apartment on Airbnb in Korea.

Was it wise to put my trust in such a person? Someone who lost money left and right, who was so cavalier about engaging in illegitimate business transactions?

The small instalment savings I had diligently built up over ten years of part-time jobs, and the other instalment savings I had started after getting my job at Maron and deferring money from my pay check, were both about to reach maturity. Though I had no idea what a blockchain or cryptocurrency were, I was considering doing what Eun-sang told me by throwing my entire life savings into Ethereum. I didn't care that Ethereum was some revolutionary new technology. But it did bother me that I couldn't hold it in my hand. It was just a bunch of 1s and 0s. Should something happen, I would be left high and dry, my entire life savings lost to the ether, so to speak. I would have to start over from scratch. I still hadn't even paid off all my student loans. So I'd be in a hole. Perhaps Jisong was right: maybe Eun-sang was a troublemaker. Perhaps if I followed her, I'd get into a lot of trouble, too.

But, just this once, I decided to trust Eun-sang.

And it was all because of the graph Eun-sang had shown me two days earlier, a beautiful curve that only went up.

# J-curve

*2 May 2017*

I met Eun-sang in Cabin 3 at Coffee Bean just before the three-day weekend for the Buddha's birthday.

Lying on the table in front of her was a slab of light gold, soft, elegant and shiny.

'Is that the new iPad?'

'Yup.' Eun-sang gave a haughty look as she folded her arms and nodded.

Still standing, I picked up the iPad and ran my fingers over the round yet sharp edges, and the Apple logo on the back which sparkled like a well-polished mirror.

'It's so pretty. When did you buy it?'

'Take a seat.'

After grabbing me by my shirt and sitting me down next to her, Eun-sang rolled her iPad cover into a triangular pillar, *click-click*, and propped it up on the table. She then opened a spreadsheet called 'My Ethereum'. Recorded in this document were all of Eun-sang's investments, updated in real-time. Column A was the purchase date, column B was the price at time of purchase, and column C was the amount she had deposited. According to the spreadsheet, Eun-sang had bought 2,000,000 won's worth of Ethereum when one ether was worth just 7,252 won; she bought another 7,000,000 won's worth when the price hit 9,000 won, and it was at that point that she closed her instalment savings account. When the price passed 10,000 won, she invested the remaining 3,000,000 won of her savings. After that, there was a continuous stream of small investments. Eun-sang explained that she used her monthly pay checks to buy even more ether, taking only the minimum amount for living expenses and loan payments. As I stared at her screen, unable to peel my eyes away from the sesame seed-sized numbers, Eun-sang asked me a question.

'Do you know how much Ethereum is worth now?'

I shook my head, afraid of the answer. But instead of telling me directly, Eun-sang double-tapped the home button on her iPad and opened the web browser. The dense, white grid on her screen turned black, as though day had turned to night.

Arranged in a row on the browser's jet-black background were colourful bars of irregular heights, sporadically going up and down. Red and green bars. The two colours pierced my eyes like neon lights. Each time Eun-sang moved her thumb right or left across the screen, the colourful bars would flicker as they dashed across the display, like tiny flashing lights on a rapidly spinning Christmas tree. The red and green lights were jumping up and down chaotically. As I stared into the high-contrast colour scheme, I felt like I was starting to get tunnel vision. I didn't know where to focus, but then, finally, Eun-sang brought her screen to a stop and kindly directed my attention to a single number.

'92,350 won,' she said in a low voice. 'That's how much it's worth.'

I sat there for a second in awe, feeling the immense gap between this number and the original number of 7,252. Eun-sang made a wide V-shape with her thumb and index finger and touched them to the screen. She then quickly brought her two fingers together. As the distance between her fingers shortened, the graph zoomed out suddenly. The time range increased, and the bars became small and clustered. Then, out of the seemingly endless and random back and forth of red and green, a shape started to appear: a single large, steep curve that was shooting up as though it had been given enough energy to go stratospheric. It looked exponential. It looked like a J-curve.

I felt my stomach drop. The impact when it landed sent a shock wave through every cell in my body.

I was imagining myself at a fireworks show. A glowing firecracker had been shot up into the darkness. It was so high I had to look straight up to see it. Bursting with a *pop*, it sent a shower of orange sparks in every direction. But as the flashing fragments fell back down to earth, instead of sizzling, they jingled like tiny gold coins. I had yet to invest a single penny, but looking at this graph was enough to make me feel like I'd hit the jackpot. I was so overwhelmed by these images and emotions that I couldn't move.

Never in my life had I wished for something so much and not known until I'd seen it. This is what I'd been dreaming of. The letter J. This was what I so badly needed. The realisation that the thing I had been waiting for was none other than this geometrical shape, this curve, hit me like a defibrillator.

Day after day, I'd toiled away accumulating small, futile, pebble-like amounts of money. And yet I knew I wouldn't get anywhere building up my wealth one pebble at a time. I only persisted because it brought me comfort to know that I was participating in the daily grind and not quitting. Although I tried not to think about it too often, I was well aware of the fact that all it would take was some passer-by sneezing for everything I had built to come crashing down.

When I entered college and moved to Seoul for the first time, I lived in a three-person dorm room. Because I felt awkward and claustrophobic sharing a room with people I had just met for the first time and who were different from me in every way – major, background, personality, tastes, life patterns – I literally only went to that room to sleep. And even though I was only ever unconscious in that room, it still felt uncomfortable. I just could never get used to it.

The next year when I didn't get into the dorms, I found a boarding house behind campus. The place was located on the top floor of a commercial building, which had been partitioned into several smaller spaces. There were six rooms, one communal kitchen space, and two bathrooms. Eight students lived there, five girls and three boys, and there was only one toilet in the girls' bathroom. I never imagined that the chronic constipation I developed then would follow me to this day.

The bathroom alone convinced me it was definitely a downgrade from the dorms. At least in the dorms there were only three people to a toilet and not five.

The year after that, I moved to a 'premium' goshi-won. This was a bit of an oxymoron because goshiwons were by definition cheap studio apartments targeting students preparing for exams who didn't have money to spare. The reason I went a bit beyond my means and looked for a 'premium' goshiwon was that I absolutely had to have my own bathroom. To this day, I still don't understand why the barrier between that room and its bathroom wasn't a wall but a section of clear glass, as though it was some love hotel. Thanks to that, I realised a truth that few stop to think about: toilets don't have sizes. Technically, the shape of toilet openings can either be round or elongated, but their dimensions are basically the same. There's no such thing as an XL or XS toilet. Everyone, regardless of size, has to sit on the same sized toilet. Another way to look at it is that no matter how little space you have in a room, there's no way to shrink the toilet. Because of this, the smaller the room, the more one feels the presence of their toilet.

In that 140-square-foot room, it was impossible to escape that toilet behind the glass wall. It was always with me – when I woke up in the morning, when I drank water, when I changed clothes, when I ate, when I did homework or studied for tests. It was even with me up to the last second of the day as I lay waiting to fall asleep. I could always see out of the corner of my eye that glossy white object. I tried covering it, of course.

I bought all-purpose suction hooks, used the moisture from my breath to firmly adhere them to the glass, and hung up a large towel that just barely covered the toilet. But every other day or so, usually in the middle of the night, the pole would come crashing to the floor.

When I started earning a pay check, I was able to move into my current apartment. Up to that point, it was the biggest room I had lived in. It had a large window, and a bonus feature was that it was a perfect square, as opposed to a tight rectangle. Indeed, it was only after moving into my current place that I realised how strange my previous squished pentagon-shaped boarding room was. It had so many angles, and each of its sides was a different length. In fact, the room was such a disorienting shape that I often had nightmares of a large, ugly polygon crushing me and stabbing me with its sharp vertices. That's why I so appreciated this neat square of a room. The only problem was those damned thresholds! No area to take off my shoes, no lip in front of the bathroom. No boundaries, nothing to stop the trespassing dirt from my shoes, or the bath water seeping out from under the bathroom door.

But I was definitely heading in the right direction. Each new place had at least three improvements to one drawback – progress of a kind. But it wasn't just my living situation. My whole life felt that way. With each year that passed, from the time I was born to now, my life was always getting a little better – or perhaps a little less bad. My life was like poor-quality back-stitching. A clumsy back and forth that nevertheless trudged forward. In that way, at least I wasn't stuck in place. But the progress. It was so slow. Little by little. Piece by piece. Day by day. But would I dare ask for more?

Yes! I was sick and tired of being a shitty seamstress. I wanted to strap a booster rocket to my back and get to my dreams already. I wanted to skip the tedium. I wanted to leap! I needed exponential growth. I had never been allowed to skip the line like that – such a thing had never even seemed like a possibility – and because of this, I had never expected it, let alone desired it. But now here it was, flickering right before my eyes.

J.

As soon as I saw it, I immediately recognised it as the thing I wanted.

Eun-sang pressed the home button on her iPad again. This time, she selected the app icon with a dark purple graduated background and the word 'GO' in white text. She showed me her cryptocurrency wallet, how much Ethereum she had, and how much that equated to in real money.

136,000,000 KRW.

'This is insane.' These words escaped my mouth.

'Dahae, you're exactly right. This *is* insane.'

Eun-sang's voice was shaking slightly, as though she really couldn't believe how much money she'd made. She told me that she hadn't been able to focus on work all day because Ethereum had been going through the roof since the morning. She also told me that this had happened several times this week already. Sudden spike, after sudden spike, after sudden spike.

When I heard this, I felt depressed. Perhaps it was already too late for me. Eun-sang read my mind and insisted that if I was going to get in, now was the time to start. She told me that this was how it always was; that the more it shot up, the more you had to buy, that you got rich by riding the upward trend, that the dumbest thing you could do was buy when it was on the way down, that once it started falling, the only thing that was going to happen was more falling, that you needed to chase the upward trend, that it was going to keep rising because it had momentum, that it still had a long way to go.

I later learned that Eun-sang read about crypto-currency every day on an internet forum. Not only that, she also kept abreast of the latest breakthroughs in technology by religiously reading (with the help of an online translator) the newsletters sent out by Ethereum's founder, Vitalik Buterin. And according to her own judgement, Ethereum wasn't just going to be as valuable as Bitcoin, it was going to surpass it.

After a while of my not responding, Eun-sang repeatedly waved her hand in the air as if she were call-ing someone in the distance to come quickly. As she did this, she nodded her head in time with her hand and whispered furtively:

'Jump in. Before it's too late.'

Perhaps because of her choice of words, I imagined myself standing on the edge of a precipice. My toes were dangling over the threshold of a door that led from a world of endless toil to a world of leisure and luxury.

But even so, I was reluctantly leaning backward, into the world I'd always known.

'Dahae. Look.'

She paused for a moment before continuing.

'I'm going to pay off my debt. Right now.'

Eun-sang took out her phone and opened her mobile banking app. She showed me her bank account. Yesterday, she told me, she had withdrawn 15,000,000 won from her Ethereum wallet and transferred it to her bank account. As she told me this, she navigated on the bank's app to loans, and then payments. Finally, she selected the option to pay off the loan in full, all 14,000,000 won of it, and pressed confirm. A one-line message appeared on her screen:

**Your loan has been paid off in full.**

'Look. Now I'm debt-free.'

She paused before asking:

'Didn't you say you have student loans too?'

I did. So what? From what I could tell, Eun-sang had only borrowed just enough to pay for tuition. I on the other hand had taken out loans for both my tuition and all my living expenses. I would need a lot more than 14,000,000 won to pay off my debt.

'Make the jump already. Can I be honest with you? People like us... this is all we've got.'

As I sat there lost in thought and unable to respond, Eun-sang asked me another, this time somewhat random, question. She wanted to know if I watched that old cartoon show when I was a kid, the one about time travel.

'You know, that one with the weird kettle that wore sunglasses?'

*Time Travel Tondekeman.* Of course, I remembered. The anime about kids who discovered a tea kettle called Tondekeman made by a genius scientist from the future, which magically created a portal allowing the main characters to travel through space and time. Eun-sang then asked me to remember where those portals led.

'They always took them to random, unexpected places. Places they could never have imagined. And the portal always closed after ten minutes.'

Eun-sang then pointed to the Ethereum graph on her iPad screen and said that this was no different. This portal to a world beyond our wildest imaginations was going to close just as quickly as it opened. Just like the flashing blue tunnel in *Time Travel Tondekeman*, this tunnel from one world to another was only going to get smaller as more people passed through it. And eventually it would seal shut with a *sha-sha-sha*. If we didn't take it as soon as it opened, we would miss our chance forever.

'For people like us, this is a once-in-a-lifetime opportunity. It's temporary and completely coincidental.'

The words 'people like us' continued to echo in my ears.

The reason why Eun-sang, Jisong and I were able to become so close so quickly was because we had a tacit understanding that we were of the same ilk. One of the many things I learned over the past few years was that just because you worked at the same company and received the same pay check did not mean you lived the same life. Between people was a line, an invisible change in elevation, like a hierarchical staircase. And people could only talk about work-related things for so long; eventually, people had to reveal things about their personal life. It could be anywhere: by the water cooler, at lunch, in the elevator or the lobby, during office parties or over post-work drinks, on the commute home. I also couldn't help but eavesdrop on conversations as I walked past people. I would pick up on small, revealing bits of information, and then realise that they existed in a space above me. I didn't do this on purpose; it was just something that happened.

Through small talk, people revealed if they came from money or not: in what neighbourhood they grew up; whether they drove or took public transportation to work; what they did on the weekends; where they went for their vacations; what their parents did for a living. I would learn that they lived in Gangnam; that they were educated abroad; that their parents were professors or doctors. Once I knew their background, I couldn't help but feel something inside me shrivel up every time I was around them. Indeed, it was this feeling of atrophy that I felt first, even before I could put a clichéd or embarrassing name to the emotion, like jealousy or envy. Of course, I hated that I felt like this, but I couldn't help it. This wasn't one of those things you could control. Even though we worked at the same company and earned the same pay check, even though on the outside we didn't look that different, everyone existed in a completely different reality from me — everyone but Eun-sang and Jisong. And every once in a while, it even felt like that chasm was getting larger.

People who revealed such things about themselves, of course, had no ill intent. They were only having normal conversations about everyday happenings. They probably didn't even realise that revealing such information could make someone else feel small. They probably didn't judge people on where they lived, what their parents did, or how much money they had. If they knew there was someone that judged others' backgrounds, they would think them uncultured. In other words, they would judge them on their character, instead.

I couldn't do that. Even though I knew it was a bad attitude to have, I couldn't help but catch every little secret someone revealed about themselves and where they came from. I couldn't help but draw a line, and place myself beneath it, making myself small and distancing myself from them.

Then one day, I had a realisation. All of a sudden, I understood how some people could work at such a miserly company with such a happy look on their face all the time. Now I understood how they could have fun at their job, feel accomplished after working overtime, and be so passionate about everything. Some people didn't need to worry about working for pennies, because they knew that when they got married, their parents would still buy them a house and a car. And even if their parents didn't pay for everything, they would still pay for part of it. How comfortable a life that must have been. Not having a care in the world. If only I could live like that. I'd feel so secure. I bet they didn't even know how petty I was. Who knows, they might even have thought I was one of their own. I was less jealous that they grew up with means, and more jealous of the fact that they had the positive disposition to accept people as they were. People like me only brooded and sulked from envy, and struggled to make friends.

But when I talked with Eun-sang and Jisong, I didn't feel these things. From the first day we met each other, I intuitively knew we came from the same reality. This formed the basis of our friendship; meeting and talking more only made us more certain of our similarities. No matter how much we revealed about our lives, there was nothing that set one of us apart from the others. Our parents hadn't gone to college; they didn't work for the government; they were blue-collar workers. Because of this, none of us was able to receive financial help from our parents. All our families had debts they couldn't pay off. We lived in cheap housing in unpopular neighbourhoods; we could only afford small studio apartments. I could let my guard down and be friends with people like Eun-sang and Jisong. When I was with them, I could forget how crummy my life was compared to other people's. The only thing I thought while meeting them was that we were all trying our hardest to get by. Until now.

However, as things currently stood, only Eun-sang had cut the iron chains from her ankles and jumped through that glowing portal that had suddenly punched a hole through time and space. She was just on the other side, waving her hand to me, seconds away from moving farther into the beyond. I wanted to enter too, if only I could. I wanted to cut the heavy shackles from my legs and leap into that world. And there it was, flickering in front of my eyes, that perfect 1.2-room apartment with its mini bedroom and vaulted ceiling.

On my way home from the cafe, I called the realtor.

'That apartment we looked at. I want to move in there when the renovations are over. I'll send the money now.'

I opened my mobile banking app and sent her the holding deposit. I then downloaded BitGo, the app Eun-sang had told me about. As I waited for the app to install, I checked my bank account. My instalment savings account had already reached maturity, and the balance had been transferred automatically to my regular savings account.

I spent two more days biting my nails before finally buying 3,000,000 won's worth of Ethereum.

# Part Two

# To the Moon

*5 May 2017*

The price of one ether hit 149,980 won. I'd been worried that this was the end of the J-curve, but it turned out that we were at the beginning of yet another spike in prices. In fact, my entire investment in cryptocurrency went from 3,000,000 won to 4,000,000 won overnight. But my initial excitement was short-lived. Why had I only put in three million? Thankfully, I had enough money in my savings account to buy another 4,000,000 won's worth of Ethereum.

*19 May 2017*

One ether was now 164,850 won, and my virtual assets totalled 8,890,000 won.

I'd thought I would be calling myself crazy for investing in something as dangerous as cryptocurrency. I'd thought I would need time to self-reflect because I'd lost my mind and all my money. It was this anticipation of failure that prevented me from going all in like Eun-sang had advocated. But now I felt crazy for not buying more at the beginning. I should have thrown in my entire life savings. Why hadn't I? Why was I so timid?

I tossed and turned every night. I knew there was only one way to put my regret to rest. I had to take the money from all my accounts and buy more ether. I would set aside only the bare minimum each month for living expenses.

*21 May 2017*

1 ETH = 204,300 KRW
Virtual assets = 19,690,000 KRW

Strangely, the more money I made, the happier and angrier I became. I was happier for obvious reasons, but I was angry at myself, perhaps even furious, for not being more confident. I'd already put all my money into Ethereum, but I lamented the fact that I hadn't done it sooner. If I'd invested 30,000,000 won when one ether had been 100,000 won, I would have 60,000,000 won by now. And if I'd had 100,000,000 won to invest, I'd have 200,000,000 won by now. These were the kinds of pointless hypotheticals I painted in my mind. As it was, I had already made a respectable profit, but I rarely thought about *that* money. All I could think about was the money I could have made had I invested more and earlier.

*22 May 2017*

1 ETH = 269,400 KRW
Virtual assets = 25,970,000 KRW

I was anxious. This seemed like the upward trend Eun-sang had told me about. And if what she'd said was true, the only thing left for it to do was continue rising. I needed to buy more before that happened. I prematurely withdrew everything from my instalment savings accounts, into which I paid 50,000 won every month, so I could buy more ether. And still, all I could think about was how I wished I had more money to invest.

I even noticed a post on the company bulletin board that I normally wouldn't have given the time of day. The notice said that the company had found a new securities firm to manage employee severance pay, and that those interested could receive an interim settlement. That night, I got a message from Eun-sang. She told me to apply for the interim settlement because it was a good chance to get a large sum of cash.

**Dahae**
I already did.
**Eun-sang**
That's my girl.

As soon as the money was deposited into my account, I was going to buy more ether.

*23 May 2017*

1 ETH = 246,400 KRW
Virtual assets = 25,580,000 KRW

*24 May 2017*

1 ETH = 270,200 KRW
Virtual assets = 28,000,000 KRW

*27 May 2017*

1 ETH = 200,400 KRW
Virtual assets = 21,000,000 KRW

That day, I received my interim severance package. It wasn't a huge amount of money, but it was a lot to me. I used all of it to buy more ether.

*1 June 2017*

1 ETH = 304,000 KRW
Virtual assets: 49,700,000 KRW

Eun-sang told me that her virtual assets now totalled 390,000,000 won. Even though I had turned a large profit, all I could think about was that I needed more money. I tried opening another line of credit at my old bank, but they told me that I couldn't because I had too many unpaid loans and debts. So I borrowed 3,000,000 won from a savings bank, and used all of it to, of course, buy more ether.

*2 June 2017*

Of course, it wasn't all smooth sailing. The price didn't always increase; sometimes it fell. Every time this happened, I felt like I might die of a panic attack. Sometimes it only lasted for two days, but other times it fell for ten days straight. And every time, I considered pulling out while I was ahead. Perhaps it was time to cash in. After all, what if it tanked and I lost all my money overnight? Whenever I worried like this, I always went to Eun-sang for advice.

'Dahae, it fell for an entire month last December. It's called a nosedive. It's unpredictable by nature. Ethereum almost went back to its opening price. Do you know what I was thinking at the time? I was thinking the same thing you're thinking right now. I wanted to sell everything and get out, like when I used to invest in stocks. But I couldn't bring myself to press the sell button.'

Eun-sang told me the reason she held was because of a newsletter Vitalik Buterin had sent out. After poring over the letter, she realised this couldn't be the end of Ethereum, and she decided not to sell. Eun-sang asked me a question:

'If I hadn't held, if I'd sold everything and got out, what would I be thinking now?'

There was only one right answer. She would be kicking herself in regret.

'Just hold. You need diamond hands if you want to get rich.'

Time proved Eun-sang right. Even though it was nerve-racking to hold, it was only a few days before the price started to rise again. Indeed, the coin was volatile. All I had to do was endure it for a little while; soon I would realise that this period of uncertainty and decline was nothing but the start of another J-curve. From one all-time high to a new all-time high. A period of unimpeded growth. And every time the y-axis of the graph had to expand to accommodate the soaring green bars, Eun-sang and I would take a screenshot of the graph and post it in the NOR(3) group chat. I would check my phone as soon as I opened my eyes in the morning, and the first thing I would do when I got into the office was turn on my computer and open up our group chat. Sometimes I was first, other times it was Eun-sang. Unable to hold back our delight, we would scream everyday:

**Dahae**
Let's go!
**Eun-sang**
Let's gooo!
**Dahae**
Come on, 1,000,000!

Once one ether surpassed 400,000 won, I started calling Eun-sang 'Captain'.

**Dahae**
Captain Kang! I believe in you!
**Eun-sang**
Come on, 1,000,000,000 won.
**Dahae**
O Captain! My Captain!

Jisong, however, was always quiet. She didn't even respond to our messages. But then one day, after being silent for so long, Jisong finally spoke up, saying she couldn't hold it back any longer.

**Jisong**
How long are you guys going to keep this up? Would you please stop?

She then posted a notice in the chat.

**Jisong**

[NOTICE] Banned words and phrases in NOR(3): coin, Ethereum, Captain, let's go and any variant spellings, and diamond hands. Any screenshots of BitGo are prohibited.

**Jisong**

Last warning. If you send any more messages about cryptocurrency, I'm leaving the chat.

**Dahae**

O Captain! I believe in my Captain!

**Eun-sang**

And where are we going?

**Dahae**

To the moon!

**Jisong**

Have you two lost your minds? Is this really how it's going to be?

**Eun-sang**

But you should stop complaining and join us!
*Jisong Kim has left the chat.*

Afraid that we'd gone too far, I frantically reinvited her.

**Dahae**

All right, I'm sorry.

**Dahae**

We won't talk about cryptocurrency any more in front of you, I guess...

Jisong berated Eun-sang and me as soon as she re-entered the chat. She said she had held her tongue until now, but that the two of us looked silly to her, getting so excited over how much money we were making.

Jisong was drawing attention to the fact our wallets weren't 'real' in the traditional sense of the word. She said it was just a number on our phones; that the digits hadn't turned into real money; that the two of us looked so foolish staring all day every day at our virtual wallets as if we had real cash in our hands, when our coins could very well become worthless overnight; that she'd thought we were doing it just for fun, but after seeing us repeat the same routine day in day out over the last several weeks she'd realised it was not just for fun.

She only laughed at first, she said, but now she was worried because it seemed like we really believed that our virtual wallets and real wallets were the same. She said she wasn't interested in investing, regardless of how much we made, of how much was in our virtual wallets. She didn't want to hear about it any more and wanted us to stop talking about such things in front of her.

Perhaps most importantly, Jisong said listening to us made her uncomfortable because it gave her the feeling of missing out. Being so close to us as we talked all day about earning ridiculous amounts of money, she felt like she had incurred a huge loss even though her life hadn't changed at all. We were making her feel dumb for not being interested in financial independence, guilty for not taking action when she could be making a fortune.

**Jisong**
I hate myself for being unable to stop myself from thinking these things. It upsets and bothers me. Why do I have to experience such discomfort because of you two?

94

**Eun-sang**

Jisong, didn't you say earlier that you weren't interested in how much we make?

Jisong didn't answer.

**Eun-sang**

I thought you weren't interested. But... I think you are interested. That feeling, that feeling of being deprived of something... that means you're interested. You want to earn money just like us. Don't deny it. And I think there's something you've got wrong. The money in your virtual wallet can immediately be turned into cash. The only reason we haven't yet is because we want to make more money... This money is our money.

Eun-sang shared a link in the chat.

**Eun-sang**

You can do it with us. It's not too late. Just click on the link. It's an article posted two days ago by Vitalik Buterin.

**Jisong**

Stop it! Just stop! I told you already I'm not going to do that stuff.

Jisong then brought up something from several years ago. She asked us if we remembered how Eun-sang and I had almost lost our minds investing in the stock market, if we remembered how after weeks of day trading, we barely broke even, if we remembered how we attempted to sugarcoat things by saying, 'At least we didn't *lose* money.' She said she didn't want to be stressed all day looking at graphs. She just didn't have the time or energy.

Then out of nowhere, she changed the subject.

**Jisong**
It's already 10. Don't you guys have work to do? I've got a lot of things to do today, so don't message me.

After a few minutes, Jisong sent one last message.

**Jisong**
To be honest, I think you two are playing with fire.

I closed the chat without responding. Just as I was about to get back into the flow of work, my taskbar started flashing. It was Eun-sang. But this time, she was messaging me not through NOR(3) but our private chat.

**Eun-sang**
Should we talk here for now?

Even after the fight, Eun-sang and I didn't change our behaviour. Whenever we had a spare moment, we would share screenshots of Ethereum's price graph, and scream, 'O Captain! Let's go! Let's gooo!' Eun-sang changed the name of our new group chat to 'To the Moon'. It was then that we promised each other not to sell until we'd made it to the moon.

My daily life revolved around that graph.

An orange line that connected bars of red and blue. Above that thin line was my life savings, every penny I'd saved up over the last ten years. My life, my fate, was riding that line.

Over those two months, the price fluctuated wildly on a daily basis. As a result, it felt like my mental state was riding a see-saw. The price of Ethereum went as high as 480,000 won and as low as 130,000 won. As a result, my life savings went from 90,000,000 won to 20,000,000 won.

A sum of money larger than I had ever experienced was popping in and out of existence right before my eyes. Every day I felt like my entire soul was being shaken to its core.

I spent most of my days thinking regretfully, 'I should have sold when it hit 480,000 won...' Even when I tried to focus on other things, these words of regret repeated themselves in the back of my mind. Of course, at the time, I had wanted to hold out until it hit 500,000 won. It was so strange. Technically, I hadn't lost any money, but I couldn't help but feel like someone had stolen 70,000,000 won from me. I often felt anger directed at some unknown entity, and for this I pitied myself.


Thankfully, Ethereum was again showing an upward trend. The price was fluctuating around 300,000 won. I pressed the minus button several times and zoomed out of the graph. The bars, which rose and fell like the heart rate of someone high on adrenaline, suddenly shrank, tracing out the silhouette of the side of a large mountain. No longer visible was that tiny valley; the only thing that I could see was a large upward trend emerging from minuscule valleys and peaks.

It was clear to me now.

The price of Ethereum had decisively jumped to a new level. I was certain that now, no matter how steep of a nosedive it took, it was going to be nearly impossible for it to drop below 100,000 won, the price at which I had bought in.

We were in high gear now.

It probably started around that time. As I drafted proposals, wrote up reports, and sent obsequious emails to client companies, a single word, tantalisingly cozy, was crawling on the surface of my mind: quit.

I'd had enough. I knew it might seem ridiculous of me to say this as someone who hadn't even been around long enough to be promoted to assistant manager, but I'd truly had enough. I was sick of this conservative company, its moronic bosses, the measly wages, and my lack of influential connections to elevate me. I was sick of doing meaningless work that didn't lead to personal growth. I was sick of this stubborn industry that showed no intention of ever changing or innovating or trying to push itself. I could no longer see my future here.

I closed the weekly report spreadsheet I was working on and opened a new one. In it, I wrote a formula to calculate based on the current value of Ethereum how much my virtual assets were worth in won, and the per cent return I had earned on my initial investments. At the same time, I thought of the big picture. My initial plan was to get out when one ether hit 500,000 won, but even if it did hit that mark, would I have enough to quit my job? I would have about 100,000,000 won, but what was I going to do with 100,000,000 won and no job? Could I move to a one-bedroom apartment, one with a real bedroom separate from the kitchen? Oh, how nice would that be! I could have a decent couch, not a mini sofa, and even room for a TV.

But if all that money was tied up in a large security deposit, which was probably going to be in the tens of millions of won, what would I survive on?

It seemed I had reached an impasse. I would need to set higher goals. What about 1,000,000 won for one ether? Would that be enough? How much would I be worth then?

But then again, would that day really come?

Once when I expressed doubt like this, Eun-sang reassured me in an unusually fervent manner:

**Eun-sang**
That day will come.
**Dahae**
Really?
**Eun-sang**
I said it will, didn't I? As long as you have diamond hands.

Eun-sang then sent me a JPEG file. The image was the famous movie poster from Steven Spielberg's *E.T.*, but the bike in front of the moon had been replaced with the image of a sports car. Beneath the picture were these words:

How to turn a Prius into a Lamborghini:

1. Sell Prius
2. Buy Ethereum
3. Hold Ethereum
4. Sell Ethereum
5. Buy Lamborghini

A large, brilliant, round moon in an indigo blue sky, behind which were the words 'To the Moon' in cursive. I downloaded the image and set it as the chatroom wallpaper. I opened the Excel spreadsheet I had been working on in an attempt to get some work done. But as soon as I did this, I was seized once again by the monotony of it all. I was so fed up that I was fed up with being fed up. With every passing day, I had less desire to work. My time at the office was an endless series of Ctrl + Ws and Ctrl + Shift + Ts. I had never been particularly passionate about work, but over the last two months of spending hours every day staring at rising and falling graphs, my job had become even less of a priority. Perhaps this was why I started doing things I normally wouldn't touch with a ten-foot pole.

# Madam Yeonwol

*18 July 2017*

I couldn't remember the last time our entire team had gone out for lunch at the local tonkatsu restaurant. I was enjoying my meal in peace when out of nowhere Team Leader Koh began talking about fortune-telling.

'Is there anyone who wants to visit a fortune-teller near the office this week?'

'A fortune-teller?'

'There's an excellent fortune-teller around here named Madam Yeonwol who does house calls. A travelling fortune-teller of sorts. All the other departments are going in groups to see her. It's 60,000 won per person if you visit her shop, but 30,000 won per person if you want her to come to you. The only catch is you need a group of at least three people for that. Is there anyone who wants to go with me?'

I had heard of this before, while sitting with Jisong and Eun-sang in Cabin 1 at Coffee Bean a few months ago. In the corner of the cafe was an elderly woman scribbling furiously in a journal. This in itself wouldn't have been that strange if it weren't for the fact that the person sitting across from her changed every fifteen minutes. After each person's fifteen minutes was up, they would get up and be replaced by a new face. The only thing the people who came to see her had in common was that they were wearing the same company badge around their neck. Everything else – their gender, age, even the colour of the badge – was different.

It was Eun-sang who explained to me that the old woman was a travelling fortune-teller. Travelling fortune-tellers usually worked in areas with a lot of companies. So naturally, they were popular in our neighbourhood, which was home to all of Korea's best confectionary companies. And each fortune-teller had their own turf. Sangam-dong, where all the broadcasting companies were located, had its own resident travelling fortune-teller, and so did the finance hub Yeouido, and Pangyo, the Silicon Valley of Korea. Employees came to these fortune-tellers with all manner of questions: if they should get married to their current partner; when they were going to get that promotion; what to name their ambitious new product; whose side to take in the bloody struggle for power in the company; what direction their company was headed in; whether they should quit and find a new job or start their own business. The advantages of a travelling fortune-teller were that sessions were short, which meant you could get quick answers to the questions you wanted, and, of course, that the fortune-teller would come to you. In general, they specialised in reading fortunes based on the Four Pillars of Destiny, which were determined by a person's birth year, month, day and hour, but these days they also did tarot cards. In particular, they would analyse your current plight with the Four Pillars of Destiny, and then use tarot cards to offer solutions. And those who were skilled made people think they actually had supernatural powers. All they had to do was get one consequential thing right and rumours would do the rest of the work until they had a monopoly on the entire neighbourhood.

'They usually charge 50,000 won for walk-ins at their shop,' Eun-sang explained. 'But if you call them to your neighbourhood, they read your fortunes for about 20,000 to 30,000 won.'

'How can it be cheaper if they're coming to you?' I asked.

Eun-sang rubbed her thumb and fingers together.

'I don't know, but it must be profitable if they're doing it.' She then added, 'Small profits, quick returns, I guess.'

Now I was hearing that same explanation, but from Team Leader Koh. Why of all places had I chosen to sit right across from him, where I had a front row seat to the inside of his blabbering mouth and a mass of half-digested tonkatsu?

'In general, they specialise in the Four Pillars of Destiny, but this person pairs it with tarot. Is there anyone who wants to join me?'

Much to my surprise, almost everyone raised their hand. I was shocked that *anyone* raised their hand, let alone everyone. I was especially shocked to see Assistant Manager Park, who as far as I knew was a devout Christian. Everyone looked so happy on the outside, but I guess they all had their own worries. But what could they be? The hand that surprised me the most, however, was my own; it went in the air once it realised it was the odd one out. Dahae, who never had her fortune read and who didn't believe in the supernatural.

I thought about what I would ask the fortune-teller. Recently, I had been feeling a bit uneasy, but I couldn't imagine being able to explain it to anyone, especially not a fortune-teller. Is this what my life had come to? Here I was; I'd thrown my entire life savings into cryptocurrency and was dreaming of quitting my job, and now I was going to ask a fortune-teller for advice? The absurdity of it all made me want to laugh.

I unlocked my phone under the table, which was sticky from a light film of mysterious dried liquid (probably either tonkatsu sauce or salad dressing). BitGo was already open. I glanced furtively at the graph. Just this morning it was above 300,000 won, but now it was below 300,000 again. My chest felt tight with anxiety. I became nauseous, like something was working its way up my oesophagus. It was the first time I hadn't been able to finish a plate of cheese-stuffed tonkatsu.

A little more than a week later, it was time for our scheduled lunchtime appointment with Madam Yeonwol. But as noon approached, one after another, all the people who had raised their hands at the tonkatsu restaurant started sending messages saying they couldn't make it. A norovirus infection, a sudden meeting with a client company, a religious conflict – everyone had their reason. The only ones left were Team Leader Koh, soon-to-be married General Manager Yun, and poor little me. To say I was uncomfortable would be a gross understatement. Spending time outside the office with them, two people way above my rank and age, sounded like torture. Not to mention the fact that I was the only female. But I had no choice. If I cancelled and prevented them from achieving the minimum group size of three people, I would put them in a difficult situation. Now that I thought about it, I should have known that it was best to avoid something I felt uneasy about.

At ten minutes to noon, I went to my team leader to ask him a question.

'What time should I arrive at the cafe?'

'Twelve o'clock sharp,' he answered without looking away from his monitor. 'We'll go together.'

'Together?'

'Yes, the three of us. Don't tell me you were planning on going by yourself?'

'I... thought each of us had our own time slot.'

'It's only the three of us now. There's no need for that. And besides, I'll be bored if I go alone.'

He then lowered his voice as he added:

'Actually, I heard this fortune-teller has real psychic powers. I want to go together because I'm afraid I might be overwhelmed by her aura.'

But even then, I didn't fully understand what he meant by 'all together'. I had thought that we would go to the cafe as a group but talk with the fortune-teller one at a time. Because of this, I didn't press the issue. It felt like common sense. But there was something I had overlooked: people with common sense were rare.

I had also forgotten that my standard for common sense was probably too high.

Indeed, what my manager had meant by 'all together' was not what I had thought he'd meant. What he wanted was for us to sit at one table together and have our fortunes read aloud for everyone to hear. He wanted us to expose our inner troubles not just to the fortune-teller, but to our work colleagues as well. If I'd known this was going to happen, I'd never have volunteered to go, group discount or not. I'd much rather go on my own and pay the full price or go with Eun-sang and Jisong.

I wanted to cry as I sat there and learned more than I had ever wanted to know about General Manager Yun's personal life: his marriage preparations, the likelihood of his engagement being broken off, the tension within their family. And General Manager Yun probably wanted to cry just as much as I, if not more. After all, was there anyone on this planet who would want to reveal such shameful and private family matters in front of their subordinate and team leader? And yet, it seemed like he wanted to get his money's worth; he asked a lot of questions, revealed all his worries, and followed all the fortune-teller's instructions as he chose tarot cards and diligently took notes. He even got choked up at one point.

Next was my turn.

Madam Yeonwol turned to a new page in her journal and looked me in the eye. Her hair was pulled back in a tight bun, a traditional Korean hairstyle called jjok-jin meori. Her terrifyingly defined middle parting was stark white and contrasted with her jet black eyebrow tattoos. Her eyes had a bright sparkle. She had such a striking appearance that I felt intimidated just making eye contact.

'What was the date and time of your birth?'

I timidly gave her the numbers, and she wrote them down in her journal with a black felt-tip pen. As she did this, she used her fingers to calculate something, then scribbled down a few Chinese characters beneath my date and time of birth. She took out a red felt-tip pen from the pocket of her white shirt and started making check marks according to what seemed like some detailed system.

'Young lady, you're smart, aren't you? But despite your brains, you couldn't go to a good university, am I right?'

How could she know that? I felt like she'd started by grabbing me by the nape of my neck and forcing me to my knees. I didn't show any reaction to this because I didn't want to seem surprised.

'Your health was poor the year you took the CSAT, am I right?'

I wasn't sick the entire year, but on the day of the test, I did suffer from really bad body aches. I had to go to the testing centre with a high fever. Only after a few seconds did I respond to her with a nod.

'I knew it. That's why you weren't able to get into a good university. Listen to me carefully. You are fire. Look. In your Four Pillars of Destiny there are four fireballs. That means you have a lot of anger. But look at the year you took the CSAT. These characters represent a large flowing river. What happens to fire when it jumps into a river?'

She had an intimidating aura. She wasn't blinking, and her pupils were completely still. I was beginning to wonder if she was even human. Gazing into her unwavering eyes, I felt like we were having a staring contest, so I uncomfortably diverted my eyes towards her journal. As she overwhelmed me with questions, she continued to write down characters in her journal that I couldn't read. The sound of her felt-tip pen on the paper sounded like the slithering of a snake on the ground. I felt myself being overpowered by this mesmerising sound and the strong energy she was emitting. I was being swept along, unable to catch my breath. Finally, I answered her hesitantly:

'It... goes out?'

'Exactly. Your opportunity went out because you met the wrong current. In other words, it wasn't your fault, young lady. Even if you had tried harder, there was no way a ball of fire like yourself could do anything against a surging river. But the year after would have been a good year for you. If you had deferred a year and taken the CSAT again, you probably would have gone to an even better college than you thought you could. If you had been a bit more ambitious, you could have gone here...'

The fortune-teller then wrote a capital 'E' on her paper and underscored it twice. Anyone would know that this referred to Ewha Womans University, but she seemed to feel the need to make it ambiguous, like someone not wanting to boast about the fact they went to a top university.

'But it wasn't like you to retake the CSAT, am I right? You're not the wilful type, someone who tries to change their circumstances. You just go where things take you... You let things take you wherever... You've just floated your way through life, haven't you? You're not completely satisfied with your circumstances, but life is already difficult enough. You don't have the energy to stop what's already been put in motion. Going with the flow is what's comfortable for you. Am I right?'

I could feel pins and needles on my skin all the way down to the bottom of my feet. It was the first time anyone – including myself – had so decisively, and in such concrete language, described my personality and attitude towards life. It was at this time that Team Leader Koh injected himself into the conversation.

'Please, tell us about her future with the company. She's an important part of our team.'

He was giving me false praise to hide his true intentions.

'Let's see. Yes, the company.'

Madam Yeonwol was looking down at her journal. She circled in red the bundle of Chinese characters she had written beneath my date and time of birth.

'It says here that this young lady doesn't work very hard.'

'What?' I screamed out.

'You only use about 70 per cent of your abilities. You are after all very intelligent. It says you only use 70 per cent but pretend like you're working hard and using 100 per cent.'

How did she know? My heart was pounding out of my chest. I'm ruined. Acutely aware of Team Leader Koh's gaze which was locked onto the side of my head like a missile, I raised my voice:

'What are you talking about!'

'Did I say something?'

'I'm not like that.'

'Why are you getting mad at me? I'm just telling you what I see. It's all here. Look, it says here that you don't work hard. It says you're a lazy person who takes short cuts. It's not a bad thing. Because you're smart and fast, you can work at your own pace and things will still come out well. But you can still give more. Am I right? Or am I wrong?'

This was getting out of control. And with every second and every accurate description, I was getting more and more creeped out. I was trying to avoid my team leader's gaze, but I could feel every movement of his intense eyes as though they were tracing bull's-eyes around my temples. It was a mistake coming here. This is not what I wanted. As I sat there flustered, the fortune-teller took her deck of tarot cards, tapped their edges on the table to organise them, and then spread them out in a semicircle on the navy blue mat she had prepared earlier.

'Pick three cards. And while you do that, think about your work.'

No, anything but that. I knew something bad was going to happen if I picked those cards.

'Enough. I'm done.'

I hurriedly took out three 10,000-won bills from my wallet and handed them to the fortune-teller. She didn't hesitate for even a moment, swiftly taking the bills and putting them into her red patent leather wallet. She took out a business card with her picture on it, pinched it with her thumb and middle finger, and extended it towards me, slanted downward.

'I offer post-consulting as well. Send me a message through KakaoTalk.'

She then turned to my manager as if to say, 'It's your turn next, right?' I had planned on storming out of the session, but realising it was Team Leader Koh's turn, I changed my mind. I didn't want to let him off the hook that easily. If nothing else, I wanted to hear his embarrassing fortune before leaving. That was the only thing that was going to make me feel better. General Manager Yun was staring intently at our team leader's lips as though he had the same idea. But then, out of nowhere, Team Leader Koh looked at us and said with a stern look on his face:

'You two can leave now. I have some things I want to ask in private.'

The nerve! Did he think he was the only one who had a private life? What about me? I should have known. My manager was anything but normal. That lying, scheming, back-stabbing son of a bitch! General Manager Yun and I exchanged frustrated looks as we slowly collected our belongings. General Manager Yun opened the glass door and exited first. I was about to follow him out when I heard the high-pitched voice of my manager.

'Dahae Jeong!'

Startled, I turned around.

'Yes?'

'I know you're trying hard—'

He paused for a moment before continuing.

'But I also know you can do better.'

'...'

'Try harder, OK?'

'... Yes, sir.'

When I came out of the cafe, I was hit by air so warm it was almost suffocating. General Manager Yun, who unsurprisingly was in a bad mood, told me that I should go back first because he was going to have a smoke. Holding my stomach, which was empty because I'd skipped lunch, I started slowly walking back to the office in the unbearable heat of the midsummer afternoon sun.

I hadn't done anything wrong. But for some reason, my cheeks were burning. At first, I thought it was because I had been exposed for not being passionate about my job and not working my hardest, but after walking a bit farther, I realised it wasn't just that.

I had always thought that my team leader was just an ignorant puppet who was dependent on other people doing the heavy lifting. He entered the company when it was easy to get hired and was stubborn enough to stay around until he became someone whose seniority mattered. He was stupid. Stupid and lazy. And I had thought I could see right through him.

But now I realised that might not be quite true. Perhaps he knew that I thought I could see right through him. In that sense, it was I who had been seen through. Perhaps he was just pretending not to notice. Perhaps he knew that if he played stupid, his subordinates would take on all his responsibilities and work for him. That way, he could have an easy time in the company and do nothing all day long. Perhaps it was my manager, and not me, who was the lazy one, the one who always looked for short cuts. Perhaps I was the stupid one. Was this really what it was?

The more I walked, the hungrier I became. There were only thirteen minutes left in my lunch break. Team Leader Koh would probably return late from his session with Madam Yeonwol, but I knew it would look bad if I got lunch and came back even later than him. Not to mention the fact that I was already on thin ice because of what the fortune-teller had told us. Maybe I could have a ten-minute bowl of bean sprout soup? If I ate fast and ran, I could probably get back before 1 p.m. As I thought this, I passed by a corn dog shop. A few corn dogs would be perfect – maybe even better than bean sprout soup. I could order three, eat two there, and eat the last one while walking back. As I thought this, my mood improved. I opened the glass door to the shop, entered, and shouted out in a hurry:

'One potato corn dog, one cheddar cheese corn dog, and one sweet potato and cheese corn dog.'

Now it was time for me to hear those words that I wanted to hear so badly:

'You want sugar on that?'

I nodded my head furiously.

'Yes. Extra sugar, please.'

# The Taste of a New Product

I once set up an account on a job search site when I was trying to change companies. The site required new users to first submit a review of their current company before they could see other reviews. A give and take, so to speak. To get information, you had to give information. I guess there's no such thing as a free lunch.

I sat there for a while, unable to fill in the 'company strengths' field. I had already reached the maximum character count for 'company weaknesses', so my conscience told me I should include at least one strength. But for some reason I couldn't think of anything. After an eternity, I finally thought of one perk of working at Maron Confectionaries:

Free snacks.

I pressed continue but received a message:

Your answer must be at least 20 characters long.

I changed it to:

Unlimited free snacks.

This was perhaps the company's greatest strength. Indeed, there were boxes filled with snacks stacked all through the company building – in meeting rooms, beneath desks, inside cabinets, outside cabinets, along the walls, and in the hallways. There were so many boxes of snacks that you could trip over them if you weren't careful.

About fifteen minutes after everyone left for home, I had the urge to nibble on something. But I wasn't hungry, per se; in fact, I had just finished a big dinner. I figured it was that stress-induced pseudo hunger I'd read about on the internet the other day. But knowing that my body didn't need more food didn't change the fact that I was still craving something. But when I looked at my surroundings, all I found were the same old snacks I had been munching on all day: Maron's snacks. They weren't bad, but I already knew what they tasted like.

Unable to find anything new among the stacks of snacks, my desire to go home became even more desperate. My cozy bedroom was waiting for me at my new apartment, which I had moved into just over two months ago. All I wanted to do was turn on the air conditioner, hop into bed, and pull over my head the fluffy duvet with its new summer linen cover.

I stared at the title of the PowerPoint document on my monitor. 'Major Beach Convenience Store Summer Break Promotional Event Proposal' (a mouthful, I know). This proposal was actually Ice Cream's, but our team helped with it every year. And yet, it was *I* who had to work late on it. Perhaps it was my fault, though. After all, I was the one who first proposed the joint promotion two years ago. I'd wanted to do my part to increase sales. But what good had it done me? My performance was still just 'Mid'. Why was I working so hard? Thinking like this did nothing for my motivation. But I wasn't going to stop. Ever since that incident with the travelling fortune-teller, I had been working my ass off to please my team leader.

I sent a message to the NOR(3) group chat. I knew there was a high probability that Eun-sang and Jisong were also working late. The end of the month was always the busiest time for people in Management Support.

**Dahae**
Are either of you still at the office?
**Jisong**
We just ate and are heading back to the office now.
**Dahae**
I'm alone. Stop by the third floor. I'm bored.

A few minutes later, Eun-sang and Jisong arrived at my cubicle, their hands on their full bellies. Eun-sang had a small box of snacks.

'Have you tried this? We don't have it on our floor.'

It looked like the new product that Biscuits, the team right next to ours, had just released.

'No. This is the first time I've seen it in person. Where did you get it?'

'They're scattered all around this floor. Look, there's even some at your feet.'

I looked down to the left of my cubicle in disbelief. Just as she said, stacked on the floor were several boxes of the new product. Jisong knelt in front of the stack and licked her lips as she took out several boxes. Red, green, yellow – each coloured box had a different flavour.

'Hot and spicy chicken, seaweed, and honey peanut,' Jisong mumbled as she examined the packaging.

She opened the box of hot and spicy chicken biscuits, took out one bag, ripped it open, took out a single biscuit wrapped in transparent plastic, and inspected it. The biscuit was a longish rectangular shape, the width of two fingers. It was a dark brown colour with a glossy coating and smelled, unsurprisingly, like hot and spicy chicken. The biscuit was wrapped in a single layer of dried seaweed.

Eun-sang peeled the wrapping back halfway and bit into the biscuit. There was a satisfying crunch as the biscuit fell apart in her mouth. Her eyes opened wide with surprise.

'Mmm!' she exclaimed as she popped the rest of the biscuit in her mouth. 'This would be perfect as a bar snack.'

Hearing this, Jisong and I each took a biscuit and nibbled on it.

'You're right. It tastes just like snacks at a bar.'

'I bet this would go well with a cold beer.'

'You know, I heard there's a new brewpub next to the soup place...' Jisong said, the end of her sentence trailing off.

'Where the old dumpling restaurant used to be, right?' Eun-sang asked.

'Last time I checked they were still under construction,' I said. 'Have they already opened?'

'I think they're open. I heard their ale is really good.' Jisong then added, 'And there's a 30 per cent discount if you do takeout...'

Before we knew it, we were walking towards the new bar with one of the branded tote bags our company often handed out. We got our ale in these plastic bottles that had special caps for tap beer. It only took three one-litre bottles to completely fill the bag. We felt like queens walking out of the bar.

Back at the office, we set up in one of the small meeting rooms. We still had work to do, after all. We often did this – made a shared workspace in one of the small meeting rooms so that we could work late together – but today was special, what with the abundance of beer we had in our heavy reusable bag. We went to the office pantry and put the entire bag and all its contents in the fridge. After washing two mugs and a tumbler, we took two bottles of beer out of the fridge and returned to the meeting room.

We brought our laptops and shared – like the good friends we were – a single power strip for all our electricity needs. We sat around the square table, each taking one side. Out of Eun-sang's laptop bag came several bags of butter-grilled dried squid snacks. Each of the plastic bags was connected to the next, as though they had been snatched right off the production line. My jaw dropped in surprise.

'We had some left over,' she said with a somewhat embarrassed look. She inspected the back of the packaging and added: 'The expiration date wasn't too long ago.'

We poured beer into the two mugs and tumbler, and then began working as we sampled the new biscuits and Eun-sang's butter-grilled dried squid.

Unfortunately, we were more productive when we worked alone. But this didn't stop us from getting together like this. If a sigh escaped my lips while I was working alone, I would usually stop working and take a short nap on my desk, but if a sigh escaped my lips while I was working with Eun-sang and Jisong, one of them would always ask what was wrong. This gave me the chance to go on a stormy rant about how I was working late because I had to clean up someone else's mess or because one of our clients was pushing us around. Eun-sang and Jisong were already well acquainted with all the characters in my story, so they could bad-mouth everyone with me, which was just the kind of therapy I needed. In fact, we never let each other's sighs, grumbles or downtrodden faces go unnoticed; we always took each other's side and gave words of encouragement. Of course, constantly going back and forth between chatting and working wasn't particularly efficient, but it was always a great stress reliever and helped me fall asleep at night when I got home.

Before I knew it, my laptop keyboard was shiny with oil and covered in biscuit crumbs. After flipping it upside down and shaking off the crumbs, I looked around for a tissue to wipe the keyboard clean. I spotted Eun-sang glancing at her phone as she took a sip of beer. I couldn't see her screen from where I was sitting, but I knew she was checking the BitGo graphs; after all, she did that hundreds of times a day. She gave a nonchalant look as she put her phone face down on the table.

'Should we go to Jeju Island next month?' she asked out of nowhere.

'Jeju Island? What for?' Jisong asked.

'It's vacation season, isn't it? How about sometime in the middle of next month? We can swim, eat great food, go on long drives.'

'I was planning on going to Taiwan to meet Wei Lin around that time. I might not be able to go with you if it overlaps.'

'You're still seeing him?' Eun-sang said as she frowned angrily. 'Do you even have long-term plans with him?'

'What do you mean?'

'Come on, Jisong,' Eun-sang said with a sigh. 'Dahae and I aren't sure if we want to get married yet, but you... You know what you want. You always talk about how you want to get married young and become a mother of three. That's your life goal, isn't it? To become a good wife and mother? Time is running out. And here you are, acting like you're going to save up money and get married to that Taiwanese guy as soon as he graduates. Tell me, where are you going to live if you two do get married? Seoul? Taipei? You don't even know each other that well. I bet you've only spent a month at most physically together. You're not thinking about the future. You can have a long-distance relationship with some foreign boy if you want. But if you really want to achieve that dream of yours, this isn't how you get there. You can't have it both ways, Jisong. Just choose one already.'

Jisong, who had been rolling her eyes during this mini-lecture, turned to Eun-sang when she was done and looked her in the eye.

'You think I'm clinging onto him, don't you?' she asked.

'Yes.'

Jisong tilted her head back and let out a laugh.

'You're wrong,' she said. 'I'm just having some fun with Wei Lin. When I'm ready to get married, I'm going to go with the safe choice.'

Eun-sang didn't look convinced, and neither was I. Even to me, Jisong appeared crazy in love with that handsome Taiwanese boy, as though she were nineteen and experiencing love for the first time. Just seeing the way her eyes sparkled every time she said his name was enough to convince me of this. Jisong went on the offensive:

'What about you, Eun-sang? Are you happy now that you sent Dong-jun to dental school? How did that big-picture planning go for you?'

'Whoa there. What does he have to do with this?'

Dong-jun was Eun-sang's ex-boyfriend whom she met when she was twenty. When I first met Eun-sang, Dong-jun was on his fourth attempt at passing the certificate examination for junior high chemistry teachers. And Eun-sang was already several months into trying to convince him that he might not be cut out for it, that he might need to consider re-evaluating his career path.

Eun-sang told him that he needed to think carefully because he had already failed three times, never once moving onto the second round. Everyone had different strengths. It didn't mean he was stupid; it just meant he wasn't cut out for this particular test. Besides, despite what people thought, being a teacher wasn't as stable a job as it used to be. Birth rates were low, and the number of open positions was on the decline. The door was already narrow enough as it was. And because he wasn't teaching something in high demand like Korean, English or maths, even if he got his certification, he would probably need to wait several years before he found a job. 'You really need to think about whether this is worth giving up your entire twenties for.' She wasn't wrong.

Eun-sang's suggestion was DEET, the Dental Education Eligibility Test. The way Eun-sang saw it, Dong-jun wasn't stupid; he just wasn't good at tests. And the teaching certificate exam was notoriously difficult. Rather, she thought he might do better on the entrance exam for dental school. 'Just take the exam and see how you do. If I'd been a science major, that's what I would have done. You're smart; make use of your schooling!' Dong-jun, who was easily convinced by Eun-sang, took DEET that year. Surprisingly, he passed first time and was accepted by a dental school in North Gyeongsang Province. However, in his first year of dental school he cheated on Eun-sang with another first-year, and with that their six-year-long relationship ended. Every time Dong-jun came up in conversation, Eun-sang always said the same thing. Today was no exception.

'If that man had a conscience, he would pay me what he owes me for saving his career,' Eun-sang said angrily. 'I hear people charge millions of won per hour for career consulting. Ungrateful prick!'

Jisong rested her chin on her hand and looked up at Eun-sang who was sitting diagonally across from her.

'I thought you said you didn't need a boyfriend,' she said. 'But you look kind of lonely to me these days.'

'Me? No. Why do you say that?'

'Are you fighting with me because you're jealous that I'm in an intimate relationship with a handsome, younger man?'

'You wish.' Eun-sang made a straight face as she added, 'And for your information, scrawny guys aren't my type.'

'Excuse me!'

Jisong took out her phone, opened her photos, and started frantically scrolling. Once she found a picture she liked, she enlarged it so that it filled her screen and showed it to Eun-sang. In the picture, Jisong and Wei Lin were embracing each other on the beach. Their wetsuits were opened and hanging from their waists, exposing his chest and her bikini top. Their tanned, young physiques were set against picturesque palm trees and a sea of emerald. You'd be forgiven for mistaking them for swimsuit models.

'Does this look scrawny to you?' Jisong said in a somewhat dignified manner as she held her phone in front of Eun-sang's face.

Eun-sang lightly grabbed her chin between her thumb and index finger as she looked carefully at the screen.

'Ooh, he has a nicer body than I thought.'

'Right?'

The two of them locked fingers and shook their hands in the air as they giggled. It was as if their quarrel had never happened. Jisong and Eun-sang enjoyed drinking despite both being lightweights. They got like this whenever they got even a little drunk, picking fights and pointing out what they didn't like about each other. And just when it seemed like the night was ruined, they would make up, sometimes even high-fiving loudly and laughing. I realised it would be best if I was the one to finish the rest of the beer.

At this moment, the door to the meeting room burst open without warning. It was Jisong's team leader from Accounting. He was holding the handle and standing with only the top half of his body through the door. He looked just as surprised as us.

'You nearly gave me a heart attack,' he said. 'I thought someone had left the lights on.'

The three of us were flustered, but still managed to greet him in unison.

'Hello.'

'Are you three not going home? What are you doing here anyway? Are you working late together?'

'Yes.'

Looking surprised, he tilted his head to the side.

'I didn't know you three were close.'

We said yes and nodded our heads, but he still seemed confused.

'And Dahae, what are you doing here?' he asked hesitantly. 'I never would have guessed. The three of you. How do you know each other anyway?'

'We entered the company at the same time.'

Still with a suspicious look in his eyes, he slowly looked around the table at us.

'So like donggi? I see…' he said, mulling over this new bit of information. 'Anyway, strong work. Make sure you take a break.'

'Yes, sir!'

Before leaving, he extended his index finger and pointed at something.

'By the way, what's that?'

We realised immediately that his finger had found the plastic bottle, which was still a fifth full of ale. I could feel beads of sweat making their way towards my forehead through the hair on my scalp.

'Oh, this?'

It was Jisong who answered him. She lifted her tumbler with its stainless steel straw high in the air, as though she was making a toast, and brazenly stared her manager in the eye.

'Apple juice.'

Eun-sang and I looked at each other at the same time. When our eyes met, it was all we could do to hold in our laughter. Seeing Eun-sang's nostrils tremble faintly, I had to bite the tip of my tongue and stare up at the ceiling.

'Nice,' he said. 'Anyway, it's good to see that you three are so close. Fighting!' Jisong's manager gave us his usual good-natured smile and pumped his fist in the air as he closed the door.

We sat in silence for about ten seconds, holding our breath. When the coast was clear we all broke out in laughter. Before long we were face down on the table and laughing with our entire bodies. The alcohol seemed to be contributing to our good mood. Every time we managed to calm down and stop laughing, one of us would start giggling again, causing the other two to burst out laughing. It was like we were singing an endless round. After what seemed like an eternity of senseless laughter, Eun-sang suddenly waved both arms in the air and stopped Jisong and me. *Shhh*, she hushed as she brought her finger to her lips. Not long after this, we could hear footsteps coming closer and closer. *No way…* The moment I said this to myself, the door flung back open.

'Also—'

It was Jisong's team leader again.

'Turn off the lights when you leave.'

He pointed to the worn-out red sticker above the light switch.

'Gotta save energy.'

'Of course,' Jisong answered enthusiastically. 'Take care.'

The door closed, and the sound of Jisong's team leader's footsteps slowly got farther away. Once we couldn't hear him any more, we burst into another round of uncontrollable laughter. Jisong, who was nearly choking, quickly soothed her throat by slurping up the apple juice-coloured beer with her straw. Eun-sang leaned back in her chair at a forty-five-degree angle and dabbed her tears with her pinky fingers as she stared up at the ceiling.

This scene was so silly and ridiculous that I wanted to take a mental photo and hold onto it for later. But

I quickly realised it was already ingrained in my memory.

I could almost imagine myself looking back on this moment many years in the future. I didn't know when I would leave this company, but I had a hunch that when it was time for me to miss this place, it would be this precise feeling that I would miss the most. As I sat there, all I could think about was how I never wanted our friendship to end.

# Final Boarding Call

*29 August 2017*

I arrived early at Gimpo Airport. I thought I would be the first one there, but Eun-sang arrived even earlier than I did. She was sitting on her suitcase in front of the check-in desk in an unusual outfit for her – buckled sandals, white shorts and a loose T-shirt. When I called out to her, she took off her sunglasses, placed them atop her head, and turned around. As soon as she saw it was me, she produced a smile as bright and brilliant as the summer sun. We had only ever seen each other at the office in our suits, so it was odd to see each other at the airport like this, dressed so casually. Eun-sang seemed to welcome this new feeling just as much as I did.

She got up from her suitcase and grabbed the handle. The suitcase had a smooth telescopic handle, a silver exterior with a faint sheen, and sturdy, rounded corners. It looked like a Rimowa suitcase, the original model. From far away I couldn't be sure, but now that I was closer, my suspicions were confirmed. Even when I wasn't looking in its direction, I could feel the aura – that's the only way I could describe it – that the case was giving off. It was exuding that effortless beauty that only brand names had. Is that really a Rimowa Original? I tried my hardest not to stare, but my eyes kept drifting in its direction. Eventually, my eyes found the Rimowa logo. My suitcase was also silver, but it was only a cheap knockoff of a Rimowa. In fact, I'd only ever seen knock-offs, so the authenticity of Eun-sang's case intimidated me. There really was a difference. It then occurred to me that Eun-sang must be doing very well for herself.

We had gone back and forth about the holiday plans, but in the end it was Eun-sang's insistence that played the biggest role in our decision to go to Jeju Island. On our way home that night, after finishing late at the office, Eun-sang made a suggestion:

'Dahae, if you purchase the plane tickets, I'll cover the hotel and everything else.'

'What about me?' Jisong said with wide eyes.

'All you need to do is come along for the ride,' Eun-sang said as she put one arm around Jisong.

'You really mean it?'

'Of course.'

Jisong's lips were trying their hardest to stifle the smile that was spreading across her face.

'But still...' she said, 'I'll feel bad if I just tag along like that. I should do *something*.'

'It's fine. As long as you come along and have fun, that's enough. The three of us have never had a proper trip together. We always have this stupid leash around our neck whenever we're together.'

Eun-sang grabbed the company badge hanging from her neck and tugged at it violently as though she was going to tear it off. 'Why am I still wearing this?' she said angrily. She took off the badge, took the lanyard – which was partially grey where it had touched her neck – and wrapped it around the rectangular badge. The headshot on your company badge was the same one you submitted when you first entered the company. That picture was used for everything, even the intranet organisational chart and company messenger. The picture was never updated; it would follow you to your grave unless you left the company. Because of this, it was common not to recognise someone you had only communicated with over the company messenger. Not only did people submit heavily photoshopped images of themselves, but everyone gained weight working at Maron. But there was another difference between a person's picture and their real face that couldn't be explained by just an increase in weight and sagging cheeks. After working at this company for a while, the contours of people's faces started to change. After a while, their faces started to look empty, depressed, hollow. And that was despite the weight gain. In fact, I'd gained a bit of weight, and so had Section Chief Yun, but we both showed this hollowness. Even Team Leader Koh, who never seemed to age or gain weight, looked defeated. Not even Jisong's team leader, who was always so happy, was spared. An empty void is created in people when they lose something they never knew they had. A face of nothing but shells. The face of someone who depends on a monthly pay check.

When Eun-sang first entered the company, did she know what she would look like in five years? Now, as she spun her wrist round and round, her young face with its awkward smile was being covered up layer by layer by the lanyard. First her neck, then her chin, lips and eyes. Like a mummy being buried alive, unaware of the horrors to come. And finally, after two layers around her forehead, she was done. Eun-sang stuck the remaining length of lanyard underneath the tight coil and tossed the entire thing in her shoulder bag. She gave me a single, furtive glance, then turned to Jisong and whispered as though she was telling her a secret:

'Don't worry about paying us back. We couldn't tell you because you forbade it, but we've both made a lot of money. We're sort of rich now.'

Rich? Me? I flinched like I'd just been addressed by the wrong name. But once I thought about it a bit more, I realised she wasn't completely wrong. The money in my virtual wallet was almost 40,000,000 won. This large sum of money was one I'd never experienced before entering the world of cryptocurrency. But having said that, could I really say anything had changed? Was it really my money? But what was I talking about! If it wasn't mine, then whose was it? Thinking like this made me want to hold out even longer. But if I had 40,000,000 won, how much did Eun-sang have? I didn't have a calculator, but I tried doing the maths in my head even though I knew I wasn't very good at it. If my calculations were correct... although I couldn't be sure... Eun-sang would have about 400,000,000 won. I may or may not be 'rich', but Captain Kang certainly was.

Before buying the plane tickets for this trip to Jeju Island, I had never exchanged any of the ether in my virtual wallet for real cash. Not once. I only allowed myself to use the money from my monthly pay checks. In that sense, the amount of money I had at my disposal technically hadn't increased. And yet, I felt like my life had become noticeably posher. The simple fact that there were eight figures in the virtual wallet on my phone made me feel like I really had become 'sort of rich', as Eun-sang put it. Even though it was just a 'virtual' wallet, that virtual wallet felt to me just as real as a bona fide bank account. It was a fundamentally different mindset knowing I had 40,000,000 won that I could take out in an emergency as opposed to just 4,000,000. And this mindset had seeped into every aspect of my daily life.

Even though my new apartment was still a studio apartment, my sleeping area was now somewhat separated from the main living space. The security deposit was 20,000,000 won more expensive than my last place, and the rent was 150,000 won more, too. Had I not learned about Ethereum just three months before moving, had I resigned myself as always to the fact that my bank account wasn't going to see a significant change in growth, I would never have dared moving into such an expensive place. But now I could buy those organic melons at the supermarket, and premium detergent. I no longer needed to look at the last two digits of price tags. I started drinking organic milk. Before now, I had always only bought the cheapest brand on the shelf that day. I even used to buy products from unethical companies. I did this despite knowing that all the rumours surrounding their shady practices were true; after all, I worked in the same industry. This was, you could say, my default mode of consumption. I always picked the cheapest products, as though I were hardwired to do so. But not any more. Of course, the taste of my first glass of organic milk was great, but more than that, I felt satisfied knowing that I had finally become a consumer who could afford a conscience. As I put the organic milk with its understated, refined logo into my shopping basket, I imagined the CEO of that unethical company being put behind bars and forced to step down because of the financial difficulties the company was having. I thought of cows being released from their pens, allowed to romp around in open pastures, as well as the content smiles of honest farmers in straw hats. I'd never imagined being a consumer with a conscience could be so rewarding.

After closing my instalment savings account to invest in Ethereum, I didn't bother opening another one. In the past, a significant portion of my monthly pay check was automatically deposited into those accounts. Because of this, I was always tight for money by the end of the month. And the last three or four days before payday were always a struggle, as I had to resist the urge to buy coffee or bread. So now that I wasn't beholden to my monthly instalments, it felt like I had more money, even though my monthly pay check hadn't changed. After paying all my bills, I used the remaining money to buy more ether.

I even sent what you might call an allowance to my mother who was living alone in my hometown of Asan. It was only after sending this money that I learned my mother – who for the last twelve years had been driving Bus 09, the only one that circled the town – was taking a break from work because she had broken her leg. Now I knew why she had so adamantly told me not to come home last time I said I wanted to visit. Apparently, she had fallen on her way down the hill to the market and fractured her right hip joint and ankle.

I'd never imagined anyone but my mother driving Bus 09. Then again, what she drove wasn't really a bus. It was an ivory-coloured Kia Carnival with a 'Town Bus' sticker on the hood and door. The bus only ran once an hour, but because there was only one driver, my mother had to circle the town all day long. Whenever I saw the bus, it was always my mother who was behind the wheel. There were no signs demarcating the bus stops, but the locals all knew where to stand. All they needed to do was wave their hand and make eye contact. They didn't even need to press the bell to be let off. Asking politely was enough. Because of this, I always thought of Bus 09 as my mother's personal vehicle.

'Who's going to drive Bus 09?' I asked.

'Someone will,' she said in a matter-of-fact tone of voice from the other end.

I wanted to ask whether they would let her drive the route again when she was better, but I couldn't. I didn't want to think about what would happen if the answer was no. I didn't want to think about what would happen if she were no longer receiving a monthly pay check. I sent my mother money to cover her living expenses and hospital bills while she convalesced. My mother used to refuse my money, saying she had never done anything for me. Even if I tried to buy her herbal medicine, she would stubbornly refuse and tell me to keep my money for myself, which always hurt my feelings. But now, she just accepted my help and took the money I sent her every month. What if this had happened and I hadn't invested in cryptocurrency? What if this had happened and all I had was 10,000,000 won? Thinking about such things made me sick with dread.

A while back after buying the plane tickets, I exchanged some of the ether in my virtual wallet for some more cash. I traded thirty-eight ether for about 15,000,000 won and put that into my bank account. And with that money, the very first thing I did was pay off my student debt in one fell swoop.

[You have a new message.]
KOSAF-20**. First Semester principal (plus interest) payment due 9 August 2017. UB Bank.

[You have a new message.]
KOSAF-20**. Second Semester principal (plus interest) payment due 10 August 2017. UB Bank.

[You have a new message.]
KOSAF-20**. Third Semester principal (plus interest) payment due 11 August 2017. UB Bank.

[You have a new message.]
KOSAF-20**. Fourth Semester principal (plus interest) payment due 12 August 2017. UB Bank.

Four times a month I received a message reminding me I was in debt. The amount I paid off each month was so minuscule compared to the amount I had yet to pay. I sometimes wondered what it would be like to pay off such a large, imposing debt with one transaction. And now those messages that had harangued me every month, those repetitive, never-ending obligations, had finally stopped. It felt like I'd cut some corner, used some cheat code. But that's not to say I felt bad or guilty about it. I was simply thankful that someone had taught me the cheat code.

Student loan (tuition and living expenses)
Principal:          ₩ 2*,***,000
Loan balance:       ₩ 0
Per cent repaid:    100.00%

I gazed for a long time at the number o.

0

This oval felt to me like a portal to a new world. I felt like a gate that had been shut tight was finally and noisily being thrown open, and I had just taken my first weightless step on the other side. This wasn't just a figure of speech; my body truly felt lighter. I started to think about the people who lived like this all the time, carefree and with no debt to weigh them down. What was it like to live such a life? It felt so faint and distant to me. With the money I earned from selling my ether, I had paid off my student debt, paid for my mother's living expenses and hospital bills, and bought round-trip tickets for me and my two friends to Jeju Island.

After all of that, there was no doubt in my mind that this money was mine, that I truly had a mini fortune. This trip to Jeju Island was a sort of ceremony, one that was going to assure me of what I was just starting to realise.

After Eun-sang and I said we would pay for everything, Jisong, who must have felt somewhat guilty, was constantly trying to make it up to us.

'Maybe I can pay for the return tickets,' she said.

'No, it's fine,' I said. 'You just make the reservation for the rental car.'

'OK!' Jisong said with a large smile on her face. 'I'll get us a convertible!'

Unfortunately, it was looking like Jisong might not be able to enjoy the convertible she had rented. But perhaps we didn't need a convertible any more because Eun-sang looked like she was about to blow the top off her own lid. Indeed, we were fast approaching boarding time, and Jisong was nowhere to be found.

Thirty minutes before our departure, we called Jisong, who picked up in sobs. She had planned to take the express Line 1 subway train to Noryangjin, transfer to Line 9, and then transfer again to the Airport Railroad. She had even calculated her route exactly so that she would arrive on time. But all that careful planning went out the window when she missed the train to Noryangjin. I couldn't understand why she'd thought it was a good idea to predicate her calculations on the assumption that she would be able to catch the express subway train, which didn't come very often. But sensing that she was more disappointed in herself than I was, I decided not to add to her misery and just told her in an encouraging tone to come as quickly as possible. Eun-sang, who was listening in on the conversation, let out a big sigh. After hanging up, we sent messages every five minutes asking for updates, but soon she stopped reading our messages all together. It was now ten minutes before departure.

We stood at the gate as the last passengers who hadn't boarded. Eun-sang, who had an intense frown on her face, let out a deep sigh as she looked up the next plane for Jeju Island on her phone. As she was doing this, there was an announcement over the PA.

'This is the final boarding call for passenger Jisong Kim, Jisong Kim, booked for Asian Airlines flight OZ8945 to Jeju Island, departing at 1:05. Please proceed to Gate 21 immediately. Again, this is the final boarding call for—'

Even if Jisong arrived at the airport right now, it would still take her time to check in, get through security, and run to the gate. By this point, we had half given up and were just waiting for Jisong to acknowledge that we'd be departing without her.

As this was our last chance, Eun-sang and I finally boarded the plane. Based on Eun-sang's search, all of today's flights to Jeju Island were fully booked. It was after all peak season. Maybe she could book a flight tomorrow. But I had my doubts.

'I can't believe this.'

Eun-sang finally spoke up after spending the last several minutes in fuming silence. Because we were inside a plane, she didn't talk in her usual loud voice. Instead, she spoke in a voice that was somewhere between a whisper and a yell.

'Jisong is always doing things like this! She was late that time we went to see a late-night movie, and she was late that time we went to see a musical with tickets we got from the company.'

Eun-sang shook her head back and forth as she continued to grumble.

'I just don't get it. You should give yourself plenty of time on a day like today and leave early. Why was she so certain she could catch the express subway train? It's not like the Line 1 express subway train comes that often. Doesn't it only come like two or three times an hour? How can she not know that? Why was she so confident she wouldn't miss it? Didn't she consider what would happen if her only chance of being on time left without her? Did she not have a backup plan? I'll never understand her.'

Eun-sang was being harsh, but she wasn't wrong. Although I didn't say anything, I agreed with her. Just thinking about how our first trip together was already falling apart before it even started was putting me in a bad mood. It was at this moment that I heard someone wheezing in the distance.

Standing at the end of the aisle was Jisong in a floppy-brimmed large straw hat and a floral-pattern dress that was fluttering in the wind. I was too shocked to even rejoice about the fact she'd finally made it.

'She looks like she's going on her honeymoon,' Eun-sang said as she scoffed in disbelief.

Jisong rushed down the aisle noisily dragging her carry-on suitcase behind her. As she did this, her floppy hat flew backward, but because it was tied beneath her chin with ivory-coloured lace, it just dangled from her neck without falling to the ground, like a turtle shell on her back. With one hand she dragged her hot pink suitcase behind her, and with the other she made a peace sign and held it at shoulder height.

*Clap... clap... clap... clap clap clap.*

For some reason, the other people in the plane started applauding. One person even yelled out from behind me, 'Safe!' It felt like we were cheering on the last runner in a marathon, and I couldn't help but join the ovation, albeit slower than everyone else. Well, she made it in the end. That was all that mattered. Glancing to my side, I discovered Eun-sang was clapping just as slowly as I was.

Jisong put her suitcase in the overhead locker, crab-walked over us, and finally took her seat.

'I had no idea the subway was going to come so late. Sorry.'

'You don't need to say sorry to us,' Eun-sang said. Her mood was noticeably improved. 'You're the one who was going to miss the flight. What matters is that you made it.'

Jisong took off her hat, rolled it up, and used it to fan her flushed cheeks. All the while, she was panting shallowly and giggling to herself.

# Infinity

*29 August 2017*

A landscape of palm trees unfurled before our eyes as we exited the airport. The shape of the large, exotic fronds gave me the inspiration of sweet relaxation. Soon, an intense warmth reached my skin. I closed my eyes, inhaled deeply, and enjoyed the excitement of this getaway.

Suddenly, I heard a crash and a shriek behind me. I turned towards the sound. Jisong was on the ground, holding herself up with both hands. Rolling around on the ground were the casters from her suitcase.

'Are you OK?' Eun-sang and I screamed in unison.

Eun-sang tossed her own luggage aside and ran over to Jisong. I took Eun-sang's suitcase and mine, one in each hand, and walked over slowly. As I took my first step, it was impossible to not be surprised by the vast difference between Eun-sang's authentic Rimowa Original suitcase and my knock-off. Eun-sang's suitcase glided elegantly and effortlessly along the concrete, like an Olympic ice skater. The casters had 360 degrees of rotational freedom and changed direction with the slightest push. It felt gravity-defying. The whole of the luggage felt like one solid piece of material, and it was precisely this that made it feel so smooth. The casters on my suitcase, on the other hand, didn't have the ability to swivel, and because of this, they loudly skipped and skidded every time I changed direction. Just dragging it for a few minutes was enough to hurt my wrists.

As I marvelled at Eun-sang's suitcase, Jisong got to her feet and dusted off the skirt of her dress. She lifted the hem slightly to see where she had been hurt, exposing a swollen kneecap.

'It's not bleeding. But it stings so much, I thought for sure it would be.'

'That's a relief.'

As the two of them inspected her injury, I picked up each of the escapees. I found a total of four casters, which meant there were none on her suitcase. How hard would one need to fall to damage their suitcase like this? But maybe I had the order of causation wrong. Perhaps it wasn't that the casters broke because she fell, but rather that she fell because the casters broke. Realising I had no way of figuring out which came first, I decided it didn't matter. Either way, one couldn't happen without the other. I walked up to Eun-sang and Jisong and showed her the casters, two in each hand.

'Should we try putting them back on?' I asked.

But as soon as I asked this, I realised it was impossible. The pieces of plastic that had connected the casters to the suitcase were completely shattered. Eun-sang seemed to have realised the same thing. When our eyes met, she knitted her brow and shook her head.

'I think I need to buy a new one,' Jisong said in a downtrodden tone. 'For now, I'll just carry it in my arms.'

'How are you going to do that? You've got sticks for arms,' Eun-sang said.

Eun-sang offered to put Jisong's stuff in her suitcase since she had some room left over. And if that wasn't enough, we would use my suitcase as well. But I had a hunch that wouldn't be necessary.

Eun-sang took her suitcase from my hand and began the process of transferring Jisong's belongings. Her case as she opened and fiddled with it was like a symphony of satisfying swooshes and clicks. Every flowing, elegant movement – from when she rolled the case towards her and laid it down on the floor, to when she entered the combination into the lock and released the spring-loaded buckles – reverberated with a refreshingly deep, effortless, natural sound. Nothing required excessive force. It was like the case was water and would do whatever she wanted so long as she willed it. I was starting to realise what it took to live life effortlessly.

Eun-sang unzipped the suitcase, splitting it in half. The inside was neatly divided into separate sections. One shell of the case was deeper than the other, and she had used thin dividers to make sure things stayed in their place. She had also used the straps and buckles inside to secure everything. It was so organised it felt therapeutic.

Jisong and I opened her suitcase and began picking up her things. People passing by glanced over at us. Jisong's embarrassed smile told us she was sorry for all the hassle she was putting us through. Seeing this, Eun-sang asked an intentionally playful question to lighten the mood.

'Jisong, what are you? A model? You've got enough clothes and make-up for ten photo shoots.'

Eun-sang pulled out a hefty object wrapped round and round in an electric cord.

'And why did you bring your straighteners?' she asked.

Jisong finally smiled.

'Don't come to me when you want to borrow them!' she said.

'Oh, but I've always wanted to try these straighteners.'

'Well, since you let me use your suitcase... I guess I can let you borrow them,' Jisong said with a wry smile.

Because Jisong had so much stuff, we had to put all of it in the larger half of Eun-sang's suitcase and move the rest of Eun-sang's clothes to the smaller half. We rolled the clothes into tight bundles instead of folding them, to reduce volume, and we were able to easily fit it all in. The zipper closed with ease, suggesting the suitcase could take even more.

'Useless piece of shit!' Jisong said as she kicked her empty suitcase. The wheel-less suitcase skidded across the ground, letting out a hollow, shabby sound.

I picked up the suitcase, which was beginning to fray at the seams.

'We can't throw this away here. It won't fit in the garbage bin,' I said.

'Let's just take it with us for now,' Eun-sang said. 'We can ask what we should do with it when we get to the hotel.'

Jisong nodded as she took the suitcase from me. It was a vibrant hot pink, but because it was made of fabric, it looked somewhat worn-out and grungy. Carrying her suitcase by the handle, Jisong took the lead. As she walked in front of us, she had her hat hanging from her neck, a selfie stick tucked under her arm, and her empty suitcase in one hand swinging back and forth. Despite having just lost her suitcase, her footsteps were light and carefree.

The hotel Eun-sang had booked was a new 'luxury' hotel in Seogwipo. But I had no idea just how luxurious it was until we got there. Indeed, I felt intimidated as soon as we entered the hotel. I was nicer than any hotel I'd ever stayed at – or even imagined staying at, for that matter. At the entrance, hotel staff dressed in freshly ironed uniforms approached us and took our bags. As Eun-sang checked us in, another one of the lobby staff came over to Jisong and me.

'Please take a seat and enjoy a glass of champagne,' he said with a kind smile.

Jisong, whose shoulders were hunched over, picked up her wheel-less, empty suitcase and showed it to the employee.

'Actually, I was wondering where I should throw this away—' she mumbled.

'You can leave it with me. I'll dispose of it for you, ma'am.'

The hotel employee took the bag, grungy with soot, turned around, and left. As soon as he was gone, Jisong and I exchanged glances. We were both dumbstruck by the great service and couldn't hold back our excitement. Soon after that, another hotel employee came over with a small silver cart. A dark green bottle was lying at a forty-five-degree angle inside a large, transparent glass bowl filled with ice. As the cart's wheels rolled towards us, we could hear the sloshing of ice cubes. The cart stopped in front of us, and the employee placed three pear-shaped champagne glasses on the table. The refreshing sound of the cork popping, the glugging of the wine flowing out of the bottle neck into the glasses, and the fizzing as the glittering bubbles met the air – all these sounds harmonised like music.

I took the long delicate stem of the champagne glass and slowly lifted it. The fresh, effervescent scent of grapes rose through the narrow opening. I tilted the glass a bit further and took a sip. Ice-cold and sweet. The carbonated bubbles burst as they tumbled across my tongue and down the back of my throat. Once the sweet, refreshing taste of fizzing champagne left my mouth, I immediately wanted to take another sip. Before I knew it, I had guzzled the entire glass. Jisong, who had also finished her glass in one shot, looked a bit ruddy.

'This is so nice,' she said. 'Too nice.'

She was right. This hotel was much nicer than I'd expected, and we hadn't even been shown to our rooms yet. I was certain that I would love everything this place had to offer, that everything I was about to experience here was going to be way above my standards. This was too fancy for me, and that frightened me. What if I was experiencing things that were too good too soon?

What if I had taken too quick a short cut? What if this was going to give me unreasonably high expectations? Eun-sang had said she would take care of the hotel, so I hadn't bothered to check her choice. I simply never imagined she would book such a fancy hotel. Jisong seemed to be thinking the same thing. From the marble floors and walls to the high ceilings and the myriad of chandeliers that sparkled like the Milky Way – Jisong's head was spinning as she marvelled at the hotel's interior. And all she could say the whole time was: 'This is *too* nice.'

In the elevator up to our room, Eun-sang told us that this was a 'seven-star hotel'.

'A seven-star hotel? Does that even exist? I thought five was the max.'

'It is. Traditionally the highest you can go is five stars. This place just gave itself seven.'

'They can do that?'

'Well,' Eun-sang said as she fiddled with the room key, 'it's obviously better than other five-star hotels. That's why it's more expensive. If they called themselves a five-star hotel like everyone else, there'd be no differentiation. I guess that's why. Maybe? I like the idea of it, though. Why should there be a limit? Things can *always* be better. The world has an endless supply of luxurious things. It would be unfair to both customers and owners to give two hotels the same five-star rating when one is twice as good as the other.'

The elevators stopped at the tenth floor. The top floor. Eun-sang got out first and led the way as though this were her house. Jisong and I followed her like zombies. Eventually we arrived at the door to our suite. When Eun-sang opened the door, the curtains inside the room automatically began to retract, lifting the veil of darkness shrouding the room's interior.

I'll never forget that moment.

I'd never seen a view like that before.

The wall opposite the entrance to the room was a giant, seamless window, as if someone had taken a cross-section of the horizon and framed it in our room. The emerald water was glimmering in the afternoon sun like sparkling jewels. There was absolutely nothing to ruin our view. I found myself agreeing with Eun-sang. It *would* be inadequate to stop at five stars. This hotel deserved those extra two stars.

We dived into beds which were neatly wrapped in bright white sheets. The sheets smelled subtly of expensive detergent and rustled like a pile of autumn leaves as we fell into them. I was suddenly overwhelmed with a mellow drowsiness. The bed was so cozy and plush that I never wanted to leave. How nice would that be? But then Eun-sang got to her feet and said, 'This isn't the time to be taking a nap.' We changed into our swimsuits – all different colours – put on robes made of thick microfibre cloth, and walked up to the rooftop swimming pool through the 'suite guests-only' staircase located conveniently next to our room.

The swimming pool was situated at the edge of an expansive rooftop. Because the pool was designed without a railing along the outer edge, it gave the illusion that it extended to the open ocean. Beyond the pool, the blue ocean water transitioned seamlessly into a clear sky. The line separating the pool water and ocean was almost imperceptible. This was an infinity pool, something I had only seen on Instagram and never actually experienced in person.

I took off my robe, tossed it on the beach chair, and crouched at the edge of the pool to dip my feet in. I sat down and dunked my shins in the water, which sparkled like blue Gatorade. The water wasn't too cold, nor was it lukewarm. It was perfectly refreshing. It was such an ideal temperature that it made me wonder if there was a scientist on staff who constantly tested the water. It seemed to me that the words 'perfect' and 'just right' were made for moments like this. Now that I was in the pool and closer to the surface, the optical illusion was even more convincing. Pool, ocean, sky – each transitioning into the other like a smooth gradation. It truly felt like I could reach the ocean if I swam far enough in that direction. I was soaking my legs in a virtual estuary.

On Instagram, I'd seen models pose in pools like this. But I always scrolled past those pictures thinking that such beautiful landscapes didn't have anything to do with me. But now that this landscape was before me, I couldn't help but think that maybe it did after all. In fact, I even felt like I should have experienced this sooner, that it was my right to experience it.

But there was something else, too, in the back of my mind. I was becoming more and more enamoured with this seven-star hotel, yet at the same time a deep sense of dread was growing in my mind, the way a tree's roots dig deep into the ground as it grows. Now that I had experienced a seven-star hotel, I didn't feel like I could ever go back to those cheap motels I'd stayed in to save money. I was only here because of Eun-sang and her money; I didn't have the means to come here on my own. But I was already hooked on this feeling. What was I going to do?

In the distance I could see Jisong and Eun-sang with their hair tied up, holding their phones so that they wouldn't get wet and carefully walking through the water, bobbing up and down. They were, it seemed, attempting to take the same kind of photo I'd seen on Instagram. They took turns photographing each other. They would turn around with their waist underwater and lean against the edge of the infinity pool with the breathtaking gradation of pool, ocean and sky as a backdrop.

As I watched, I thought about the word infinity.

Infinity meant both something that was limitless as well as something that was untouchably distant. Infinity was like an unattainably distant reality. Fate had allowed me to step foot momentarily in that distant world, but I knew this wasn't the end of my journey. People's greed was limitless. Once you had one thing, you wanted more. And once you had that, you wanted even more. My stomach felt uneasy. From the other side of the pool, I could hear Eun-sang calling me.

'Dahae!'

Eun-sang was cutting through the water effortlessly towards me in her vibrant green swimsuit. She placed both wet palms on my dry knees.

'What's on your mind?' she asked me.

'It's noth—'

Before I even finished talking, Eun-sang pulled me towards the water. I let out a half laugh, half squeal as I flopped into the pool.

The water wasn't deep, but I was immediately in up to my neck. My entire body, which had been toasting in the heat, was now being embraced by a cool current. I chased after Eun-sang, who splashed water everywhere as she fled from me. Eventually I arrived at the edge of the pool. Without thinking, I had already folded my elbows and lifted my arms onto the ledge. I rested my chin on my arms and stared out at the waves. The noise in my head subsided, and all I could think about was how beautiful and perfect the view was. I relaxed my legs, and my body started to lightly float on the surface of the water. Before long, the landscape before me was painted red by the sunset.

Once it got dark, several hotel employees appeared and started setting up by the pool. The lights in the rooftop bar beyond the glass wall turned on, and the terrace area was cleared out. On one side of the pool, they set up a machine that looked like a cannon. As Jisong and I looked on in confusion, Eun-sang took out six long, thin pieces of paper from her robe pocket and waved them in the air. They were three admission wristbands for the pool party, which she had bought beforehand, as well as three eighteen-and-over wristbands. We peeled the stickers off the ends of the wristbands and wrapped one wristband around each wrist.

Before long, the pool party started.

It was still the same infinity pool, but it felt like we'd been transported to a new place. The pool's blue undulating water and rows of sky blue tiles were nowhere to be found. The lights between the tiles had all turned on, and the water of the pool was now cycling through a rainbow of colours. Yellow, orange, bright pink, deep blue, blinding kiwi green. I felt like I was in an oversized tropical cocktail. Soon I heard a machine being turned on. When I looked towards the source of the sound, I saw bubbles spraying from the muzzle of the cannon. The soap bubbles, which smelled of tropical fruit, flew high into the sky, scattered in the wind like falling snow, and came to rest on the surface of the water. The people in the pool let out screams of excitement. At one end of the pool, a DJ was playing music. I could feel the vibrations of the speakers deep in my bones. Chilled champagne, draft beer, and every cocktail known to man and then some were all available for free at the bar. There was also a buffet set up on the tables on the terrace. Among these was a large glass container filled with skewers, each piercing three fat marshmallows. In the centre of the table was a burner to roast the marshmallows, next to which was a five-tiered chocolate fountain. Glossy chocolate poured out of the top fountain and cascaded down the tiers. I picked up a marshmallow skewer, roasted it over the flame until it was perfectly brown, rolled it under the falling chocolate to give it a thick coating, and popped it in my mouth. The warm chocolate and fluffy marshmallow caressed the tip of my tongue as an overwhelmingly sweet taste exploded in my mouth.

At one point, we realised that each of us had in our hands three different colours of glow sticks, but we weren't sure who had given them to us. We took the glow sticks and tied one around our wrist and stuck the other two in our hair. We jumped into the water and danced as we played with beach balls and our glow sticks.

I hadn't noticed at first, but they'd increased the water temperature and decreased the water level. When we felt slightly cold from the late-night breeze, we gathered around the fondue flame again, roasted more marshmallows, and then went into the jacuzzi at the corner of the rooftop with more drinks. As we sat there, we allowed the hot jets of water, which were just the right pressure, to massage our tight backs and shoulders. When we felt completely recharged, we got another round of drinks and food as if we had just got to the party and jumped into the pool again. Jisong got out of the pool saying she'd already finished her drink. She seemed somewhat in a hurry because, instead of using the stairs, she simply lifted herself out of the pool and ran through the puddles of water. Water dripped from the tip of her tied-up hair.

Eun-sang was saying something to me. But because the music was so loud, or perhaps because we were so drunk, we had to lean towards each other and scream just to hear.

'Dahae, are you cold?'

'No. Why?'

'You look uncomfortable. Should we go in the jacuzzi?'

'No, it's not that. I just feel kind of guilty.'

'What do you mean?'

'I really appreciate your bringing us here. I really do. But I'm not sure if I should be enjoying myself this much. I don't know. In the back of my head, I keep thinking that this doesn't suit someone like me. I don't know if I have the right to enjoy myself like this. And to be honest, I know this will sound lame and overdramatic, but I've been thinking a lot about my mom.'

'I know what you're feeling.'

Eun-sang put her arm around me and gave me a big smile.

'You really think I don't know what you're going through? My parents have never gone to the beach to play, let alone stay at a hotel. There's nothing people like us can do about that.'

*People like us.* Strangely, every time Eun-sang said these three words, I felt both happy and sad. It felt like I was pressing a bruise on my body. It ached, but in a good way. It felt like I was being mean, but only to myself. And thus, it felt like I could forgive it all.

Eun-sang pinched the long glow stick about a third of the way down its length. She held it sideways and slowly shook the thing up and down in front of my eyes, as though she were trying to hypnotise me. I knew it was probably an optical illusion, but when she did this, the glow stick started to flop as though it were a pliable piece of rubber. As I stared at the bendy glow stick, Eun-sang suddenly hit me in the forehead with it.

'Hey,' she said. 'I didn't invite you here to start stinking up the place with your depressing talk. Just enjoy yourself.'

Then she yelled out in slurred speech:

'And besides! Why don't you have the right to enjoy yourself? You do! Everyone has the right to enjoy something good, something better. There's no one on this planet who doesn't have that right. You, me, even our parents. We're all the same. There's no end to how good things can get. And now you know it!'

Eun-sang pointed her glow stick at the sky as she leaned into my ear and whispered to me:

'Don't worry. We'll get there.'

Her yellow glow stick was pointing at the moon in the night sky. One half of the moon was shrouded in darkness, and the other half shone coolly. It was a perfect half-moon.

# Golden Wave

We woke up late the next morning. I couldn't remember the last time I had woken up like that: without an alarm, through the mere feeling that it was morning and time to rise. The summer sun, which was extending into the room through the large ocean-view window, was dulled by a thin layer of chiffon curtain. Without completely waking up, I lay on my side and looked around the room. Off-white ceilings and walls. High-quality furniture made of hardwood. My eyes traced the beams of light that touched every corner of the room. It was only after studying the room for a while that I learned the reason I'd been able to wake up without an alarm: the light. In fact, this was the first time I'd experienced a morning like this. All my rooms since I was young faced either north or northwest. Well, technically my current room faced south, but because the view from the window was blocked by a building I could only see the sun from a very small, specific angle. Waking up to the sun in the east might seem like a natural thing to do, but not everyone could enjoy such naturalness.

Sheet covers of blinding white entered my vision as I glanced down. The way the sheets seemed to hover above the mattress reminded me of the view from the plane yesterday. They were still fresh, despite all my tossing and turning. A few feet away, I saw Eun-sang and Jisong still fast asleep. There were three beds arranged side by side, but when you looked at them from this angle, they merged into one gigantic bed.

I extended my arms and squeezed the cotton duvet, the plushness almost sending me back to sleep. I could hear a dry rustling with every movement. It seemed like the air conditioner, which we put on low last night, had made both the air and the blankets cool and crisp. I wish I could feel like this more often. How nice would it be to stay at a seven-star hotel once every season? The words Eun-sang said to me last night were echoing inside my head: Everyone has the right to enjoy themselves.

I reached up towards the headboard and let out a low groan. I then reached further, my arms above my head, groaning louder. Only after sitting up in bed did I finally begin to wake up. The sound of my rising caused the other two to turn over and open their eyes.

'Now that's the face of someone who's had a fantastic night's sleep,' Jisong said.

She was right. I felt recharged and light as a feather.


We headed to the lounge for breakfast. Our first plate from the buffet was European style, the second was American, and our last was Korean. Once we were done, we got three different slices of cake, to share. The mango mousse, something I'd never tried before, was creamy and sweet.

After breakfast, we went back to our room to shower. I stared vacantly at the droplets of water that occasionally fell from the three swimsuits hanging beyond the glass divider. A smile formed on my lips as I thought of the infinity pool from last night.

When it was almost noon, we got dressed in the outfits we picked out for each other and headed down to the parking lot. We all had licences, but none of us were used to driving. After all, none of us owned a car. We agreed to take turns. Eun-sang had driven us to the hotel on the first day, so today was my turn. I could hear Eun-sang's voice from the back seat as I entered the address into the GPS.

'Did you guys know? Tourists are the number one cause of big accidents on Jeju Island. People like us.'

'What do you mean *people like us?*'

'People with driver's licences but who are inexperienced because they don't own a car. People who think it's safe to drive just because it's Jeju Island and not a big city like Seoul.'

'Don't talk like that.'

'Just make sure you pay attention.'

I shrugged my shoulders. 'Don't you know? My mom's a bus driver.'

As Eun-sang and I bickered, Jisong connected her phone to the car's audio system and put on some Ariana Grande. 'Greedy!' Jisong sang out in falsetto. When the drop hit, the three of us screamed out and began dancing in our seats. Unfortunately, Jisong could only get a compact car instead of the convertible she'd promised, as those were all booked up. 'You know, Jeju Island is really windy,' Eun-sang said when she first saw the car. 'Are you sure this won't tip over in a storm?' I realised she had a point. The car was so small that the whole thing was shaking as the three of us jumped up and down. But I had no complaints. After all, this shaking wasn't because of the wind but because of our cheerful dancing.

We headed for a cafe with an ocean view. On the way, Jisong played DJ while Eun-sang made song requests. Yesterday when we landed in Jeju Airport, we promised each other we wouldn't talk about work, but the more we chatted, the more we realised that work was the most interesting thing to talk about. Eun-sang even used a VPN to connect to her work email to show us a fight between two team leaders from Branding over the marketing budget.

But things quietened down as Eun-sang became preoccupied with something on her phone. Jisong turned around to look at Eun-sang in the back seat.

'Eun-sang, stop looking at your phone.'

'Fine.'

'What's so interesting, anyway? I hope you're not working.'

I knew what Eun-sang was looking at, but I didn't say anything.

'It's nothing.'

As Eun-sang said this, my phone, which was placed in the car's central cup holder, began to vibrate. I was fairly certain that it was a message from Eun-sang and that it was about Ethereum. It was either great news or terrible news. My heart was racing as I went back and forth between feelings of excitement and dread. It felt like my phone was trying to get my attention as it buzzed urgently four more times. When we hit a traffic light, I took out my phone to check. Eun-sang had sent me a screenshot. It was a picture of a sharply rising graph.

**Eun-sang**
Omg.
**Eun-sang**
It's skyrocketing.
**Eun-sang**
400,000 won. It's on fire!
**Eun-sang**
Come on, 1,000,000!!!

After checking to make sure the light was still red, I opened BitGo and checked my virtual wallet.

One, two, three... seven, eight. Eight zeros.

100,000,000 won.

One hundred million won.

I couldn't believe my eyes. I started counting the zeros again. But there was no doubt about it. Nine figures. One more than before. 1 followed by eight 0s. I took my hand from the wheel and cupped my mouth. I glanced out of the corner of my eye at the front passenger seat. Jisong was leaning out the window with her arms crossed and her chin resting on her forearms as she gazed out at the scenery. The light changed. I calmly placed my phone back in the cup holder and accelerated as I tried to keep the corners of my mouth from forming a smile. But I couldn't control my facial expressions well. Looking up at the rearview mirror, I could see Eun-sang gnawing on the inside of her cheeks, barely able to hold back her excitement.

'Look!' Jisong yelled out suddenly. 'On the right.'

There beyond a small hill of lush green were ripples of yellow so deep it was almost an orange. It was an endless field of mysterious yellow flowers. The farther we drove, the farther the dark yellow landscape expanded, until it completely dominated our field of view. As this happened, I could sense a single thin, low-hanging cloud, which had been hanging overhead, starting to move rapidly across the sky. The field of yellow, which was now receiving the direct sunlight, was even more vivid than before. Captivated by the landscape, I turned the wheel in the direction of the field of flowers.

'Should I pull over?'

'Yes.'

The GPS took a moment before it started warning us that we were off track.

With my eyes fixed on the field of yellow, I extended my hand and blindly pressed buttons until I eventually turned off the navigation.

We parked in the nearest lay-by and got out of the car. The yellow field before us looked like one giant wave. The stems of the flowers were all gently leaning in one direction. And every time the direction of the wind changed, a wave would ripple through the vast field. Eun-sang bent over, put a flower between her two fingers, and inspected it.

'What kind of flower do you think these are?' she asked.

'Isn't it rapeseed?' I said.

Eun-sang looked up at me and scoffed.

'You don't know anything about flowers, do you?'

'You don't either.'

'At least I know this isn't rapeseed.'

Eun-sang took out her phone from her satchel and took a close-up of the flower. It seemed like she had an app that could tell you the name of the flower based on a picture of its petals.

'It says it's called Golden Wave. It belongs to the daisy family and there are annual and biennial species.'

'That name's perfect. It's so mesmerising. I bet it would make for a great picture.'

'That's an idea!'

We all looked at each other in agreement. Because it was peak season, all the famous spots were packed with tourists. But here, there were barely any people. We couldn't not take a picture. We took turns taking photos in pairs, a sun-bathed field of sparkling Golden Wave behind us. Finally, it was Jisong's turn to take a picture of Eun-sang and me. As Jisong ran with her back to us so she could get a wide angle, Eun-sang whispered something to me in a low voice:

'It hit 430,000.'

Jisong stopped running as soon as Eun-sang said this. We flinched, afraid that she'd heard us, but she seemed to have missed it. She turned around and held up her phone as she shouted, 'You're gorgeous!'

Jisong's voice was almost inaudible due to the sound of hundreds of thousands of flowers swaying in the breeze.

'The lighting is perfect. You two look so happy.'

Did we? Eun-sang and I, who were still posing for Jisong, looked at each other. When our eyes met, our smiles grew even larger. Just as Jisong had said, Eun-sang looked ecstatic. I guess Jisong was right. But did I look as happy? As if she'd read my mind, Eun-sang extended her left hand slightly behind her butt, put her palm in mine, and locked fingers with me. I squeezed her hand. I couldn't hold back my smile any longer.

'So natural! Just like that!'

We let ourselves go and smiled from ear to ear. A strong gust of wind blew, causing my short hair to stick to my cheek. I grabbed the hair and tucked it behind my ears as I squeezed Eun-sang's hand a bit tighter. She squeezed my hand back. She squeezed so tight that I almost cried out in pain. We were still looking each other in the eye, and our smiles were so wide we could see all our teeth. In the distance, we could hear Jisong shout out to us: 'Now look at me.' When we turned to look at her, she was crouching to get a better angle. With her eyes focused on the phone screen, she was raising one hand high above her head and giving us a thumbs up.

# Double O

*30 August 2017*

We arrived at the ocean-view cafe a bit later than we would have liked. The building was large, more of a mansion than a cafe. We crossed the parking lot, and when we entered the building through the back entrance we couldn't help but gasp. We were surprised first by the panoramic view and next by the throngs of people sitting along the window.

'Look at all those people.'

We waded through the crowd of people, which was dense despite all the space in the cafe. There were no seats next to the window – in fact, there were no empty tables at all inside. I was regretting our decision to have a relaxing morning when I realised that Eun-sang was no longer with us. I turned around and found her standing back at the entrance. I waved, raising my eyebrows to ask what she was doing over there. Only then did she slowly start walking over to us, all the while marvelling at the packed cafe.

'They must be rolling in money,' she said. 'But I'm not surprised. This is a great location.'

Jisong's sideways glance was saying, 'There she goes again, talking about money.' Jisong took the lead and started looking for an empty table. The crowd was densest towards the window. Outside they had a lawn speckled with beanbags and camping chairs, and beyond that was the ocean. At first, we tried sitting on the grass, but it was so hot that we came right back inside. Coincidentally a group was leaving just as we passed them, releasing a table in the right-most corner of the cafe.

I finally was able to take in the sights once we sat down. Eun-sang was right. This location *was* perfect. Despite being in the corner of the cafe, there was nothing obstructing our view of the ocean. Eun-sang went to get coffee as Jisong and I marvelled at the ocean swells. When Eun-sang came back with our drinks, Jisong took her iced coffee, lifted it up, and took a picture using the lawn and ocean as a backdrop.

'I had no idea Jeju Island was this beautiful,' she said.

'It truly is beautiful,' I chimed in.

'I used to think people were just being patriotic when they said it's the most beautiful island in the world,' Jisong said. 'But now I know what they mean. I went to Bali recently, remember? Bali's all right, but this is paradise. You know that friend of mine? The one who grew up on Jeju Island? She went on a trip to Europe recently and said that not even Europe's most famous beaches have water as blue as Jeju's.'

'Who? Your friend from college?'

'Yeah...'

Jisong's words trailed off as she watched disinterested Eun-sang pull out her phone again. I didn't have a good angle, but I knew she was looking at BitGo. My phone buzzed. It was a message from Eun-sang.

**Eun-sang**
It hit 450,000.
**Eun-sang**
It's really catching fire now.

As I glanced out of the corner of my eye at Jisong, I decided not to respond and just tapped the power button. But there was nothing I could do about the excitement raging deep inside me. Jisong was looking back and forth at Eun-sang and me with a cross look on her face.

'Is something wrong?' she asked. 'Why do you keep staring at your phones?'

'Oh? That—'

Before I could think of an excuse, Jisong cut me off:

'You guys aren't texting each other behind my back, are you?'

'No, it's not that—'

'Actually,' Eun-sang said, cutting in. 'The cryptocurrency we've invested in is skyrocketing right now. Really. Its price goes up every time we look at it. I feel like I'm losing my mind. I can't stop looking at it. Sorry.'

I didn't expect Eun-sang to be so honest. After all, for the last several months, Jisong would blow up and yell at us every time we mentioned cryptocurrency. At some point, Eun-sang and I promised each other not to mention cryptocurrency again in front of Jisong.

Back when I first started investing in Ethereum, Eun-sang was the only other person I knew who knew about it. Most people had only ever heard of Bitcoin, if even that. But in just the last few weeks, Ethereum had been featured on the evening news several times. And it wasn't just Ethereum; several new coins like Ripple and Quantum were experiencing nationwide booms. Articles, videos and editorials about cryptocurrency were being pumped out daily and dominating the finance sections of news websites. They criticised such investments as misguided and warned about the dangers of this new get-rich-quick culture. The articles sounded just like Jisong. In fact, I wouldn't be surprised if Jisong had read these articles and was repeating their arguments to us, like a parrot.

She always said to Eun-sang and me that if we wanted to invest in anything, we should be investing in stocks — that stocks had actual value and real companies behind them, that cryptocurrency had no value, that our money could disappear overnight, that we shouldn't go all in on something so volatile without a backup plan, that she couldn't understand why we were doing this, that we were so much smarter than this, that we should stop recommending cryptocurrency to her. Whenever she went on like this, Eun-sang would also turn into a broken record, 'That's not true. It has value. Blockchain is the banking system of the future!' But Jisong would always reply, 'I don't even know what that means! Whatever, I'm not getting into it. So, stop talking about it!'

Jisong wore a look of disapproval as she stirred her iced coffee with a straw. Behind her was a backdrop of tropical waters. Deep contempt flashed across her eyes as she glared at us and shook her head. Her brow furrowed as though she were looking at an irksome speck of dirt.

'You two are losing your minds,' she said. 'You're losing your minds over that damn cryptocurrency.'

She paused before adding with emphasis:

'You're like two lunatics.'

'What's your problem?' Eun-sang said as she slammed her phone down on the table. 'I should be allowed to look at my investments as often as I want.'

'Is it normal to look at your phone all day when you're on vacation in Jeju Island? Just look at this view!'

'So what? I'm not telling you to do it. Feel free to look at the ocean all you want.'

'We're finally hanging out, just the three of us. But all you two are interested in is your phones. How do you think I feel? Not to mention the fact that you're sending messages to each other behind my back. I'm like a third wheel.'

Jisong took a deep breath then continued to lecture us:

'You guys have been doing this since yesterday. Did you really think I wouldn't notice? If you were going to be like this, why did you invite me?'

Starting to feel a bit guilty, I slipped my phone into my pocket.

'I'm sorry you feel that way,' Eun-sang said apologetically. 'But you must understand. We've put our entire life savings into this. And right now, it's skyrocketing. It's making it so hard not to look. I don't know how to quite explain it. If you'd invested, you'd understand.'

At this point, I thought Eun-sang had said just enough to make her point. Any more and she would ruin it. But just as I feared, she couldn't stop herself and ended up crossing the line.

'What I'm trying to say is, it would've been perfect if you'd started when I first invited you. If you only knew how much Dahae has earned because she listened to me, you wouldn't be talking like this.'

'Just stop!' Jisong shouted.

Everyone sitting near us turned to stare at us.

'I said I'm not investing.'

Jisong's face was fuming red.

'Please, stop. You two don't know how ridiculous you look. You two have absolutely lost your minds over that damn crypto-whatever. If you love money that much, you should make it honestly with hard work and sweat. Using money to make more money is dishonest. It's no better than gambling!'

She opened her arms and pointed to the ocean beyond the window.

'All you guys think about is money. But you know what? There are more important things in this world than money. Just look at that water. That emerald green. Have you no shame?'

Jisong paused a moment before continuing:

'It's a bad look. It's disgusting.'

172

Suddenly, Eun-sang started to chuckle. Her laughter started quietly but slowly got louder and louder. It made me feel uncomfortable. Then just as suddenly as it started, the smile on her face disappeared completely.

'Jisong,' Eun-sang began. 'You're one to talk. Isn't that right, Dahae?'

Eun-sang turned to me. Not knowing what she was trying to get at, I just sat there silently. She returned to Jisong.

'If it weren't for us, you wouldn't have been able to afford any of this. Did you forget where all that money came from?'

Jisong avoided Eun-sang's eyes by turning towards the ocean. It seemed Eun-sang's words had hit a nerve.

'You came here because Dahae and I paid for everything. With the money we got from Ethereum. You came here with nothing. You didn't pay a single penny.'

Eun-sang pointed over her shoulder towards the parking lot with her thumb.

'Oh, sorry. I almost forgot,' Eun-sang said with a scoff. 'You rented that piece-of-shit compact. Thank you so much.'

Eun-sang had crossed the line. She wasn't showing any signs of stopping, but I didn't know what I could do.

'You paid jack squat. Not the plane ticket you almost wasted by being late. Not the raw fish platter from yesterday, which you ate the most of, may I remind you. Not our hotel or the admission fee to the pool party. Not this outrageously expensive coffee. Nothing!'

Eun-sang picked up her phone, launched BitGo, and shoved the screen in Jisong's face. As the phone dangled in front of her eyes, the price of Ethereum shot up again in real time.

'We've paid for everything with this thing you called "disgusting". What do you have to say about that?'

'Eun-sang,' I said, unable to stand by any longer. 'Why are you being like this? We do cryptocurrency because we want to. It's OK if Jisong doesn't.'

'You're right.' Eun-sang lowered her gaze and nodded her head for a moment before suddenly looking up again and lifting her head. 'But I'm not the one who started it. She's the one who called us lunatics. She thinks we're just two money-grabbers.'

I didn't know who was at fault. I didn't want our first trip together to be ruined like this. It had been less than a day. I grabbed Eun-sang's arm with both hands and forced it and her phone beneath the table in a desperate attempt to return things to the way they'd been. I patted the back of her hand and shook it up and down trying to placate her.

'Let's not do this. I know you're angry; Jisong shouldn't have said what she said. But she only reacted like that because you asked her to do cryptocurrency with us again. She already said she didn't care what we did as long as we didn't try to drag her into it. And we already promised each other we would stop.'

Jisong, who was still staring out the window at the ocean, didn't look in our direction, but she did slowly nod her head as if she agreed with what I said. Eun-sang, on the other hand, looked like she thought I was being unfair.

'Is wanting her to join us such a crime? This isn't some pyramid scheme. It's not like I will get any money if she starts doing it. I just feel bad that it's just us who are making the money. I want Jisong to be rich like us. I'm doing this for you, Jisong, not for me. I can teach you. I can help—'

'No. I don't need your help,' Jisong said brusquely.

'Actually, you need it the most.'

Jisong shot Eun-sang a glare.

'Let's be real. We all agree that we live hopeless lives, right? But out of the three of us, your life is the most hopeless, Jisong. You must know this.'

Jisong bit her lip, as though deep down she knew this was true.

'You know it. I know it. You're a double O.'

Double O? What did that even mean?

'You, me, Dahae. Right now, we have the same job rank and earn the same pay check. But how long do you think we can be friends like this as if nothing is wrong? In about a year or two, assuming we continue working like we have been, Dahae and I will have been promoted to assistant managers and will be taking on more responsibilities. We'll be working our way up the pay scale. And while the two of us get promotions, you're going to be stuck in the same place doing the same work every day, without a proper job title. You'll be called 'Ms Jisong' for the rest of your life.'

It seemed like Eun-sang knew something about Jisong that I didn't.

'We know we have nothing to lean on. We know we're poor and weren't born with silver spoons in our mouths. Our spoons were dirty, and so are we. If you don't have the will to improve your circumstances on your own, then please, at least marry a man with a stable job, not some college freshman from Taiwan. Don't you see yourself! You waste half your money on plane tickets to go and see him, and the other half going to Yangyang for surfing lessons every weekend. You've completely lost touch with reality. How do you expect to continue living like this? Do you even save any more? And at the same time, you're always asking me to introduce you to someone so you can get married. Can you see now why you're such a headache to deal with?'

As Jisong continued to stare out at the ocean, tears started gushing from her eyes.

'Eun-sang,' I said, grabbing her shoulder. 'You should apologise to Jisong.'

Eun-sang turned to look at Jisong and saw the tears that were making puddles in the lap of her dress. A look of remorse flashed across her face for a second before she folded her arms and looked the other way. Jisong was sobbing now. She quickly wiped away the tears, which were hanging from her chin like icicles hanging from eaves, and dabbed her eyes. Her eye make-up, which she'd put so much effort into, was now all over her fingertips and the back of her hand. She picked up her floppy straw hat from the windowsill, folded it, and stormed out of the cafe.

Staring at her as she left the cafe, I regretted not saying anything.

I couldn't hear the murmur of the people in the cafe any more. All I could hear was the flip-flopping of Jisong's sandals as she walked off, her yellow dress fluttering.

My chair let out a screeching sound as I pushed it back and got up. Eun-sang grabbed me by the wrist.

'Eun-sang, why did you have to be so mean?' I said as I swatted her hand away.

'I know. I'm a mean bitch.'

Jisong had already disappeared from sight. I strung the rattan bag Jisong had left on the chair over my shoulder and started running after her.

# A Table for You and Me

*30 August 2017*

I couldn't find Jisong even though I came out right after her. As I called her name and wandered through the labyrinth of cars in the parking lot, my heart sank and moisture started to form in my eyes. I'd sat there doing nothing while Eun-sang verbally abused Jisong. Why hadn't I stopped her? Perhaps I secretly agreed with Eun-sang. And what was double O? My head hurt as though someone was squeezing it.

Once I crossed the parking lot, I discovered Jisong in the distance walking away from me, the image of her no larger than a fingernail. Thankfully I was able to recognise her immediately from the large hat hanging around her neck. I was about to call out to her but stopped myself. I decided instead to follow her slowly and keep my distance. I felt like I was trying to approach a skittish stray cat.

The sun was beating down on the sidewalk. I continued to shadow Jisong along the empty road. Without a spot of shade to hide in, my back became drenched in sweat after just a few minutes. I took the rubber hair-band from my wrist and tied up the hair that was sticking to the back of my neck. As I fanned my burning cheeks, I gazed at Jisong in the distance and wished for her sake that she would put her hat properly on her head. At least that way, one of us would be spared sunburn. If only I could protect her from the sun's rays. If only she were not so far away. I imagined Jisong walking directly in front of me. I was reaching out, gently grabbing the brim of her straw hat, and sliding it over her head. And Jisong would then turn around and look at me.

As I imagined this, Jisong suddenly changed direction. She stepped off the sidewalk and onto the grass. After a while, she disappeared into the bush. It seemed she had found a path through the tall grass and trees, one that I couldn't see from where I was. I quickened my pace and chased after her.


I followed the narrow dirt path Jisong had taken into a forest. A green smell filled my nostrils. The deeper I went, the denser the surrounding trees became. With each step came a new species of tree, each with a different shape of leaf.

What was this small, dense forest? It didn't seem man-made. It felt natural, but I couldn't be certain. I continued to follow the path farther into the forest, albeit hesitantly. Seeing the occasional plant label in the ground, I realised the forest had to be cared for. And yet aside from those labels, the forest felt untouched, almost primal.

I could hear cuckoos and crows, as well as the call of a bird I couldn't quite identify. Crickets chirping, leaves rustling in the wind, and ocean waves breaking. I must have been just steps away from the shore. These sounds were like a soundtrack to our footsteps as we treaded the dirt path. The sound of Jisong's flip-flops with their bright white straps was getting louder. Jisong might also be taking in nature's symphony. I started walking a bit faster. I closed the distance between us, without making it too obvious. Before I knew it, Jisong turned around and looked at me.

'This place is really beautiful, isn't it?' she asked.

She seemed to know I'd been following her. I tried to hide my surprise.

'Yeah, it really is.'

'Dahae, you didn't know I was a double O, did you?' Jisong asked nonchalantly.

'I didn't. I don't even know what that is.'

Jisong turned again and showed me her back. About three steps still separated us. Jisong tilted her head back slightly and began to walk again as she looked up at the sky. She then began to explain to me what a 'double O' was, in a calm, even kind, voice.

As well as full-time employees, Maron also hired interns who had the chance to become permanent employees, and contract workers who were limited to working for a maximum of two years with the company. Double Os however, were somewhere in between these two, a type of indefinite contract worker. The work double Os did was simpler and more limited than that of other permanent employees, but needed more skill to complete than a typical intern or contract worker could offer. When the company needed someone to manage such duties for an indefinite amount of time, they would hire a double O. 'Double O', or 'OO', came from the term 'office operator'. It turned out that Jisong hadn't gone to college, only graduating from high school with a specialty in accounting. She'd immediately found a job as an accountant at a small company where she worked for the next five years before being hired by Maron as a double O. Because there were no double Os in Branding where I worked, I had no idea that such a position existed. But apparently, each team in Management Support had one or two of them. Jisong was the only double O in Accounting.

Jisong was hired as a double O because Accounting needed someone just to balance accounts. On the surface, she looked like any other employee. Her company badge was the same shape and colour as everyone else's, and obviously there was no 'OO' recorded next to her name in the company's organisational chart. Jisong's status as a double O was only known by people with special clearance, like people from HR or the hiring manager. She worked in the same office, did more or less the same work as everyone else, and received just as much overtime and vacation. She was also evaluated yearly against the same standards, just like everyone else. But there was one decisive difference between her and the rest of us: money. Even if she received the same performance evaluations as me, her raise was applied differently. This pay scale was set in stone when she entered the company and had a much slower rate of growth. She was also excluded from being considered for bonuses or incentives. This was the first time I learned that she had never received the

50,000-won gift card that the company passed out twice a year on Chuseok and Lunar New Year. Most important, no matter how long she worked at the company, she was never going to be given an official job title, like assistant manager or general manager. So she would always be referred to as 'Ms Jisong' instead of something like Assistant Manager Kim.

Another thing Jisong told me, although I found it hard to believe, was that the people in her department refused to eat with her. They would invite her to the monthly or bi-monthly office dinner party or to the quarterly workshop, but they never invited her to lunch during the week.

'Well, I doubt they do it on purpose—'

Her department rarely ate together, she tried to explain, and people usually ate separately. There were always one or two people who had their own plans, and her team had a lot of small cliques. But because Jisong was the only one without any friends in the team, she always ate lunch and dinner by herself. That was, at least, until she started eating with Eun-sang, who was in the team next to hers. And once a week, I would break off from my own team to join them. Meals were her favourite time of the day, she said, the thing she always looked forward to.

'What will I do if you guys leave the company?' Jisong asked. 'Just thinking about that frightens me.'

Jisong slowly turned around to look at me.

'Please stay with me for as long as you can,' she said. 'And promise me you'll get promoted to assistant manager and general manager and department manager.'

She then asked me if she could continue calling me by my name instead of Assistant Manager Jeong, even after I became an assistant manager next year. 'What are you talking about? Of course you can,' I said, intentionally raising my voice. When she asked me if she would have to call me Department Manager Jeong when I got that promotion, I yelled even louder, almost angrily, 'Of course not!'

'Department Manager Dahae Jeong… Department Manager Jeong…' Jisong repeated this to herself several times before laughing about how strange and icky it sounded.

'Do you think you'll stay that long?' she asked me.

I didn't say anything.

'I have no idea where my life is headed,' Jisong continued. 'I know I need to save up money. I know dating Wei Lin isn't good for me. But I just want to live in the moment, without thinking about the consequences. And at the same time, that makes me uneasy… I don't know what I should do.'

'Just do what you want. Not everyone can live like Eun-sang, always planning and calculating. Eun-sang's just a bit different.'

'You think so, too?'

'Yes.'

With this short and definite agreement, we stopped talking and finally started walking side by side.

How far did we walk? As we rounded a bend in the forest path, I tilted my head back to follow the trunk of one tree all the way up to the canopy. Despite not touching each other, the branches were dense enough to fill the gaps between the trees and shield us from the sun. The canopy was like a fine yet chaotic fishing net made from blue silk that had been cast over the sky. It even looked like the palm of someone whose fortune had been etched in sky blue ink. Thin beams of light scattered as they passed through the cracks. I leaned back and soaked in the sun's faint rays.

'What is all this?' Jisong was pointing to several towers of rocks in the distance.

Black-grey stones, both big and small, were stacked to form tall, pointy spires. The base of each tower was just wide enough to prevent a single person from wrapping their arms around it. The towers were tall enough to dwarf most adults. There was something awe-inspiring about them. How could such precarious stacks of rocks stand upright without falling over on this windy island?

The towers received the light shining through the canopy and twinkled like Broadway actors under a spotlight.

There were several similarly shaped rock towers of different sizes, forming a small colony. I quickly counted about a dozen of them. I wasn't sure whether to describe them as 'beautiful and elegant' or 'totally awesome'. Regardless, the way these towers were so perfectly balanced was enough to instill wonder in me even from a distance. Jisong seemed mesmerised as she approached the towers.

As we got closer, I slowly realised the towers were much larger than I'd initially estimated. Utterly magnificent. They were nothing more than piles of rocks, but they were somehow glamorous. What were they called? Wishing towers? Cairns? How long had they been here? Did one person stack all these rocks in the hope that all their wishes would come true? Or perhaps they were built over a long time by different people, one rock for each wish. Although I knew nothing about these rock towers, I could imagine someone stacking rocks one at a time towards the tall sky, and conveyed with that image was a sense of the sublime and sanctity.

Placed at the base like cornerstones were hefty boulders too large for one person to lift. Stacked above were similarly shaped rocks of smaller size. And above those were rocks the size of bricks. As you went higher up the tower, the rocks became smaller in a regular, uniform manner, as though they were following some geometric series. And even though each rock was angular and shaped differently, they all fit together perfectly, like a picture that had been broken apart and pieced back together. I lifted my head and looked up to the top of one of the towers. A flat, round chestnut-sized rock was placed at the top as though it were balancing the entire pile. The tower next to it was the same. Although they were of slightly different heights and breadths, they shared the same shape. Each was like a miniature or magnified version of the other. The balance of each individual tower and the balance of the towers as a group was so perfect and thus beautiful.

*Sparkle, sparkle.* Twinkling small rocks receiving individual specks of light. Small rocks at different heights each with their own place.

Jisong strode over to the closest tower.

'They're so beautiful, Dahae.'

'They really are. I feel like I should show respect.'

'Me, too. It's like I'm in the presence of something magnificent.'

Jisong took a step closer, extended her arm, and was about to touch it. Afraid the tower would fall over, I quickly grabbed her sleeve from behind and pulled her back.

'Hey, hey. Be careful.'

As I said this, I discovered that the edges of Jisong's shoulders were shaking minutely. As though the sound wave of my voice had set her body vibrating at the same frequency and amplitude.

'You've got to be kidding me,' she said.

'What's wrong?'

Jisong turned around and glared at me. As I thought about what to say, the expression on Jisong's face changed.

'They're being held together.'

'Come again?'

'It's all held together by cement.'

Jisong reached out towards the surface of the rock tower without hesitation and stuck her finger between the rocks angrily.

'Look! Look at this. It's cement! Cement!'

I brought my face right up to the rock tower to get a good look. Indeed, filling the gaps between the sharp rocks was dark grey cement.

No way.

It wasn't just these mysterious rock towers that I couldn't believe. It was also the emotions I'd felt while looking at them. It was so strange. Even though I knew now that the rocks were standing up with help, even though the sublimity from earlier had been somewhat reduced, I still couldn't stop admiring their beauty. Jisong kicked the base of one of the towers.

'Oh, fuck!'

This was the first time I had ever heard Jisong swear.

'Argh!'

Jisong let out an ear-splitting scream. She grabbed her foot with both hands, fell to the ground, and started rolling in the dirt. My stomach dropped. The entirety of this small, tranquil forest was suddenly echoing with her terrifying screams. Before the echoes even stopped, something even more terrifying caught my eye, causing my heart to start pounding out of my chest.

Jisong's foot, which she was holding, was covered in blood. I was as surprised by the blood as I was by the speed with which it had covered her entire foot. I didn't think it was possible for blood to come out of one's foot that fast. The bleeding didn't look like it was going to stop. She was squeezing her foot to stop the bleeding, but blood continued to seep through her fingers. Tears started falling from my eyes as fast as blood was pouring out of her foot. I knelt in front of Jisong, who was still rolling around on the ground in pain, and squeezed her bloody flip flops with my hands hoping it would stop the bleeding. 'Oh my god, oh my god,' I screamed again and again. I fumbled through my bag with bloody, shaking hands and pulled out my phone. I was terrified by the pungent smell of blood that had reached my nose. After two failed attempts, I finally managed to dial for help.

'This is the fire department. What is your emergency?'

'My friend. She's hurt. Like, there's blood.'

I couldn't get the words out because I was sobbing.

'She hit it. A giant rock... Yes, that's right. We're near Ocean Shine Cafe... No, we can't walk. My friend can't walk... She's, like, bleeding. A lot.'

The dispatcher told us the ambulance was on its way. She told me I could tell her our exact location when the ambulance got closer.

'But we're not at the cafe. We're in some remote forest!

'I don't know the name. There's this rock tower... No, this rock-tower-like thing... We're in front of it.'

Admitting this fact made me feel even worse, and another bout of tears started to pour out of my eyes.

# New Birthday

Jisong received stitches in the emergency room for over an hour. She was unfortunate enough to have kicked the only sharp rock protruding from the tower. And because of that, she had a gash in her foot ten centimetres deep and a fracture that would require surgery when we got back to Seoul.

Eun-sang only arrived at the hospital once the initial chaos was over. There was no need to fill her in, however, because I'd already told her the whole story over the phone. Eun-sang tiptoed into the room, knelt at the edge of Jisong's bed, and placed her palm next to Jisong's foot wrapped in thick bandages. She didn't lift her head once while doing this.

My opinion was that Jisong deserved an apology. That was the right thing to do. And this was the perfect time. I was expecting the words 'I'm sorry' to come out of Eun-sang's mouth, but she kept us waiting. To my surprise, it was Jisong, not Eun-sang, who was the first to offer an apology.

'Eun-sang, I'm sorry.'

Jisong, who had been propping herself up on the bed, was now lying flat on her back and staring at the ceiling. She spoke as if she were talking to herself.

'You're right, Eun-sang. Everything you said is right. I've known it, too. I've known it all along. If I don't break this pattern, I'm going to be earning pennies for the rest of my life. I'm going to end up spending every penny I have with nothing left in my savings. I have nothing and no one to rely on. I'm the only one responsible for my life. And looking after myself is only going to get harder. My parents have no retirement plan. I'm probably going to have to take care of them. In four years, I'm going to be thirty. If I'm lucky, I'll be able to move out of my studio apartment and into a proper home by the time I'm forty. I might even be able to achieve my lifelong goal of getting married and having three children. But for that to happen, I need to start studying for the civil service exam. And if I can't manage that, I need to at least meet a man with a stable job who can support a family. All of this, I know.'

When she finished, Jisong nodded her head a few times as if to convince herself one more time of her reality. After a momentary pause, her determined facial expression was overtaken by sadness.

'But Eun-sang, I don't want to marry some man who's way older than me and unattractive.'

Jisong started weeping. Her tears flowed straight down her temple and fell onto the pillow cover, on which were printed the words 'Seogwipo Medical Centre'. Jisong was now weeping with her entire body. Eun-sang and I were caught off guard and unable to say anything. We just sat there and listened to Jisong's sobbing in silence.

'I've never cared about looks before. They say girls need to date guys who like them, that happiness comes from *being* loved. We were always told this when we were younger, remember? So, that's all I considered when dating. Not whether I liked a guy, but whether he liked me and how much. That seemed most important to me. Even if I didn't like him, even if he wasn't my type, I would still date him so long as he said he liked me. And if he was good to me, I saw no reason to break it off. After a while of being together, they would start to grow on me. My affection for them was contingent on their affection for me. Even if I didn't like them, I'd start liking them for the sole reason that they liked me. Of course, even I have my own preferences. There are some guys I feel more attracted to. But I've always lived my life ignoring those things.'

Jisong was getting the words out despite her tight throat.

'But I don't want to date someone just because they like me. I want to date someone because *I* like them. And what I like... what I like is a pretty face. I like Wei Lin's face. I know myself now. There are all kinds of people in the world, and I... and I am someone who likes handsome men. I don't think I can meet anyone else. No matter how much he likes me, if I don't like him, if he doesn't have a pretty face, I'm not going to date him.'

Jisong wiped the corners of her eyes with her scratched-up hands and tried to catch her breath.

'And, most importantly,' she continued, 'Wei Lin likes me as much as I like him. He really *really* likes me. After he graduates, he's going to come to Korea and look for work. He's learning Korean right now, too. Do you know how cute it is to watch him reciting the Korean alphabet? I know there are a lot of things working against us, but I've finally found someone who I like as much as he likes me. He's not someone I like just because they like me. Something as lucky and improbable as this won't happen twice. I can't live without this.'

I had no idea that looks were so important to Jisong. So, when I heard this confession, which flowed out of her like water from a burst dam, I couldn't help but pity her. Eun-sang took out two travel tissues from her bag and wiped Jisong's tears as she patted her on the back.

'There you go. It's OK. You'll find a handsome man. Now that you know what you want, you can stop crying. You'll wear off the anaesthetic if you continue sobbing.'

This didn't sound scientifically accurate to me, but Jisong followed Eun-sang's advice nevertheless. She took a long, deep breath in through her snotty nose as she tried to get a hold of herself.

'So, Eun-sang—' Jisong began. 'How do you do that thing?'

'Do what thing?'

'That thing you do. Cryptocurrency.'

Eun-sang and I turned to each other in surprise.

'I want to join you two,' Jisong said, this time with more confidence.

Before Jisong could ask again, Eun-sang snatched up Jisong's phone from the corner of the bed and put it in Jisong's hands.

'First, you need to download the app. Once you open an account, I'll send you ten, no, twenty ether. I started way before you; I can spare that much.'

Jisong and I blinked our eyes in disbelief.

'Are you serious?' we both shouted.

'Think of it as a birthday present. Twenty ether is worth 8,700,000 won based on today's prices. We won't sell until—'

Eun-sang paused for a moment as she caught her breath.

'Until it reaches 87,000,000 won. No! 100,000,000!'

Right at that moment, Eun-sang seemed like the coolest person in the world to me. I was somewhat envious of Jisong, too. And I felt ashamed for feeling this way. Eun-sang was sharing her immense wealth. Perhaps I should have given Jisong three of my own ether, too. Jisong's face, which had been a mottled mess of regret, shame, sadness and despair, was gradually being overrun with joy.

'But my birthday is in November—'

Jisong lifted herself up and propped up her pillow to lean against. She wiped both cheeks with the palm of her hand before glancing at the lock screen of her phone and declaring in a barely audible voice:

'From this day forward, *today* is my birthday. August 30th.'

# Is It Greed or Is It Desire?

*13 September 2017*

There's a Korean proverb, but I can't quite remember how it goes. Was it 'The scariest kind of thief is a late bloomer'? Whatever the saying is, Jisong embodied it by losing herself in cryptocurrency as soon as we got back from Jeju Island.

Eun-sang worried for nothing that Jisong didn't have any money to invest. She had a small amount in her savings and was also able to make a deal with her landlord to increase her rent in return for getting a large portion of her security deposit back early. She even opened a line of credit. She took this money and dumped all of it into Ethereum.

If only Ethereum had kept going up.

The problem was that the sharp upward trend we experienced from July to August turned upside down in September. And unfortunately for Jisong, August 30th, her new birthday, was the day that Ethereum peaked. In fact, when we woke up the next day, it had already fallen several per cent, and this only continued through breakfast. It was sharp fall after sharp fall, with no sign of stopping. The dreaded nosedive.

But Jisong wasn't deterred. Quite the contrary; even as prices were falling, she used part of her monthly pay check to buy even more ether. Then again, Eun-sang *had* taught us that when cryptocurrency prices dropped this much, it was a sign that you should buy even more. Textbook scale trading. But whether Jisong was following Eun-sang's teachings because she really believed them, or because she was simply desperate to earn back what she'd lost, was uncertain. Every morning in the NOR(3) group chat, Jisong and Eun-sang would exchange messages like the following:

**Jisong**
Omg... It's down again.
**Eun-sang**
Don't worry! You have nothing to worry about.
**Jisong**
Captain Kang, do you think I should buy more?
**Eun-sang**
Yes. Go, go, go!
**Jisong**
To the moon!

After this, the two of them both sent the angel emoji, complete with a halo and that smiley face that looked like it belonged to someone who'd achieved nirvana. But I was getting a bad feeling about the whole thing. If I were her, I would consider pulling out, but Jisong must have been braver than I thought, because she was holding steady. She'd probably learned over months of silently watching Eun-sang and me.

For several months, Eun-sang and I had been on an emotional rollercoaster as Ethereum's prices went up and down, never enjoying a single day of peace. And yet, in the end, when we came out on the other side, we were on a mountain top. So, it seemed Jisong was expecting she would also hit the jackpot if only she followed Eun-sang's advice: buy more when the price nosedives and then hold on for dear life.

Of course, I had faith that things would turn around. I was going to be like that American teenager who invested in Bitcoin when one coin was the price of a pizza. Of course, Ethereum was worth more like five or six pizzas when I first got in. Regardless, I was looking forward to the day I would cash in and finally quit my job.

But this was just a hopeful dream. There was no guarantee it would actually happen.

On the surface, Jisong was behaving as though everything was all right as she told herself over and over that Ethereum would turn around, that all she had to do was believe in Captain Kang's teachings. But I knew that she was biting her nails in secret because all ten of her fingertips had turned stubby and bloody. Eun-sang, who shared a cubicle wall with Jisong, said the dry tapping of hardened blood on Jisong's keyboard made her feel guilty. Even though she was encouraging Jisong to buy more and more ether, I could sense her anxiety and dread on the inside. She even told me that, from the way things were trending, the prices in August might be as good as they were going to get. And if that was the case, it would be smart to cash out as soon as possible.

I also had a feeling that this time things were different. Usually, the ups and downs of Ethereum only lasted for a few days at a time. Such a long dip was unprecedented.

Things were different now, after all. Unlike earlier this year, everyone had heard about cryptocurrencies like Ethereum and Bitcoin. Every gathering had at least one person who pretended to be well-informed on the topic. At the start when people warned of get-rich-quick fever and the inevitable crash of cryptocurrency, it was easy to tune out the noise. But I couldn't ignore these voices any more. And that was because there was serious talk about government regulations. It was no longer something we could pretend not to listen to.

Then the worst happened when, just a few days ago, China released new regulations targeting cryptocurrencies. With that, every coin in the cryptocurrency market took a nosedive unlike anything the market had seen before. Ethereum itself was down no less than 60 per cent. The price of one ether, which had been so close to 500,000 won when we were in Jeju Island, had now done a one-eighty and dropped as low as 200,000 won. I stared vacantly at the price of Ethereum for a while, which looked like it had just ended its life by jumping off a cliff, before shaking myself out of it and sending Eun-sang a message.

**Dahae**
Did you see the article about China?
**Eun-sang**
Yeah. Things don't look too good.

A week after the news of China's new regulations broke, I ran into Eun-sang in front of the elevator on the third floor. We went to the end of the hallway, leaned against the wall and started talking with looks of gloom on our faces.

'I'd been holding out in hope that it would start rising again,' Eun-sang said. 'But I don't know if there's a point in waiting any longer.'

She confessed that she regretted getting Jisong into cryptocurrency. Because Jisong had bought in at the peak, she'd only lost money. The twenty ether Eun-sang had given her wasn't even enough to cover the losses. Because we got in earlier, we would still make a profit if we sold now. I desperately wished that Jisong's ether would increase in value, even if ours didn't. Of course, I knew this to be impossible. We'd boarded the same ship. Our destinies were interlocked. And right now, we were in the middle of a storm, faced with the dilemma of whether to abandon the ship or go down with it.

Eun-sang was considering selling all her ether as soon as she got the chance. With the money she earned, she would give Jisong enough to cover her losses. After all, it was she who had egged Jisong on, so it was she who should take responsibility.

'If Korea starts regulating cryptocurrency too, this current nosedive will be nothing compared to the crash that's headed our way. Honestly, I've been looking for the right time to get out for some time now.'

It wasn't that Eun-sang disagreed with regulation. But she did think it would be best to stop investing in cryptocurrency once regulations were put in place because that would cause prices to fall. And if Eun-sang was going to exit this virtual world, I needed to exit too. After all, when it came to money, I trusted Eun-sang's judgement. She was the only captain for me.

Deep down, though, I didn't want to accept that this was the end.

I thought for sure we'd go higher. I thought we were headed for the moon. I didn't want to leave. Not yet. This wasn't enough! It was far from enough. With prices as they were right now, the balance in my virtual wallet was a mere 50,000,000 won. Combining everything I'd put into Ethereum until now – the money from my savings account, my severance pay, the dangerous loan, and each pay check I earned – I had invested a total of 20,000,000 won. That meant I'd only made 30,000,000 investing in Ethereum. Sure, it was more than I earned in a year, but I didn't want to accept that the effortless fortune I'd dreamed of for the last six months was never going to manifest.

I was angry. This was so unfair. At the same time, I wondered how I could be so shameless, so entitled, so greedy. But it couldn't be helped. People's greed was always shameless and limitless. Make one million, and you'll want ten million. Make ten million, and you'll want one hundred million. More and more, your greed would demand. Back on Jeju Island, I had 100,000,000 won. Having already imagined all the things I could do with 100,000,000 won, 30,000,000 felt pitifully insufficient.

Now that I had a 1.2-room apartment, now that I could lie in my bed and not see my front door or kitchen, all I could think about was not having bed sheets that smelt like my cooking. I wanted more separation, more windows, better ventilation. Was that being greedy? Was wanting to sleep outside of your kitchen being greedy? Whether it was greed or simple human desire, I knew now that I wanted to live, not in a one-room apartment, but a one-*bedroom* apartment, where the bedroom and living space were separated. The street to my house from the bus stop was filled with eateries and bars. At night when the restaurants closed, there were always garbage bags lining the sidewalk. And that line of garbage didn't end when I entered my apartment. Every time I opened the window, the smell of food and the voices of drunkards would invade my space, something I hadn't realised would happen when I first saw the place. I knew for certain now that I was sensitive to smells. I hadn't known this about myself until moving here. I wanted to live in a place where I wouldn't have to smell pizza and gamjatang every time I opened my window. I didn't want a view of restaurants and karaoke bars; I wanted a view of a park, or at the very least a view with a tree or two. I wanted to move into a residential housing complex in a nice neighbourhood. I wanted the subway station to be within walking distance. Better yet, I wanted a car. Driving around Jeju Island made me realise how convenient it was to have your own vehicle. And if I bought a car, I would need to move into an apartment that had its own parking lot. I wanted to live in a family apartment complex, even if it had to be a small one. I wanted to go on frequent vacations, and I wanted to take trips abroad without having to worry about money.

I knew Eun-sang could sell right now if she wanted to. She would net 300,000,000 won if not more. That's how much I wanted. With that kind of money, I could quit my job at this dreadful company and take a much-needed — albeit short — break. I would have time to think about what my interests were and time to pursue what I was good at. I wasn't suggesting I bum around for the rest of my life. I wasn't that delusional. I just wanted to take a break for a year, no more, no less, as I searched for another career. Just one year, that was all I asked. But to do that, I needed more money than I had right now. A lot more. Perhaps this was greed after all.

Fine. I wanted money without having to work for it. I wanted a bit of leisure in my life. I'll admit it. I dreamed of getting rich quick. My pay check just wasn't enough. I needed more.

I placed my hand on Eun-sang's gloomy, hunched over shoulders and made a suggestion.

'Eun-sang, I can't stop now. Not like this. Let's seek advice before making our decision.'

'But from who?'

I rummaged through my wallet and handed Eun-sang a tattered business card.

Black hair pulled back in a traditional Korean bun, shiny forehead, dark eyebrow tattoos, bright red lipstick — printed in the middle of the business card was the striking photo of Madam Yeonwol.

# A Northwesterly
# Siberian Wind

*18 September 2017*

On the day we met at Coffee Bean, Ethereum had
slightly rebounded and was now worth 280,000 won.

Madam Yeonwol was already seated and waiting for
us, dressed in a white dress shirt with a crisp collar and her
hair pulled back into a tight bun. Open on the table was a
large notebook, and spread out next to this was a brown
mat. Madam Yeonwol was organising her tarot cards
on the mat when we arrived. I sat across from her and
greeted her with a slight nod. Jisong followed me in, then
Eun-sang. The three of us sat on the small sofa, our legs
touching. Madam Yeonwol went from right to left as she
inspected each of our faces. She greeted us with a question as she brushed off a blank page from her notebook.

'Young lady, I've seen you before, haven't I?'

'Yes, that's correct.'

Her eyes jumped back and forth between Jisong and
Eun-sang.

'And of the other young ladies, one of you is in a relationship with a foreigner it seems.'

Jisong was sitting right next to me, and I could sense her leg flinch when Madam Yeonwol said this. I glanced at Jisong through the corner of my eye; she was clearly dumbfounded. Last time I met Madam Yeonwol, with Team Leader Koh and General Manager Yun, she'd seen right through me. This time was no different. By skipping the questions and offering accurate descriptions of us, she was demonstrating her powers. Perhaps this was a business strategy of a kind. Of course, you would need at least some skill to pull off such a tactic. I looked again to my right. Judging from the look in Jisong's eyes, she was already helplessly bewitched by Madam Yeonwol.

'Yes, me. It's me,' Jisong said, going so far as to raise her hand high in the air.

'Young lady, it appears that foreign men are a good match for you.'

'Right?'

As Jisong said this with conviction, she turned to look at Eun-sang. I couldn't see her face, but I could clearly imagine the gloating smirk she must have been giving Eun-sang. 'I told you so.' Madam Yeonwol took out a black felt-tip pen from her shirt pocket and took off the cap. The cap came off with a small pop as the air trapped inside was released, echoing like an ominous gong.

'What is the date and time of your birth?' Madam Yeonwol asked as she put the cap on the back of the pen.

'1991. November—'

Jisong gave this information solemnly, as though she was making a confession. Madam Yeonwol quickly wrote the numbers into her notebook. It was lunchtime, and the cafe was filled with employees from the nearby companies. The bleak yet mysterious scratching of her felt-tip pen was floating atop a background of chatter. Beneath Jisong's date and time of birth, which was abbreviated with a few Chinese characters instead of the usual Arabic numerals, Madam Yeonwol wrote a few mysterious Chinese characters as she used the digits on her other hand to do mental maths. When she finished, she took out a red felt-tip pen and swiftly circled the characters she'd just scribbled.

'The young lady is best suited to a cold foreign country.'

'What?' Jisong blurted out with wide eyes. 'What about a warm country?'

'It says here a cold country.'

Jisong's expression suddenly turned dark.

'What about a warm*ish* country. Not a desert or anything like that.'

'That, I'm not sure. Either way, a place with freezing winds.'

Madam Yeonwol paused before continuing:

'The country is north of us.'

That settled it. Taiwan was undeniably south of Korea.

'You see,' Jisong began, 'I'm in a relationship with someone who lives in a somewhat tropical climate. I was planning to ask about that because I'm not sure what to do. If I should keep seeing him or—'

Madam Yeonwol nodded her head to indicate that she understood and picked up the deck of tarot cards from the mat. She fanned out the cards in front of Jisong.

'Would you pick three cards for me? It's important that you picture your relationship in your head as you do it.'

Jisong slowly ran her fingers over the top of the cards. I turned to look at Eun-sang who, as expected, was glancing back at me. We had reserved only forty-five minutes (fifteen minutes each), and Eun-sang and I were worried that Jisong's couple's counselling was going to use up all our time. Jisong picked one card, then another, and finally the last one. She then spent several minutes messaging Wei Lin on Facebook to ask him for the date and time of his birth. Finally, when that was done, Madam Yeonwol said she would use the Four Pillars of Destiny to determine if they should get married. Jisong was wasting all our time, but there was nothing we could do about it.

Eun-sang had finished all her iced coffee, and I could hear the sound of her crunching on the remaining ice. Then as if something had suddenly occurred to her, Eun-sang opened her eyes wide and impatiently interrupted the fortune-teller and Jisong's conversation.

'Wait! Wait! Just wait a minute.'

'Yes?'

Everyone turned to stare at Eun-sang.

'You said earlier that she's suited for a country north of here. Exactly what country is that?'

'Let's see—'

Madam Yeonwol opened her notebook and once again alternated between her red and black felt-tip pens as she wrote several Chinese characters in cursive-like handwriting. Finally, she wrote down two extremely difficult characters that I had never seen before and punctuated them with a double underscore.

'The Soviet Union,' she said.

'The Soviet Union?'

'Yes.'

'As in Russia?'

'That's the one. Let's have a look at your fortune too, young lady.'

Madam Yeonwol jotted down Eun-sang's date and time of birth on a new page.

'It's not just one of you, all three of you would do well in Russia. There are cold currents of air that come down from the north. Northwesterly Siberian winds, we call them. If you ride that current, it will take you places. Faraway places. That's what it says here.'

'All three of us? Including me?' I asked.

'Yes. Last time we met, I called you a ball of fire, remember? The fiercer the wind, the bigger the inferno.'

The more I listened, the less convinced I became. The fortune-teller took a deep breath and puffed out her cheeks. She then blew out all the air as she brought her palm down onto the table.

'The wind goes *whoosh* as the fire rages. You see what I'm saying?'

I nodded, but all I felt was doubt. At the beginning she'd swept us off our feet by guessing that Jisong's boyfriend wasn't Korean. But ever since then, she'd just been blowing smoke. Eun-sang, who was staring intently at the two Chinese characters for 'Soviet Union', had a conflicted look on her face. On second thoughts, perhaps she looked relieved. Although I couldn't understand why. Perhaps she really didn't like Wei Lin.

The session lasted a few more minutes. When we asked about investing, she said our fortunes for investing weren't particularly bad this year, but not particularly good either. And she warned us *not* to put all our eggs in one basket. But then again, wasn't this common-sense financial advice? As I sat there regretting our decision to consult a charlatan, our time suddenly ran out.

I felt somewhat disappointed as we left the cafe, unlike Eun-sang, who was staring down at the pavement with her hands deep in the pockets of her trench coat, nodding as though she was still undecided.

'I'm not selling,' she suddenly said in a low voice. 'Let's hold on just a little longer.'

'Why?'

'Vitalik Buterin, the co-founder of Ethereum—' She paused for a moment before continuing. 'He's Russian.'

At that moment, I heard a flame ignite in my mind – or was it in my heart? The flame was blazing. Without saying anything, Jisong and I took each other's hand.

We had decided to follow that northwesterly Siberian wind.

We had decided to hold on a bit longer.

# Attributes of Money

November 23th. Thursday. How could I ever forget such a numerically beautiful day? 1123.

It was a day like any other. The only difference was that it was so cold that I needed my winter woollen overcoat instead of my usual thin trench. On the sleeve of this coat, which I hadn't worn for some time, was a faint stain. It was the coffee I'd spilled in January on the way to J Mart HQ. I probably would have been able to get rid of the stain had I immediately dropped it off at the dry cleaners. But I'd made the mistake of trying to wash it myself at home. I eventually did take it to the dry cleaners when that didn't work, but by then it was too late. That was all before I started investing in Ethereum. If the same thing happened now, I'd have immediately taken it to the dry cleaners without hesitation. I found my past frugality laughable. Getting a woollen coat professionally cleaned only costs between 5,000 and 6,000 won. 10,000 at the most with spot cleaning. For what had I been so stingy?

I turned my nose up at my old mindset, but it wasn't like I'd completely forgotten what it was like.

I vividly remember spending my days with the expectation that tomorrow wasn't going to be any better than today, ignorant that improvement was even possible. I remember only wishing things wouldn't get worse. I remember living my day-to-day life neither sad nor discontent because I thought stagnancy was the way of the world. I remember clearly those squalid thoughts that had dried on my consciousness like an old stain.

I rolled up the cuff of my sleeve to hide the stain. But on the inside of my cuff were dozens of tiny insect-like pills. As I plucked off as many as I could, my eyes caught the hem of my coat, down by my knees. There, too, was a tiny infestation of pills. I bought this cream-coloured overcoat from the outlet mall nearly five years ago as a gift to myself for getting a full-time position at Maron. Before it, I'd only owned one other coat, which was a boring black. I loved this cream-coloured overcoat so much that I always wore it to important meetings. But this morning, I decided it was time to buy my third coat and started researching long coats on the subway train to work. 23 November 2017. That was the kind of day it was — at least until *it* happened.


I still don't understand why it happened on that day of all days.

I'd just finished lunch and was about to return to the office when Ethereum's price started rising as though it had suddenly met a mysterious and fast current. It was around 410,000 won that morning but broke through

440,000 won by three in the afternoon. It was then that we started sharing screenshots of BitGo in the group chat. With each successive new peak, three more screenshots arrived in NOR(3). We were secretly competing to see who could upload the image first. Our real-time reporting of Ethereum's price continued through the afternoon and even into the evening after we left work. Our messages didn't stop for anything, not even for bedtime. After all, we were too excited to fall asleep.

At around midnight, the price broke its five-month high, hitting 469,500 won. Eun-sang gave us her prediction:

**Eun-sang**
It'll hit 500,000 won tomorrow. It's picking up speed. I see it hitting 1,000,000 won this month. I believe it.
**Jisong**
Yes! Please!
**Dahae**
Let's go!
**Jisong**
O Captain!
**Dahae**
My Captain!

The next day, on the morning of the 24th of November, the price of Ethereum, which had been rising throughout the night, hit an all-time high. It finally passed 500,000 won, hitting a peak of 535,000 won. My virtual wallet was once again displaying nine figures. I couldn't believe it. It felt like great possibilities were opening themselves to me. I was standing before two steel doors that looked like they might open to a freezer.

They let out a metallic creak. And as they swung open, a beam of blinding light poured out from inside and into my eyes.

What made me the happiest was the look of joy on Jisong's face that morning. She had finally made a profit. She confessed to us that when Ethereum was falling, she hadn't been able to focus on her work because she spent all day nervously monitoring the price. But even though Ethereum had rebounded, she still couldn't focus on her work because all she wanted to do was check how much she was making now. Finally, she understood how we'd felt during our trip to Jeju Island.

**Jisong**
Can you imagine if I hadn't invested back then? Just think-ing about it makes me dizzy.

On the one hand, I was excited and happy, but on the other, I was a bit dumbstruck. We always talked about 'diamond hands', but these words now felt like some magic spell that only worked if you repeated it enough times. But there had to be a logical expla-nation for Ethereum's sudden spike. But what? Part of me didn't care, but the other part of me couldn't let it go. Prices always reflected value. Supply and demand. An explosion like this had to have been caused by something. I wondered if the regulatory risk had changed, or if experts had finally endorsed cryptocurrency. I looked for articles in my spare time, but everyone was only talking about cryptocur-rency's unexpected revitalisation. I couldn't find any detailed analysis of its cause.

**Dahae**

Why do you think it's rising like this?

**Dahae**

The risk of regulation is the same as before.

**Dahae**

Why now?

Eun-sang told us that there were no fundamental changes to cryptocurrency. At the beginning, Chinese regulations and rumours of regulations coming from the Korean government had hurt prices, but at the same time, this had given cryptocurrency a lot of media exposure. In the long run, this had had a positive effect on prices. At least according to Eun-sang's theory.

**Eun-sang**

Those people went on and on about how problematic cryptocurrency was, how it needed to be regulated, how we were going to get our just deserts.

**Eun-sang**

But by criticising it they started grabbing the attention of people who until then had no knowledge or interest in cryptocurrency.

**Eun-sang**

All they heard was 'you can get rich buying cryptocurrency'.

**Eun-sang**

That's how we got to where we are.

There were hundreds of news articles warning of the dangers of cryptocurrency, but all people remembered were the stories of people who became millionaires overnight. As a result, Eun-sang surmised, the demand for cryptocurrency actually increased. At the same time, people might have started investing their money into cryptocurrency because the housing and stock markets had become stagnant recently.

**Eun-sang**
All these things came together at the right time.

Money was a zero-sum game, so if money was taken from one pot, it had to go somewhere. Keep your eye on the money.

**Eun-sang**
I'm going to start paying closer attention.

Eun-sang had never had money to play with, so she had no idea what kind of attributes money had, where or how it flowed from one hand to the next. But soon, when she sold all her ether and was in possession of an actual fortune, she would need to know the laws that governed money in order to properly invest it.

**Eun-sang**
Where does money like to go? I want to know!

When I read this message, I was reminded of Eun-sang Kang's Mini Mart days. A woman in a dark office, hunched over her desk, illuminated by a single lamp. Her hands busily moving back and forth as she made stacks of coins from her piggy bank's punctured belly.

The way Eun-sang declared her desire to understand money's attributes terrified me. She reminded me of a super villain from a cartoon toiling away in their laboratory. But then I reminded myself that Eun-sang and I were on the same side. I felt relieved that I had the good fortune of being able to stand on her shoulder like a little crow.

# Flash

*12 December 2017*

1 ETH = 630,000 KRW
Virtual assets = 110,820,000 KRW

We met for lunch every day in Cabin 4 to have a small ceremony. Before anything else, we ordered drinks and slices of cake. Cake used to feel like a delicacy that we only splurged on when we were in a good mood, but now that we had the money we could eat it every day. Indeed, we even had enough money that if one of us was torn between ordering chocolate mousse or New York cheesecake, she would just order both. Once our drinks and cake arrived, we could officially start the ceremony. First, Eun-sang would take out her iPad and launch the BitGo app. She would press the button to convert today's price of Ethereum to won, take a screenshot, open her photo album, select the screenshot, then zoom in until the number filled the screen. Then one of us would hold up the iPad, emblazoned with its large number, and another would hold her phone out and take a selfie of the three of us. She would then share

217

the picture to the group chat, which was filled with pictures from the previous days. In every picture we were sitting around a table on which there were three drinks and three (sometimes four) pieces of cake. One person was holding the iPad with both hands – either in front of her chest, beneath her chin, or above her head. And with every picture, the number on the iPad screen was getting larger and larger.

*13 December 2017*

1 ETH = 720,000 KRW
Virtual assets = 124,970,000 KRW

I took a screenshot when Ethereum hit 690,000 won during lunch. At five that afternoon, it hit the upper circuit limit. I was in such disbelief that my hands were shaking. I didn't want to miss such an occasion. Not wasting a moment, I sent a message to the group chat:

**Dahae**
Sixth Floor. Meeting Room A.

We gathered secretly in the meeting room, quickly took a celebratory group photo, and uploaded it to the group chat. Displayed on the iPad above my head was the number 723,250. We all glowed with joy. Our smiles were growing with the numbers on the screen.

*18 December 2017*

1 ETH = 900,000 KRW
Virtual assets = 156,220,000 KRW

By now, we were sharing more than just screenshots and selfies in the group chat; we had also started sharing pictures of tattoo art.

In September, back when we'd decided to let that northwesterly Siberian wind take us wherever, we'd also agreed to get a friendship tattoo if the price of Ethereum ever hit one million won. But a tattoo of what? There was no consensus. We all seemed to want a full moon and the words 'To the Moon', but we couldn't agree on how the words should be incorporated. I wanted them written beneath the moon in cursive. Jisong wanted them written on a ribbon that tucked behind the bottom half of the moon. And Eun-sang wanted the words to form a halo around the moon. Jisong and I both thought Eun-sang's design was ridiculous and made fun of her for having bad taste. Eun-sang rejected our designs out of spite. And as there was no point in getting a friendship tattoo without a unified design, and because we couldn't ignore the opinion of our captain, we had to start over from scratch. Eventually, we settled on ditching the words all together. Instead, we added the image of a rocket.

*19 December 2017*

1 ETH = 1,000,000 KRW
Virtual assets = 173,570,000 KRW

*20 December 2017*

1 ETH = 1,020,000 KRW
Virtual assets = 179,780,000 KRW

Engraved on my body now was a small yet glorious symbol. A full moon and a rocket, neither larger than a 500-won coin. We kept the design simple, but made sure the moon had shadows and craters so people didn't think it was just a yellow circle. The rocket had to be cute too. It looked aerodynamic, and had a rounded tip. In the middle of it was a circular window, and it had three fin-like wings at the back. And finally, shooting out of the tail end of the rocket was a small flame. Eun-sang got the tattoo on her left shoulder; Jisong, on the inside of her right wrist; and I, on the inside of my right forearm, just below the elbow joint. While each of us was getting our tattoo, the other two periodically gave updates on Ethereum's price by holding up Eun-sang's iPad. I was the last to sit in the chair, and while I was getting tatted up, the price hit that day's upper circuit limit. Perhaps that was why I didn't feel any pain? Maybe getting tattoos just wasn't as painful as people made it out to be. Or maybe I had a higher pain threshold than I thought. Whatever the reason, I didn't even notice the needle's sting.

*31 December 2017*

1 ETH = 1,030,000 KRW
Virtual assets = 182,610,000 KRW

I invited Eun-sang and Jisong over to my house for New Year's Eve; it was the first time they'd visited. Jisong stepped in front of me as soon as I unlocked the door and barged into the room, hurriedly taking off her shoes.

'This is so big,' she said in awe. 'I wish my room was this big.'

She took a few more steps into the room and then turned to the right. The gasp that escaped her mouth was exactly the reaction I'd been hoping for.

'Wow! You even have a small bedroom.'

I leaned against the entrance to my bedroom and triumphantly turned the halogen light on and off. Eun-sang came over to me and perched her chin over my arm, which was extended towards the wall, and peered into my room.

'It's so pretty,' she said. 'But doesn't it get a bit cold?'

'You're right. It's because of the window. That's why I hung up two insulating curtains.'

The real problem was that the heated flooring didn't extend into the little cove, but I didn't feel the need to mention this. My apartment wasn't very large, but there was a noticeable drop in temperature when you moved from the main living space to this tiny makeshift bedroom. I only realised this several months after moving in, when the temperature started to plummet. Perhaps the real estate agent had been right when she suggested I used this room as a closet. But a little bit of teeth chattering at night wasn't going to prevent me from getting my own bedroom. The cost of an electric blanket and a slightly higher electricity bill was worth it.

Jisong ordered Domino's newest pizza, which she'd been dying to try. As we waited for it to arrive, I made a pasta bake for three with a generous helping of meatballs. Jisong and Eun-sang took out the belated housewarming gifts from their shopping bags. Jisong had got me a bottle of red wine, and Eun-sang had brought me four crystal wine glasses. I laughed when I saw Eun-sang's present.

'I live alone, you know. You didn't need to buy four wine glasses.'

'Wine glasses are always sold in pairs. And there are three of us, so I couldn't buy only two. I know it's just for today, but it'd be so tacky if two of us drank from wine glasses while the other drank from a mug.'

Eun-sang removed the wine glasses from the box and peeled off their bubble wrap. Turning the glasses upside down, she carefully peeled off the stickers on their bases with her fingernails and set them on the counter.

'And besides,' she added, 'you're supposed to buy more wine glasses than you need. They're thin and shatter easily.'

As soon as Eun-sang said this, we heard something crash to the floor in the kitchen. Jisong, who had offered to wash the glasses in the sink, had accidentally broken one. Thankfully, it broke over the sink, so there weren't many shards on the floor. But just to be safe, I gave Jisong and Eun-sang some of my socks to wear. We vacuumed the floor and used the lint roller to get any remaining pieces. As Jisong and I cleaned up the last of the broken wine glass, Eun-sang sat cross-legged on the chair with her Rudolph Christmas socks. She placed the remaining three glasses on the table.

'I told you, didn't I? People are always breaking wine glasses. Look, now we have exactly three.'

She turned to look at us and smirked.

'Perfect.'

I placed a trivet on the table, which sometimes served as a desk and other times as my kitchen table. On top of the mat, I placed the pasta bake from my mini oven. The pasta was topped with a layer of perfectly toasted cheese. I stuck two forks in the middle of the dish and pulled them apart, exposing a mix of tomato sauce, pasta and meatballs. As I looked at it, my mouth started to water. Eun-sang skilfully uncorked the wine bottle, and Jisong poured wine into each of the glasses she'd so diligently cleaned.

Time for a toast.

We lifted our crystal glasses and clinked them together. When their rims touched, they rang brightly like bells. We were so shocked by the sound that we exchanged wide-eyed looks. Before taking our first sip, we brought our glasses together several more times so we could hear the sound of bells again.

It was approaching midnight by the time we finished eating. I took out several cans of beer from my fridge, which we sacrilegiously poured into our wine glasses. The beer mixed with the few drops of wine left in the bottom of the glasses, producing a subtle rosé colour. We decided to set up the iPad on the table so we could watch the price of Ethereum as we did our New Year's countdown. Bars of red and green. The bars flashed as they danced up and down like Christmas lights wrapped around a Christmas tree.

11:59:49. Jisong propped up her phone on the windowsill, set the timer for ten seconds, and ran over to insert herself between Eun-sang and me, who were already striking our poses.

'Eight, seven, six, fix, four, three, two, one! Happy New Year!'

Jisong's camera flashed. We took our glasses filled with rosé-coloured beer and made a toast. The tiny room was once again filled with the ringing of bells. 1 January 2018. The new year was looking bright. They said 2018 was the Year of the Golden Dog. I was twenty-eight now. And the price of Ethereum had just surpassed 1,050,000 won. The graph sparkled.

# The Three Miseries of Life

*2 January 2018*

For the office New Year party, everyone at Maron including the CEO wore matching crewneck sweatshirts.

I'd never seen the auditorium, which was in the basement of the company building, look so colourful. The floor was divided into sections by department, each of which had its own colour. We looked like an assorted box of hard candies. Maron's logo, which was on the left breast of each sweatshirt, was also printed in a different colour for each team.

Last year, around the start of the fourth quarter, there was a sweatshirt design contest to celebrate Maron's fortieth anniversary. The sweatshirt had to be crewneck, but other than that teams had the freedom to choose their own logo and accent colour. Each team designed and ordered their sweatshirts and posed for a group photo – 'Make it fun!' they emphasised. Each team then uploaded their picture to the company bulletin board. The team with the most votes wouldn't have to pay for dinner at the next office party.

While slaving over my team's entry without getting paid overtime, I tried to figure out what the purpose of such events was. The executives of Maron probably wrote it on a meeting-room whiteboard as something that would 'boost employee morale' or 'promote devotion to the company'. Of course, for those not in charge of designing and ordering their team's sweatshirts, I'm sure standing together with your colleagues and wearing new-smelling, matching sweatshirts was enough to momentarily 'boost morale'. But for people like me, it only accomplished the opposite. It was always the newest team member who was tasked with assignments like this – of course, because the newest member usually had the fewest responsibilities and the smallest workload. But my team was a bit unique.

Snacks, which was like a patient on life support and was the only team in Branding that hadn't released a new product in the last several years, hadn't had a job opening since I joined the team. Because of this, I was still technically the newest member, despite having been here four, actually five years. I was only the newest member on account of a lack of fresh meat. So now, at the busiest time of the year, it was me who was invariably given the task of coming up with the design, pestering everyone for their sizes, and submitting an order to the clothing manufacturer.

To make matters worse was the fact that this year, Team Leader Koh had his own set of demands for the sweatshirt: he wanted me to design a sweatshirt that he could also wear out in public.

'We always make these team sweatshirts whenever there's a company event or workshop,' he said to everyone in the meeting room. 'But we always wear it once and then throw it away. It's such a waste. And it's bad for the environment, too.'

Up to this point, I agreed with everything Team Leader Koh had said. But the solution he arrived at was a bit puzzling.

'How about we design something that I can wear every day. You know, something that wouldn't be embarrassing even if I wore it outside the office. I want something that I can wear as part of a stylish outfit, that I can take a picture of to post online. Everyone's doing it these days. Posting pictures of their outfits online. And in front of it they put that symbol that looks like the Chinese character for a water well (井). What's that thing called again?' Team Leader Koh turned to me as he asked this question.

'You mean #OOTD?' I said, remembering that the character for well (井) kind of looked like a hashtag.

'Yeah, that's the one. What does that mean, anyway?'

'Outfit of the day, sir.'

'Anyway, that's the concept I'm going for. Hashtag OOTD. Isn't that so cool and original? I'm positive we'll get first place with this.'

Actually, posting pictures of company sweatshirts on Instagram was about the most uncool thing I could think of. Besides, he was missing the point. The higher-ups wanted this sweatshirt to create unity and camaraderie, not likes on Instagram. It was becoming clear to me why Team Leader Koh had lost favour in the company.

'Dahae, you're perfect for this because you were born in the nineties.'

This made everyone in the meeting room turn and stare at me with that look they always gave me. That glazed-over look of anticipation, as if they expected me to suggest something that might dazzle them, something bursting with life, something witty, something different, all because I was a 'millennial'. Their stares, their misplaced expectations, were such a burden to me. I was born exactly at the turn of the decade. Two more years and I would be thirty. But all of them, even those only a few years older than me, would constantly expect me to produce insights about 'millennials' and their 'hip sensibilities'. What they were asking from me was the dreaded 'innovation' that they couldn't manage themselves any more.

'Dahae, why don't you whip something up? You can present it tomorrow morning when we have our weekly meeting. Remember, something hip that I can wear outside of the office.'

I was mortified. Didn't Team Leader Koh know this was impossible? As soon as something had a company logo plastered on it, it ceased to be cool. It was a set of contradictory constraints. Or to put it in terms he might understand, it was like ordering a hot cup of iced coffee.

I had originally planned to go home on time today for the first time in a long time, but now I needed to stay late because of this impossible company sweatshirt. I drew a circle on the empty PowerPoint document on my screen. Right click. I opened the colour palette and shaded in the circle with a few different light colours.

I then pasted onto the circle a PNG file with Maron's logo on a transparent background. I used my right, left, up and down arrows to adjust the position of the logo. All the while, every breath that escaped my mouth was a sigh.

I wondered how I could make this sweatshirt wearable outside the office. Clicking on the corner of the logo, I made it as big as it could be, then dragged my wrist in the other direction, making it smaller and smaller until it was the size of a millet seed. The smaller the better. If only it would disappear completely. But that was against the rules. I fiddled and fiddled, but I just couldn't think of a solution. I couldn't believe this is what I was spending my evening on.

And then it hit me. At the moment the logo became a singularity, an idea popped into my head like a flash of lightning. Where there's a will, there's a way. These were my crisis management skills at work – skills I'd honed working for five years in this office. I felt myself carried along by an invisible force as my fingers flew across my keyboard.


The next day when we were wrapping up the weekly meeting, Team Leader Koh stopped everyone before they packed up and left.

'Oh, right! Shouldn't we see the sweatshirt design proposal?'

I connected my laptop to the meeting room monitor. A few moments later, the presentation I made last night appeared on the screen.

'First, I tried a crewneck sweatshirt in creamy white, something warm.'

I looked over at Team Leader Koh to see his reaction. He seemed content so far.

'And then I embroidered the special fortieth anniversary logo on the left breast. The logo is about this size.'

I made a circle with my index and thumb to show everyone. My team mates all nodded their heads slowly, either because they liked what they were hearing, or because they just wanted to seem like they were paying attention.

'And...' I said as I moved to the next slide, 'the thread on the embroidery will be white.'

'Hm?'

Team Leader Koh let out a strange sound as he blinked repeatedly, acting like he didn't understand what he'd just heard. I moved on to the next slide to explain further.

'Of course, getting a logo embroidered is a bit more expensive than the default option, but—'

'You want to do white on white?' Team Leader Koh said, cutting me off.

'The background is cream-coloured. The thread for the embroidery will be a similar but slightly brighter ivory colour. And because the material is different—'

'It doesn't matter what the material is. In the end, it's still white on white.'

'Yes, but—'

'So how am I supposed to see anything?'

That was the point. You're not supposed to see anything. Wasn't he the one who said he wanted to wear this outside the office? This wasn't going the way I'd expected. Last night, it felt like I'd had a eureka moment, a novel solution to my impossible problem, but now I saw it for what it was: I'd fooled myself. If my boss didn't like it, there was nothing more I could say. All I could do was wish for this moment to pass, for the team who reserved the next time slot to start knocking on the meeting room door.

'How am I supposed to see the logo if the background and font are the same colour?' he pressed me. 'It's not like I can use my mouse to drag the image from behind the background once it's printed.'

As I endured his criticism, I imagined how nice it would be if I could take my mouse and drag Team Leader Koh to the recycle bin on my desktop. I could almost hear the system sound, that rustling of paper and ping of empty aluminum whenever you emptied the trash.

A week later, a company-wide notice was sent out. The higher-ups had decided to cancel the sweatshirt design contest. Instead of leaving the design up to each team, everyone was going to be given the same sweatshirts with the same logo; the only difference would be the colour schemes for each office and team. I was sure this notice delighted all my fellow underlings. Our team ended up wearing sweatshirts with forsythia yellow lettering – the company colours – on Team Leader Koh's choice of a red background. And with this, another bulk order of single-use clothing was scheduled to be dumped in one of the many landfills polluting our planet. We still participated in the group photo contest, of course – 'Make it fun!' – but barely got a single vote.

When the New Year party was over, Team Leader Koh called me into the meeting room.

'Perhaps it's because you're young, but you looked good in yellow and red yesterday,' he said.

I laughed awkwardly, not sure how to interpret his compliment.

'I want to do another New Year party. Just the team. Schedule something for the end of this month or the first week of February. You liked the Korean BBQ place we went to last time, right? Make a reservation for a day that works for everyone.'

After that, he went on about how he would have liked to take us out for steak had we won the photo contest and prize money, but I knew he was lying. He never offered to take us out for anything as expensive as that. It wasn't that he was afraid of going over budget for office parties; rather, he was just being careful not to anger his boss. Because of this, he always made sure that our office parties cost less than other teams'. In short, he was an ass-kisser.

'Oh, right. I just thought of something—' he said hesitantly, changing the subject.

'Oh, right' implied he'd forgotten something, and 'I just thought of something' implied he hadn't. Sensing the contradiction of these two phrases, I guessed that he hadn't called me in here to talk about the office party. But then what?

'Dahae, do you by any chance know anything about… cryptocurrency?'

I'd suspected an ulterior motive, but never could I have imagined this was what he wanted to talk about. I was completely caught off guard. Not wanting to explain my long history with Ethereum, I gave him an ambiguous answer, saying I'd 'tried it once'.

'Could you show me how to do it?' he asked.

'Uh… Well, first you need to download an app.'

He handed me his phone. I went into the app store and tried downloading BitGo, but because he hadn't updated his OS in a long time, it wasn't supported.

'It can't be installed on your phone.'

'Why not?'

'You need to update your operating system first. Do you want me to do that for you?'

'Yes, as long as it allows me to buy cryptocurrency.'

'In the future, you should turn on automatic updates if you can.'

'It's such a bother. I always turn it off.'

I didn't respond to this and quietly did what I had to do. I updated his phone's OS to the latest version, downloaded and installed BitGo, made an account for him, and then wrote down in his yellowing notebook everything he needed to do in a numbered list. Only then was I finally able to escape from the meeting room.

When I left, something important occurred to me. As soon as I sat back down at my desk, I sent a message to the NOR(3) group chat.

**Dahae**
I think it's time.
**Jisong**
Time for what?
**Dahae**
Time to get out.

A few moments later, Eun-sang sent a message:

**Eun-sang**
Actually, I was just thinking the same thing. It's time to sell.

'Did you hear the rumours? They say Eun-sang Kang from Procurement is leaving the company.'

'You mean that woman who used to sell stuff in the office?'

'Yeah, that's the one. She hasn't left yet, but she's handed in her letter of resignation. She'll leave next month after she finishes handing over all her duties.'

'Doesn't she practically do everything in her team?'

'That's why they're frantically looking for a replacement.'

'I have something for her to authorise, I guess I'd better do it before she leaves.'

'But you know what, she's kind of scary, don't you think?'

'Terrifying. She always has a mean look on her face and has a sassy tone.'

'It's funny. I've never seen someone in Procurement with so much power. She acts like it's her money we're asking for.'

'It's because she's worked here just long enough to fool herself into thinking she's important.'

'I asked one of my friends from Procurement and he says she's a real scrooge. She doesn't even eat lunch with them.'

'I know. She eats with that double O from Accounting.'

'At least she was good at her job. Better than the last person.'

'For sure.'

'I couldn't believe it when she started selling stuff from her desk. It didn't seem like her. She's got such a stick up her ass most of the time.'

'It's not like she was any nicer as a saleswoman.'

'You're right. I was a regular at her store, but then one day I had to buy something with 2,500 won of credit. She sent out payment reminders once every three hours. It left such a sour taste in my mouth. I never went back.'

'Don't tell me you're the one from HR who snitched on her.'

'No, that wasn't me.'

'I wonder who did. The convenience made putting up with her bad attitude worth it.'

'She even sold Band-Aids and Febreze.'

'Where's she going anyway?'

'I heard she's not changing companies. She's going to stop working all together.'

'I heard she's leaving because she became a Bitcoin millionaire.'

'That's what it was!'

'Crazy times.'

'I heard something like that, too. Made millions on Bitcoin, bought a building in Gangnam, and drives around in a Maserati.'

'That's crazy.'

'I'm so jealous.'

'That must be so nice.'

'Damn. I should have used my money to buy Bitcoin instead of lottery tickets.'

'Should we start now before it's too late?'

'Hey, Assistant Manager Park!'

'Yes, Team Leader Koh?'

'I'm trying to have a toast, why is your table so loud? Everyone, fill your glasses if they're empty. Hey, General Manager Yun, your glass is empty. That's basically empty. Fill it up. Someone pour for Assistant Manager Park. Good, good. Does everyone have a drink now? Guys, thank you for working so hard this year. Let's make the next one just as great. Here's to a new year for Snacks! Cheers!'

'Cheers!'

'Anyway, you guys were talking about Eun-sang Kang from Procurement, right? I also heard about her, but to be honest, I'm not jealous. You think that would make you happy? I bet you think that would make you happy. But if you experienced it yourself, you'd know it's the exact opposite. There's a famous adage coined by a scholar named Cheng Yi from the Song Dynasty; it's called the Three Miseries of Life. The first is being born smart. What do you think happens when you're born with an exceptional intellect? You never have to try, that's what. And because you never try, you never grow. And in the end, your intellect suffers. All you'll do is regress. It's no good being overly talented.

'The second misery is being born to a powerful family. If you can always rely on your parents' wealth and influence, you'll never have the chance to experience the joy of cultivating your own fruit. You'll never feel the desire to apply yourself. You'll become content with living off your parents. Such an existence can't lead to growth. And if you don't grow, you fall behind.

'And the last misery, the greatest misery of all, is passing the civil service examination at a young age. Back during the Song Dynasty, passing the civil service examination was the goal of any man who wanted to make something of himself. But doing so took years of study and hardship. Young men who passed the exam at a young age became arrogant. Worse yet, they were thrown out into the world without any real-life experience. While this might seem like a short cut to happiness, it was actually a short cut to misery. There's nothing that makes someone more miserable than passing the civil service examination at a young age. Eun-sang Kang making millions? At her age? That's the modern-day equivalent of passing the civil service examination at a young age.

'If what people say is true, if it's true that she acquired a fortune without having to lift a finger, it'll be nothing but unhappiness and misery. Take it from someone who's been there before. Eun-sang needs to be careful. There will be a lot of temptation, and many people will try to take advantage of her. What I'm saying is that there are things that people her age need to experience. How old is she anyway? Twenty-nine? Fuck. At that age she should still be studying, forming connections, gaining experience. A fortune at that age will do her no good.

'Dahae! Why do you look so surprised? Aren't you close with Eun-sang? I always see you eating with her. You two are friends, right? As a friend you should give her some advice. You need to warn her not to act recklessly. I'm really worried. Kids these days don't know how scary the world is. Dahae, what are you doing? Why is your palm on your forehead? Why are you bowing to me? You're bowing like you're getting married. Thank you for the advice? Hey, don't mention it. After all, I'm your senior; it's the least I can do. Dahae? Have you had too much to drink? We only just started. How have you drunk so much already? Dahae? Dahae Jeong! What in the world? Did she fall asleep while bowing to me?'

# Part Three

# Silence and Placid Waters

*3 January 2018*

Today the price of Ethereum hit 1,310,000 won. Yesterday, after concluding that the price had reached its peak, we agreed that we would have no regrets about exiting once it hit 1,300,000 won. Part of the reason we decided on the number 1,300,000 was because it seemed like such a distant goal. But now that the price of Ethereum had broken through our initial limit in only a day, we realised that it wasn't always easy to follow through. Unsurprisingly, Eun-sang changed her mind: 'It's rising abnormally fast. This feels like another spike. At this rate, it might hit 1,500,000.' She convinced us to hold on a little longer. She asked us to trust her, as she had been riding the wave for over a year. But Eun-sang didn't need to convince me. I was already thinking the same thing. There's a saying, 'Buy the fear, sell the euphoria', but we all agreed that we hadn't reached the moment of euphoria yet. True euphoria came before you could register it. And if that was true, then right now wasn't it. We were only getting a small taste of the wonders to come. That's what we believed.

The price of Ethereum broke 1,500,000 won. Eun-sang's prediction that it would hit 1,500,000 came true in the span of a single day, but no one, not even Eun-sang, had predicted that it would get there with such speed. After work, we gathered at Cabin 4.

'Isn't it time to sell everything?' I asked.

This made Jisong start to sob.

'This is so unfair,' she said.

After a short fit of sobbing, Jisong used her middle finger to dab the trails of her tears on both cheeks.

'I know I shouldn't be saying it's unfair. But that's how I feel. Resentful, angry, disappointed.'

'Who are you angry at?' Eun-sang asked.

'I don't know.'

Jisong said she knew she shouldn't be feeling angry, but I couldn't blame her. I had felt the same way last year when I was considering exiting after making a profit of 30,000,000 won. In fact, I would be lying if I said I didn't feel that way right now. And just like Jisong, I also didn't know who my anger was directed at.

'To be honest, you two have earned everything you wished for,' Jisong said. 'But I'm just getting started. I know it's greedy of me to want more. They say you should sell when it's up and buy when it's down. I know this is the time to sell. But I just can't bring myself to do it. Eun-sang, do you really think this is the end? Do you really think it won't rise a bit more? It must. I need more money, you know that. My monthly pay check is just too small to start anything new.'

'I know what you mean,' Eun-sang said. 'I don't want it to end yet either.'

I couldn't tell if Eun-sang was saying this just to comfort Jisong or if she sincerely meant it. But I had a hunch it was the second one. I knew this because of what she said next.

'I can't sell yet either. Let's hold out a bit longer. At this rate, I think it will go up a few hundred thousand more. When that happens, I think I'll be able to sell for real.'

### 7 January 2018

When the price of Ethereum hit 1,700,000 won, we gathered and put our heads together. I was the first to speak.

'Honestly, I'm getting kind of scared.'

'But you can't pull the trigger, right?' Eun-sang asked.

Jisong and I nodded.

'Then let's decide on a specific price. We'll sell when it hits that value. We can set a limit order.'

When Jisong asked how much, Eun-sang's eyes paused for a moment on the graph in her hand.

'At exactly...' Eun-sang then raised two fingers to make a peace sign. '2,000,000. Let's sell everything at 2,000,000 won. Deal?'

'Deal?' I said.

Only Jisong didn't answer.

'What, you want higher?' Eun-sang asked.

'No... That sounds good.'

Eun-sang took two fingers and decisively waved a peace sign in front of our eyes.

*8 January 2018*

The price of Ethereum hit 2,000,000 won. It was less than ten hours after I set a limit order of 2,000,000 won on my BitGo account. Automatically, my virtual assets were sold and converted to won. I transferred the balance to my bank account. It felt so surreal. Even as I checked my profits, Ethereum continued to soar.

*9 January 2018*

The price of Ethereum hit 2,190,000 won. Eun-sang was kicking and screaming all morning.

> **Eun-sang**
> I should have held out a bit longer!
> **Jisong**
> Actually… I haven't sold yet.
> **Eun-sang**
> What? Didn't we agree to set a limit order?
> **Jisong**
> I was going to… But I'm not like you guys… It's not enough for me to stop here. Even if it's a bit risky, I want to hold out a bit longer.

That little liar. But I had to give her credit. She was braver than I thought. I was jealous out of my mind that Jisong's Ethereum was still going up and up. And it was this jealousy, not Jisong's boldness, that surprised me the most.

*10 January 2018*

The moment the price of Ethereum hit 2,380,000 won, Eun-sang sent a message to the group chat along with a screenshot of the skyrocketing graph.

**Eun-sang**
Jisong, have you still not sold?

**Jisong**
My heart is pounding... I just sold all of it...

**Eun-sang**
At what price?

**Jisong**
2,370,000.

**Eun-sang**
Good job.

**Jisong**
Yeah, thank goodness.

And with this message, the chat went silent.

The silence continued into the next day, and the day after that.

Our group chat had been buzzing constantly with chatter for the first ten days of the new year, only quietening down when we were asleep. But now, complete silence. Everything halted – the screenshots, the graphs, the chants. The roar of our greed had disappeared.

It felt like we'd reached the summit of a tall treacherous mountain and were finally catching our breath. We'd made landfall after months on a raft, being swept this way and that by high waves. The ride was over, and we were finally on solid earth. Oddly enough, only now were we experiencing vertigo.

In the end, in the span of just eight months, I had made 320,000,000 won, Jisong had made 240,000,000 won, and Eun-sang had made 3,300,000,000 won.

# Cotton Candy

There was a rumour going around the office that Eun-sang Kang had earned a fortune investing in Bitcoin, bought a building in Gangnam, and now drove around in a Maserati. Admittedly, the rumours that surrounded Eun-sang, who was due to leave the company soon, weren't completely false, but they were wrong in small yet important ways.

First, it was true that she had made a fortune doing cryptocurrency, but it was Ethereum and not Bitcoin. Second, she *was* the new owner of a building, but it wasn't some high-rise in Gangnam; it was a five-storey 'mini building' in Seongsu-dong. (I couldn't believe anyone would call something that required such a large sum of cash to buy 'mini'.) And lastly, although Eun-sang hadn't bought a Maserati, she *was* considering buying a car soon; she just wasn't sure which kind – either a BMW, a Mercedes Benz, or a Maserati. Eun-sang figured that someone must have seen her last week when she came out of a Maserati showroom with a brochure in her hand. Technically she hadn't bought one yet, so to say that she 'drove around' in a Maserati was misleading.

**Dahae**
People are saying all sorts of things about you.
**Dahae**
They say they saw it with their own eyes.
**Eun-sang**
Well, it's possible that someone saw me taking a test drive.
**Dahae**
A test drive?
**Eun-sang**
You can do test drives if you make a reservation. You two wanna come?

This was why the three of us were meeting in front of the Mercedes Benz showroom. I wanted to buy a car someday, but I wasn't planning on buying one *right now*. And I'd never imagined, not in my wildest dreams, buying such an expensive foreign import. And yet, I would be lying if I said I didn't want to take a test drive with Eun-sang. It was spring and it would be wonderful to enjoy the nice weather in a fast car.

But my biggest reason for taking Eun-sang up on her offer was simply that I missed her. I hadn't seen her for almost ten days; before that, we'd seen each other at work every Monday through Friday for the last five years. She hadn't officially left the company yet, but she had a lot of annual leave saved up, so after handing over all her responsibilities she took the remaining time off. This coming Friday was her last official day. She was planning to come to the office that day just to return her company badge and laptop.

Eun-sang was already in front of the showroom when I arrived. Her complexion was noticeably rosier than before. She looked full of life. Her pupils were clear and lucid and awake, and her facial muscles looked relaxed and recharged. A fresh, clean vibe. Her skin was unrecognisably lustrous. And her cheekbones glowed as though they'd been dipped in honey. Of course, Eun-sang was merely reflecting the light from inside the showroom, but for some reason the way her face glowed made it seem like more than just the reflection of an external light source. Her face seemed to be emitting actual photons, as though she had a tiny, golden sun inside her skull.

They say the best medicine for a burnt-out office worker is to leave their job. Eun-sang was proof of this, and she hadn't even left the company yet. How could submitting a resignation letter have such a profound effect on one's complexion?

Eun-sang noticed me approaching her and called out to me.

'Oh my god!' she said. 'You look fabulous. What happened?'

'Me?' I asked in shock. I wanted to ask her the same question.

'Yeah, you. Who else? Your skin looks positively radiant.'

Before I could respond, Jisong appeared in the distance. As she came over and stood before us, Eun-sang and I both shouted out in unison:

'Jisong! Did you get a facial?'

Our faces had never looked healthier or more radiant. It was strange. Nothing had really changed. Sure, Eun-sang had submitted her letter of resignation, but we were all still technically employed by Maron. We still received 'Mid' performance evaluations, lived in tiny studio apartments, and mostly ate in the company cafeteria. And even when we did eat out, it was nothing particularly fancy: Jeonju-style bean sprout soup, tonkatsu and udon, kimchi stew with all-you-can-eat ramen refills, cheap cake from the cafe, and street corn dogs rolled in sugar. And yet, since that moment on 8 January 2018, our entire world had changed. The change was all-encompassing and impossible to describe in a few words – just like the mysterious lustre lingering on all our faces.

'Shall we go in?' Eun-sang asked.

She took the lead like someone who had done this dozens of times before and guided us into the showroom. A dealer dressed in a clean suit walked over to us in a hurry. As he got close, his excited facial expression changed. He clearly wanted to ask us what three kids were doing in a luxury auto dealership. Was it because we looked that young? Or was it something else?

Eun-sang told the dealer that she was looking to buy a car. As they exchanged a few words, Jisong and I hesitantly glanced around the showroom. The dealer looked happy to talk with Eun-sang, who looked the least out of place.

'Do you have a model in mind?'

'Let's start with the C-Class.'

'Excellent choice. That's more than enough for the lady.'

This caused Jisong and me to wince. Eun-sang squeezed her eyelids shut, rolling back her eyes before opening them again.

'Forgive me. I misspoke,' Eun-sang said. 'I want to look at the CLS- and E-Classes. Oh, and the S-Class, too.'

The next thing she said shocked us.

'In fact, we're all planning on buying. The three of us.'

The dealer leaned in with one ear and asked Eun-sang to repeat herself as though he'd misheard her:

'I'm sorry. All three of you are buying?'

'That's right. All three of us. We won't settle for anything less than an E-Class. Isn't that right?'

Eun-sang exchanged looks with Jisong and me as she said this. Her glare was so intense that we could only nod in agreement.

I had to act like I was going to buy a car, although why that was, I couldn't be sure. Not knowing the first thing about luxury sedans, I had to follow Eun-sang's lead to play the part. If she said, 'Hm,' Jisong and I would either repeat, 'Hm,' or say, 'Wow,' or 'Ooh'. If she said, 'That's nice,' we would say, 'Not bad'. And when she felt the chassis or the leather in the car and said, 'This feels nice, doesn't it?' we would take a look at what she was inspecting and nod our heads. The dealer, who had been following the three of us around and explaining car specs and options, suddenly asked a question – and although it wasn't clear who he was addressing, it was most likely directed to all three of us.

'May I ask, if it's not too rude? Do you own your own business?'

'Nope,' Eun-sang said, acting as our representative.

'Oh, I see.'

When Eun-sang didn't explain any further, the man pursed his lips like he was holding something inside his mouth, unable to spit it out. Eun-sang looked at this, then turned away from him as she spoke in an ambiguous manner, neither addressing the man nor talking to herself.

'You're dying to know, aren't you?'

'Come again?'

'You're dying to ask us what we do for a living.'

'Hahaha! You got me. I am really curious.'

Eun-sang placed her finger momentarily on the Mercedes Benz emblem which was sticking out of the hood of an E-Class exclusive.

'We're just simple office workers,' she said.

'Is that so? You must work at a good company.'

'Does such a thing exist?'

'Hahaha, that's very true. Would you mind taking a seat and waiting for a moment? I'll be right back.'

The dealer said he was going to check when the models with the options we chose were going to be available from the warehouse. He was also going to check to see if Jisong and I could take test drives today, as Eun-sang was the only one who had made a reservation. He guided us over to one corner of the showroom where there was a low-standing glass table. We took a seat on the cushioned chairs around the table, as the dealer brought over a picnic basket and placed it in front of us.

'Please, have some refreshments.'

I froze. Filling the picnic basket were dozens of individually wrapped Mini Choco Chestnuts. These were *the* Choco Chestnuts, Maron's bestselling product and, to be quite honest, what paid our monthly salaries. There were several different sizes of Choco Chestnuts, and these bite-sized minis were the bestselling. We let out a scoff of disbelief as we stared at Maron's familiar logo atop the background of forsythia yellow. The dealer had sensed our lukewarm reaction.

'Oh, if these aren't to your liking, I can—'

'No,' Jisong said, waving her hand in the air dismissively. 'It's not that.'

The three of us started making excuses, talking over each other to speak first.

'Who doesn't like Choco Chestnuts?'

'Choco Chestnut is the best-tasting chocolate candy in the nation.'

'That's right.'

'Don't worry about it.'

Each of us took a Choco Chestnut, unwrapped it, and popped it in our mouth, as though we were trying to prove something to him. When I bit into the dark chocolate coating, a perfectly chewy milk-chocolate filling oozed into my mouth, accompanied by a nutty yet sweet single chestnut.

As soon as the dealer was out of sight, I scooted my chair up to Eun-sang and pulled her towards me.

'Eun-sang, what are you doing? Why did you say we were buying a car? I thought we just came to look.'

'I'm just pretending to buy,' Eun-sang said. 'I'm not going to sign any of their papers.'

Jisong snickered and shook her head as though she knew what Eun-sang was up to. After turning around to make sure the dealer wasn't on his way back, I leaned into Eun-sang's ear again and quietly scolded her.

'Why are you acting so mean for no reason? Are you bored now that you're not working? If you're not going to sign a contract, let's just leave.'

'That guy said the one thing I can't stand,' Eun-sang grumbled.

'What did he say?'

'He said, "That should be more than enough for you." There's nothing I hate more than someone pretending to know what's good enough for me.'

I should have known that was the issue. Eun-sang lowered her voice and continued:

'Why would anyone say something so demeaning to another human being? And they're always omitting the words at the beginning of the sentence. What they really want to say is, "It's not enough for me, but it's more than enough for you. You should be thankful for this much." It's so dishonest. If someone ever says that to you, Dahae, don't assume they think it's enough for everyone, including themselves.

'Anyway, you and Jisong should choose a Benz while we're here.'

Why was Eun-sang being such a tyrant today?

'What are you talking about? I don't have that kind of money. And I don't even have a place to park it.'

'Aren't you planning on moving? I thought you said you were looking for a place.'

'That's still a way off.'

Eun-sang took another Choco Chestnut, bit down on one end of the wrapper, and used one hand to pull the plastic down and tear it.

'You don't think you can actually buy a car and leave with it the same day, do you? Either way, you'll need to wait weeks or months before it arrives.'

'Really? That long? But even so.'

'Let's buy it together. If it's parking you're worried about, you can pay for monthly parking at a nearby lot. And if you can't do that, I'll let you park at my building for the time being.'

I thought Eun-sang was just pulling my leg.

But exactly a month later, Jisong and I had signed five-year payment plans for two small SUVs. They were smaller than the E-Class Benz that Eun-sang bought, but even so, mine cost more than I made in a year. I couldn't tell if this was backbone or bravado. My SUV was snow white, and Jisong's was blue. And we both added the option of a panoramic sunroof, making the car that much prettier.

When I finally got my hands on the keys to my first car, I bought a small pom pom keychain. Eun-sang thought it was too stuffy-looking for summer, but I liked the way it looked because of the way the end of each strand of light pink fur sparkled like cotton candy. It looked like it tasted of sweet strawberry, like the cotton candy that used to be sold every Wednesday afternoon in front of my school when I was a kid. On those days, a motorcycle carrying a machine that looked like a large tin can would be parked outside the school gate. Tied to the bike were bulbous, rainbow-coloured cotton candies wrapped in translucent plastic. These sugary cotton balls looked like they were clouds that had been plucked from the sky and tied down, ready to fly away if only you would come and cut their strings.

I remember the first time the cotton candy man came. Seeing my friends with their cotton candy, I was unable to peel myself away from that purple bike. The din of the bike's engine; the rainbow-coloured sugar being sucked into a hole one spoon at a time; the strands of sugar endlessly shooting out of the spinner; the mesmerising twirling of the paper cone; and the fluffy clouds of sugar slowly beginning to take form. But they weren't for me – not unless I had money. Just before taking a bite out of her cotton candy, my friend took a piece and generously popped it in my mouth; she must have noticed my staring. Although the sugar dissolved as soon as it touched my tongue, I'll never forget my first bite of cotton candy, so impossibly airy and sweet.

My friend took her cotton candy and slowly disappeared into the distance, but I was unable to move. I stood there and stared at the loud yet fragrant motorcycle, the cotton candy man with his fast hands and baseball cap that was squishing his white hair, his captive audience of children. I didn't move even as the pool of children replenished several times, even as the older kids (who finished school later than us) rushed onto the streets. I stood there waiting for my one chance, waiting for the moment a sweet and airy bite of sugar would fall into my mouth.

Eventually a single fragment of cotton candy was ejected from the can by inertia. As it floated down to earth, I jumped up, grabbed it, and put it in my mouth. The other kids who saw this shouted and groaned with jealousy. Those like me who didn't have money for cotton candy gathered around and started jumping up in the air with their hands outstretched, hoping to catch the fragments of cotton candy that occasionally escaped the can. The cotton candy man waved his wooden chopsticks and shooed us away. 'Scat! Little beggars.' Every time he did this, we would scream and run into the school sports field, but after a few seconds we surrounded the bike again and were jumping desperately for freebies. Every week from then on, I was drawn to the crowd where I would wait for scraps to fall into my mouth. I was a prisoner to the sugar.

# Where Does the Money Go?

*30 May 2018*

Until now, the only thing that came to mind when I thought of Gangneung was the scenic Gyeongpodae Pavilion; I had no idea the northeastern coast of Korea was also famous for its coffee shops. I guess everyone knew something I didn't. But where, I wondered, did people learn these things? Not only was I ignorant of many things, but I was also ignorant of the fact I was ignorant. I knew nothing about what or where things existed, let alone whether I liked them.

Today, we were seated not in a cabin at Coffee Bean but near a window in a beachside cafe, enjoying a view of the East Sea while smelling the fragrance of fresh hand-dripped coffee served in antique teacups. Apparently, this cafe was owned by the star pupil of a famous master barista. Of course, this star pupil had their own star pupil, who themselves had several understudies. Eun-sang stuck her fingers through the handle on her teacup and was about to take a sip when she paused and put the cup back down.

'So, Dong-jun messaged me recently.'

Even though I knew who Dong-jun was, I was so surprised that I had to confirm.

'What? The one who went to dental school?'

'Yeah, that one.'

'You're joking,' Jisong said as she wrinkled her brow. 'Has he no shame?'

'He must have heard the news,' Eun-sang said with a smirk. 'That I'm a new owner of a building.'

'Did you meet him?'

'Yeah.'

'And did you sleep with him?'

'Yeah.'

'Goodness,' Jisong sighed in disbelief.

'Did he really message you because he heard you're rich now?' I asked.

'Really. I wasn't sure at first, and I wasn't going to bring it up, but then we went for a drink. You should have heard him.'

'What'd he say?'

'He said he'd been so wrong, that he knows he hurt me, that I'm the only one for him. This much I expected. But then out of nowhere, he suggested we get married when he gets his certification. He said we could live together on the top floor of my building, and he could use the bottom floors for his dental practice. "Happily ever after", you know.'

I felt embarrassed for him, and I wasn't even there to witness it first hand. Jisong grabbed at her stomach as she laughed out loud.

'I can't believe he was so honest,' Jisong said. 'I guess he thinks he can kill two birds with one stone.'

'He was never good at hiding things. He's too easy to read. I caught him cheating the very first time, remember?'

I realised Eun-sang was more tolerant than I imagined her to be.

'But why did you sleep with him?' I asked.

'Well, we dated for so long.'

She explained that it was like falling back into a bad habit. Not to mention that she hadn't been with anyone for a while. He was an easy fix. She didn't have the energy or desire to find someone new; the usual dating procedures were so cumbersome and bothersome – pursuing someone or asking a friend to introduce you, taking the time to get to know them, gradually becoming an exclusive couple, and then beginning to dream of a future together only to have it all blow up in your face. Nor did she want a casual relationship; there were just too many weirdos these days for her to imagine herself jumping on Tinder. Dong-jun was comfortable and convenient, that was it.

'We dated for so long, and he's just so familiar. It's hard to describe. It's almost like he's family. And—'

'So you're going to raise a family together?' Jisong said, cutting Eun-sang off because she was so surprised. 'And you're going to let him into your building?'

'Are you kidding me? I'm not insane,' Eun-sang said. 'This is as far as I let him in.'

Eun-sang then asked a question as though she was trying to change the subject:

'Did you decide on your product?'

Although the company didn't know this yet, Jisong was also planning on quitting. She wanted to start her own business, and every weekend she was running around researching the market and products. To speed up the process, she was even working on weekday evenings and during her lunch breaks. She was planning on handing in her letter of resignation when she finished all the paperwork and had prepared herself mentally. Her goal was to quit by the end of the year. The last time I heard her talk about it, she said she wanted to import food products, and it seemed Eun-sang wanted to know if she had any updates. Hearing that Eun-sang was interested, Jisong's eyes started to sparkle.

'I'm thinking about importing heitang from Taiwan.'

'Heitang?'

'What's that? Brown sugar?'

'It's similar. It's Chinese for black sugar.'

'That's a bit random. Don't we have something like that in Korea? I think I've seen it at the supermarket.'

'Taiwanese black sugar is different. It has a distinct flavour. It's really good, too.'

Jisong told us she was planning on opening Korea's first black sugar milk tea specialty store. She explained that because Korean consumers weren't accustomed to the taste of black sugar, she needed to present it in its most common application: milk tea. By opening a black sugar milk tea cafe, she could open a black sugar distribution channel between Korea and Taiwan, and carve out a niche for herself. Once the demand for black sugar increased, she would be the first and fastest supplier to other retailers.

But the more I listened to Jisong, the more uneasy I felt. True to form, Jisong was predicating her whole business on the best-case scenario, just like when she planned her travel schedule to Jeju Island around the assumption she would be able to catch an express train that only came once every thirty minutes. How was she so convinced she could single-handedly manufacture a new dessert fad in Korea? I feared this project would take much more than Jisong had to offer, that Jisong was putting her money into a business that was bound to fail. Jisong had risked everything on Ethereum and made a small fortune; I wanted her to use it wisely. I wanted this more than anyone.

'But, Jisong—' I said cautiously. 'Maybe I don't know much about heitang, but aren't there already a lot of Taiwanese milk tea cafes in Korea? We even have chains selling the stuff. They're all over the place. Isn't the market saturated already? It's not just Seoul. Even places like Ansan have it.'

'Dahae.' Jisong's tone was somewhat testy. 'Black sugar milk tea isn't just any milk tea. You've never tried it, have you?'

I shook my head.

'Then you shouldn't be talking. If you tried it, you'd know just how amazing it is.'

Eun-sang was already looking up pictures of heitang milk tea from Taiwan.

'So, this is what you're talking about. It looks like translucent chocolate.'

Jisong said that through her travels to Taipei to meet Wei Lin, she had become a passionate fan of black sugar milk tea — so much so that she often drank three cups a day when she could. She liked the stuff so much that she thought she would continue visiting Taiwan just for their black sugar milk tea if she and Wei Lin ever broke up. It wasn't just milk tea; black sugar went well with coffee and jellies, too. In fact, she claimed it went well with almost everything. I was sceptical, but Eun-sang seemed to be supportive of Jisong's business venture.

'I searched it on Instagram, and there are a lot of reviews written by Korean tourists. This is a great idea. Who knows? You might even have a partnership with Maron in the future. They'll release a new flavour of Choco Chestnut made with black sugar. They already have several different flavours. How many are there again?'

'Seven,' I said reflexively.

Eun-sang took a sip of her coffee and frowned.

'Yuck. What's wrong with this coffee?'

She took another sip.

'It tastes burnt. I thought I ordered the sour bean.'

Jisong and I both took a sip of our coffee.

'Yeah, it tastes funny.'

'You're right. My coffee tastes funny, too.'

Supporting the bottom of the cups with our palms, the three of us took our coffee to the counter to complain. Someone who looked to be the owner came over, brought his nose up to the coffee, and gave it a whiff. The owner then turned around and called someone:

'Tae-young. You made these, didn't you?'

*Tae-young?* That name sounded so familiar. Standing with his back to the owner was a man with hunched shoulders and a brown apron tied behind his waist. The moment he turned around, I realised Tae-young was the name of the man I saw at work every day.

'Team Leader Koh?'

This shot out of my mouth like a sneeze.

'Oh, Dahae—'

'What are you doing here?' I asked.

Team Leader Koh hesitated for a moment before explaining that he did 'a bit of learning' on the weekends. Ha! A bit of learning. This obviously meant he was studying to become a barista. But coming all the way to Gangneung just to learn how to make coffee? It was at this moment that I realised the true extent of Team Leader Koh's coffee addiction.

No one wanted to bump into their boss while on a weekend break. Especially not in a place like this, under such awkward circumstances. When it became too much to handle, Eun-sang grabbed my arm as if to say, 'Let's go.' Team Leader Koh looked flustered.

'If you want, I can make you another cup!'

'No, it's fine,' I said.

'Let's just leave,' she said as she gave me a look.

Once we were outside, Jisong knitted her brow and asked:

'Why is he learning to become a barista?'

'Right? Clearly he's not very good.'

Eun-sang smacked her lips as though the taste of burnt coffee was still lingering in her mouth.

'I guess he wants to change careers,' she said. 'Didn't you guys hear about the company restructure?'

'What company restructure?'

'There's a rumour that Snacks and Pies are going to be combined into one team. Working-level team members like yourself don't need to worry, you'd continue doing the same work, but you can't have two team leaders, right? One of them must step down in the end. Asking a team leader to take a demotion is essentially asking them to quit. If it were up to you, who would you fire?'

I didn't answer, but it was obvious to anyone who worked in Maron that Team Leader Koh from Snacks would need to go. As I followed Eun-sang and Jisong, I turned around for a second because I wanted to check something. Through the window, I could see the side view of Team Leader Koh as he frantically pulled things out of the cupboard. I still don't know the reason for what I did next: I turned my body towards the cafe, stood up straight, brought my hands together in front of my chest, and bowed. As I stood there bent over, I closed my eyes for a few seconds. When I opened my eyes again, I stood up straight and ran after Eun-sang and Jisong. Three cars, blue and white like waves, were parked side by side with their boots facing blue ocean waters.


The late May sun was beating down on my arm, and in the distance blinding white cumulus clouds were inching across the sky. I stepped on the gas as I felt the urge to reach out and touch those cotton candy-like clouds. Zipping past by me on either side were the bright landscapes of mid-afternoon.

We were the only cars on this empty six-lane high-
way. Each of us were in our own cars, holding our own
steering wheels and with our feet on our own accelera-
tors. Sometimes I took the lead, other times I followed.
Right now, I could see Eun-sang's car in front of me,
and Jisong was passing me on the right. Once I was
staring at them from behind, I had a strange feeling —
strange, but strangely good, too.

I extended my hand towards the ceiling and pressed
a smooth, flat button. The panoramic sunroof started
to slowly open with a low hum. Sunbeams poured
into the car, and I could feel the warmth of the sun on
the back of my neck as well as a cool breeze. The silk
twilly I had tied around my right wrist fluttered in the
wind with its signature horse-drawn carriage pattern. I
stepped harder on my accelerator and sped up. Going
so fast that it felt like I was floating atop the road was
exhilarating. I turned the steering wheel to the left and
entered the passing lane. Now the three of us were side
by side. When I looked in Eun-sang's direction and
lowered the passenger-side window, Eun-sang copied
me and rolled down hers. I could hear the roar of the
wind and it rushed into the car. My hair flapped about
and stuck to my cheeks.

'I love having my own car!' I yelled as I brushed my
hair out of my face.

Eun-sang's response cut through the wildly buffeting
wind.

'I love having money!'

'Eun-sang!' I yelled in a drawn-out manner.

'What?'

'I love you!'

Eun-sang smiled with her mouth wide open. She then made a small heart with her index finger and thumb and stuck it out the window. I quickly returned the favour by blowing her a kiss. Jisong, whose car was to the right of Eun-sang's, also lowered her window. She took off her sunglasses, placed them atop her head, and then shouted to outdo me:

'Eun-sang! I love you more!'

With eyes the shape of half moons, Eun-sang turned her focus back to the road as she shouted out:

'See! I told you it was all going to turn out OK.'

Eun-sang leaned forward slightly in her seat. Her short ponytail, the silk twilly she used to tie it, and the stray hairs on either side of her head were being blown back by the wind. She put her right arm out the window, exposing the tattoo beneath the sleeve of her white T-shirt. A miniature rocket racing to the moon with a tail of fire behind it.

'Let's go!'

Eun-sang got into the passing lane. I slowed down and let Eun-sang go first. Then I stepped on the accelerator and chased after her. I smiled as I felt my torso being pushed into the back of my seat.


After driving for the better part of a day, we arrived at a rocky seaside cliff. At the top was a small, overgrown forest, and just before the edge of a sharp drop was an octagonal pavilion. Just looking at the pavilion's eight pillars, you could tell they were sturdy. The greenish-blue roof of the pavilion was just as beautiful from far away as it was when we were sitting beneath its shadow. The pavilion was large enough that the three of us could sit in one corner and not be cramped. We perched on the edge facing the ocean, and dangled our legs over the side.

Sitting there, all we could see was ocean. When we first arrived, the waves were quiet, but before long the wind started to kick up large waves. Every time a large wave crashed against the cliff rocks, white water would come spraying all the way to where we were sitting, forcing us to quickly lift our feet. Soon, the hem of my new linen trousers was spotted with tiny droplets of water. Eun-sang, who was sitting next to me, brushed the water off my trousers for me as she began to speak:

'I was thinking about how I said it would turn out OK. How I said we were going to the moon—'

Jisong and I, who were sitting to the left and right of Eun-sang, both looked at her.

'I don't know, it's almost like it was a magic spell. You had to forget about everything else and just believe that it would happen. I was always acutely aware in the back of my mind that it might not turn out OK, that there was a high probability that we might fail. Sometimes, this anxiety really got to me.'

Jisong's right cheek twitched as she put her hand on Eun-sang's.

'I know,' Jisong said. 'I knew it was dangerous too. But I wanted to try anyway. I wasn't going to blame you if it didn't turn out OK.'

I was afraid, but I risked everything for an adventure.

The three of us were each sitting somewhere between danger and adventure.

I, too, remembered the moment I decided to risk everything. I remembered the moment I realised that doubt and caution were luxuries I couldn't afford. I remembered the moment I was completely bewitched by a sweet proposition.

'Eun-sang, do you remember when you told me that this was all we had? That cryptocurrency was a portal to another world? That it would close just as suddenly as it opened? That we had to jump through even if we felt uneasy? That we didn't have time to wait around and think about how or why it had appeared? That this was a momentary, once-in-a-lifetime opportunity for people like us?'

Eun-sang nodded.

'It was when you told us this that I decided to jump into that mysterious portal. Even as you told me these things, I could see the diameter of that portal closing right before my eyes.'

I would be lying if I said I hadn't been afraid. I never imagined I would make it out the other side of this storm without having lost anything. I wished it, but I didn't think it would really happen.

I was worried. Stories like this — about people who dreamed of a life better than what Fate had ordained — always ended with the protagonist paying dearly for their greed and being punished by the heavens for going against its will. We had committed the sin of avarice, the sin of coveting riches beyond our circumstance, the sin of blindly chasing after fortune.

'I never said this, but I was really afraid back then,' I said. 'Even though I said, "Let's go to the moon", I was biting my nails every day worrying about what would happen if I lost everything.'

'What were you planning on doing if that happened?'

'I tried not to think about it. But to be honest, I couldn't help it. It wasn't much money, but it was my entire life savings after all. Not to mention I had debt. Worse yet, I took out another loan to buy more ether. Now that I think about it, what I did was completely absurd.'

'Right? If you lost everything...'

'I would rather die. That's what I thought.'

Silence fell between us.

'I felt exactly the same way,' Jisong said as she kicked at the ground with the flat bottoms of her sneakers.

A small, bean-sized pebble started to roll across the dirt. The ground looked flat at first glance, but judging from how the pebble was rolling, it must have had an imperceptible slope to it. As the pebble continued to roll, it picked up speed, finally passing under a small fence and falling off the cliff.

I had lived my entire life on a precarious slope, just like that pebble.

It always felt like I was standing at the edge of a precipice. It felt like I could fall head first at any moment, if only I or someone else made a small mistake. All it would take was a slight push or a bit of rain for me to slip and fall to my doom.

Whenever I admitted this to someone, they always said: Why do you worry about such things? You're standing with the rest of us, safe and sound. What are you so afraid of? You've got it good. Perhaps they had a point.

But the people who said this were standing close to the overgrown forest; they were yelling out to me from a safe place. And they were wrong. I wasn't safe. I could fall. The place I was standing was clearly on the edge of a cliff, and that edge was slowly being eroded with every violent wave that crashed against its face. The edge of the ground on which I stood was continuously being chipped away and broken off. It turned to dust and rolled down the cliff.

I could see all this happening right before my eyes, but I couldn't see where it fell. It just kept falling and falling, forever. I couldn't even hear it hitting the ground. It was this unfathomable abyss which frightened me the most.

There wasn't much I could do in the face of terror. All I could do was take a step back every time a layer of soil was washed away, and by doing so indefinitely postpone my fall.

I took my hand, which had been propping my body up on the pavilion's wooden floor, and brought it in front of my eyes. The outline of the wood's grain was imprinted on my skin. Straight red lines above the smooth curves of my palm lines. Overcome by a sudden dizziness, I quickly grabbed onto the edge of the pavilion. A sturdy, solid sensation entered my body through my arms. I pressed down on the wood like someone trying to assure themselves of something. When I lifted my head, Eun-sang was looking at me.

'You once said something to me, remember?' I asked. 'You said you wanted to know the attributes of money: where money goes, the direction it flows. You said you were going to study it.'

'That's right.'

'So did you get an answer to your question?'

Eun-sang turned away from me to look at a far-off point.

'Yes, I think I did.'

'So, where does it go?'

Still staring out at the ocean, Eun-sang said in a low voice as though she was quoting someone:

'Money, too, goes to the people who like it.'

A large swell crashed into the cliff. The cold foam of the sea sprayed onto our faces. We leaned back and let out a shriek. Then, seeing how soaked we had become, we burst out in laughter. And this cycle of laughter and screaming continued one more time.

# Epilogue

This was my twenty-ninth year on this planet, but each year I still experienced something for the first time. Sometimes it was something fascinating. Other times, something that put me at a loss. And every so often, it was something utterly confounding. This year, it was the heat. It wasn't my first time complaining about the heat, which invariably came every summer, but I had never experienced an inferno like this. They said it was unprecedented — the longest and hottest heat wave on record, and there were heat advisories every day. Just walking on the street for a few minutes when the sun was out was enough to leave you completely drenched in sweat. Wherever you went, you could feel the absurd heat, and wherever you went, it was all anyone could talk about.

It was because of this that on a Saturday morning, I woke up early and left the house with my laptop and diary. Three days earlier, my air conditioning unit — which was already on its way out — finally took its last breath. The repair person said they could come the next day, but they kept having to delay their visit, first by one day and then an entire week. I was at work during the day, but at night, I tossed and turned as I wallowed in the hot air. Usually, I couldn't sleep with the window open because of the loud voices of drunk people and the bright lights from the karaoke bars. But I thought this would be better than enduring the heat, so I tried opening the window for a while – but to no avail. Perhaps because of the structure of my room, which didn't allow for good ventilation, the heat that seeped into the room during the day stayed there and refused to leave. I had no choice but to rely on my mini portable fan as I drifted in and out of sleep in a bed drenched in sweat.

I had to leave this sauna of an apartment before the sun reached its zenith. As soon as I opened my eyes, I hopped in the shower, washed away the sweat, and got ready to go out. After drinking a glass of cold milk, I applied sunscreen, put on the lightest, coolest clothes I could find, and tied up my hair in the highest of ponytails. Unplugging the portable neck fan from its charger, I hung it around my neck and finally put on my Velcro sandals. I had barely done anything, but I was already sweating from my morning routine. I stepped outside without wasting another moment. I walked through the quiet Saturday morning street of restaurants, which seemed to have forgotten the loud debauchery of just a few hours ago, and quickly headed for the bus stop. I had already decided on my destination. This place was quiet, had a self-serve coffee machine, twenty-four-hour high-powered air conditioning units, and a seat cushion that was perfectly moulded for my butt. A place with large windows and a view of central Seoul.

I was headed to the office.

No one was forcing me to come in on the weekend. It was just that I had work to finish by Monday. It wasn't much; I could finish it in two or three hours if I focused. Of course, I could do the work at home, but I usually chose to come to the office on days like today. It must have been a mystery to people why I would come to the office like this on the weekend, especially when I didn't live nearby. I used to think the same way until one particularly busy period when I found myself coming in on the weekend several times. After a few times doing this, I realised something. First, the office on the weekend wasn't as soul-draining as it was during the week. And two, the office on the weekend was actually a great way to recharge. There was only one proviso: I had to be the only one there.

The office was much larger than my apartment and more pleasant because it had working air conditioning, heating and air purifiers. My monitor, chair and desk were also better than what I had at home. In fact, now that I thought about it, the thing I hated about the office wasn't the office itself but the people inside it – people who gave me extra work, treated me harshly, and said things I could never fathom saying to another human being. An office without people was like a haunted house without ghosts: there was nothing to be afraid of. When no one was in the office, I felt a pleasantness as I worked in comfortable clothes and sat with my legs criss-crossed on my rolling chair. And because there was no one to ask me for favours or talk to, I was able to focus much better.

Thankfully, today again there was no one in the office. Because I didn't have a lot of work to finish, I was planning on eating lunch before getting started. Until then, I wanted to sit beneath the air conditioning and sip on a cup of free coffee as I wrote plans in my journal about my future life, about my life after earning 320,000,000 won.

I took from my pencil holder several different coloured pens with clips on their caps and clipped them to the cover of my journal. I untied the ribbon fixing my seat cushion to my desk chair and stuck the cushion under my arm. Then, as I took my laptop and headed for the elevator, the old fridge in the office panty entered my vision, causing me to remember something. *Right! Crème caramel! I wonder if it's still there.*

I opened the refrigerator to find it full of all sorts of smells. Unfinished cartons of milk, superfood juice packs, withered salads from the convenience store, and side dishes in Tupperware. Adhered to each item was a Post-it with the owner's name written on it. I took these out one by one and temporarily placed them on the floor. Finally, I found a small, round glass jar hiding in the back of the fridge.

*Found it!* On the small but sturdy-looking glass jar was a heart-shaped Post-it with the words 'To the lovely Dahae, Have another great day!' written on it. This was the crème caramel Jisong had bought for me a few days earlier. Jisong had been to a famous dessert place with the rest of Accounting after lunch. The crème caramel was so good that she'd bought an extra one for me. I had put it in the fridge to save it for a special occasion, and completely forgotten about it until now. Once I removed the crème caramel from the back of the fridge, I returned to their rightful places all the items I had taken out, and closed the fridge door. Turning over the glass jar, I discovered a layer of dark brown caramel at the bottom. It was just past its expiration date. I turned the jar right side up, opened the lid, and brought my nose to the opening. The sweet, milky scent of custard. Just smelling the pudding was enough to make my mouth water. This still seemed edible. I found a plastic spoon in the box filled with single-use crockery left over from the last workshop. It occurred to me that this crème caramel would go perfectly with a cup of refreshing iced coffee. But for that, I would first need some ice. On the door to the freezer were several Post-it warnings.

The freezer gets crowded in the summer.

Please, one ice tray per person only!

Don't use anything larger than a 30-ice-cube tray!

PLEASE!

Give me a break. I carefully opened the door to the freezer. If I didn't use caution when opening the freezer, the buckling ice trays could all come crashing to the floor. In fact, just last week, there had been a large fight over this exact issue. It was such a large fight that people came and formed a circle to watch as soon as they heard the loud shouting that filled our floor. Perhaps because of that fight, or because of the terrifying warning messages on the door, the dozens of colourful ice trays were now packed tightly into the freezer without any empty spaces. I found the light green ice tray with my name written on it in Magic Marker, and pulled it out gently as though I were playing a game of Jenga. I took off the clear cover, grabbed both ends lengthwise, and twisted the tray, causing the ice cubes to break free from the mould. Only five were left as I had taken a few from the tray yesterday. I picked out these five ice cubes one by one and dropped them into my tumbler. I filled the now empty tray with water from the purifier, put the cover back on, gently placed the tray in its spot, making sure not to spill any water, and then closed the door. I was confronted again with the warning messages. The freezer gets crowded in the summer. Please, one ice tray per person only! Don't use anything larger than a 30-ice-cube tray! PLEASE! It was tiresome reading these messages, which were far angrier than they needed to be. On the other hand, I also felt relieved that I had my own space. Because of the heat wave, everyone had bought their own ice tray to stash in the freezer; by now, there wasn't room for even one more. So, if a new person came to our floor, they would need to go all the way to the convenience store or cafe if they wanted to make or buy iced coffee. That must be expensive. If there was someone like that, would it be so hard for those more fortunate to share their ice trays? But I doubted that these awfully selfish, faceless users of the freezer would do that. I tucked my seat cushion and diary under my arm, used my laptop as a tray for my crème caramel and tumbler, and carefully walked to the elevator. My destination was the eighth floor. The top floor.

There was a coffee machine in the lounge of each even-numbered floor. Because I worked on the third floor, I had to go to the second or fourth floor any time I wanted a cup of coffee. But Team Leader Koh used the one on the eighth floor. I once asked him why, and he told me that the coffee beans they used on the second, fourth and sixth floors were the cheapest you could buy. But on the eighth floor they used ultra-high-quality coffee beans. Indeed, the only people who worked on the eighth floor were the CEO, Professor Ham and a few high-ranking executives. Because Team Leader Koh was picky when it came to the taste of his coffee, he went all the way to the eighth floor to fill his cup – but only when there was no one in the lounge.

I didn't have the audacity to drink the eighth floor's coffee on weekdays, but the weekends were a different matter. Not only did they have better coffee, they also had a wonderful lounge. Facing a glass wall was a long, bar-style desk and several chairs. The view was stunningly beautiful.

I put my things on the table and walked over to the coffee machine with my tumbler. Even a cursory glance at the eighth floor's coffee machine was enough to know it was a different calibre from those on the lower floors. I placed my tumbler in the machine and pressed the double espresso button. A low hum and the nutty fragrance of coffee started to spread throughout the room.

Suddenly, a thunderous rumbling shook the room. I turned towards the source of the sound to find a fancy hardwood cabinet. A metal bar was installed along the top shelf, and hanging from this was a chequered curtain. The sound must have come from behind there. I slowly but confidently walked over to the cabinet. There was a continuous, low vibrating sound coming from behind the curtain. But then, as soon as I stood before the wrinkled curtain, the sound suddenly disappeared. *Hm?* I reached out and opened the curtain in one swift motion. My silhouette reflected back at me through the shiny surface of a large black machine. *What is this? No way.* When I grabbed what looked like a handle and lifted my arm, my face was hit with a cold draught.

*No way.* The interior was filled with solid cubes of ice. I stood there dumbstruck for several seconds, staring down at numerous mounds of ice. The ice maker was enormous, and there were too many ice cubes to count. Stuck in the ice was a silver scoop. It was one thing for them to keep the good coffee beans and ice maker to themselves, but hiding it behind a curtain was a bit low, even for them. As I stood there, a new batch of ice cubes poured out of the ice maker.

Instinctively, I checked behind me. When I was sure that no one was around, I scooped up a generous helping of ice and poured it into my tumbler until it was overflowing. I closed the door to the ice machine and was about to close the curtain as well but decided to leave it open. As I walked back to the table, I could hear the tumbling of ice inside the machine.

I put my cushion on the seat, sat down, and opened my diary.

Now it was time to plan out my future, a life with no more debt, a life after earning 320,000,000 won. I started writing in my diary.

1. *Apartment*

My 1.2-room apartment. I had initially chosen it because I liked the cozy extra space with the two halogen lamps hanging from the ceiling, but it was too cold in the winter and too hot in the summer. Not to mention the fact that my air conditioning unit had finally broken. And when I opened the window, my room was invaded by the voices of drunkards, lights from karaoke bars, and the smell of garbage. I had to move. I wrote down what I wanted from my next apartment:

*Forty minutes from work. At least one bedroom. A division between the living space and the kitchen. Good ventilation. Parking. Balcony if possible. New building if possible. Even better if it's a family-oriented apartment complex. A nearby park. This September.*

Eun-sang pestered me about buying a place. But the place she had in mind was a large apartment with one more bathroom and bedroom than I currently needed. Eun-sang told me that she'd been researching houses recently, too, but I quickly realised it wasn't the type of research you did sitting at your desk. No, she was running around all day and getting a leg workout. She would go into a real estate agency pretending she was moving to the neighbourhood soon, and would ask them to show her everything that was for sale. Going from neighbourhood to neighbourhood like this, she was able to get a sense of each area and find the one she liked best.

I always listened to Eun-sang when she gave me advice, but I wasn't so sure when it came to buying an apartment. Not only did I not have the courage to go around shamelessly pretending I was going to buy that day just to force them into showing me places, but I also knew that such places were too expensive for me and would require me to take out another large loan. And what if I decided I didn't like the place after living there for a while? What if I decided to sell but the price of the place had dropped? I might change my mind later, but for now I wanted a lease in which I could put down a large security deposit in exchange for not having to pay rent – I needed *jeonse*. I was so happy and excited just by the thought of this. After circling the word several times, I drew a small star next to it then turned to the next page in my diary.

### 2. *Work*

I rested my chin on my arms and stared out the window. An ivory Kia Carnival was driving through an intersection in the distance. It looked just like the bus my mother used to drive. My mother hadn't been able to get back her job driving Bus 09. So, even after recovering, she'd been forced to take a longer break.

She called me recently to tell me she had finally found work as a cashier at J Mart. Unfortunately, J Mart was quite far from her house, and ever since her fall her legs always ached whenever it so much as rained. I worried about her having to work all day on her feet, but she told me it was OK, that she was making do.

'I stand there all day and see what people are buying. I had no idea Maron was so popular. Choco Chestnuts always sell well. And when it's hot out, those Ice Choco Chestnuts fly off the shelves.'

My mother told me she felt pride every time she scanned a product from my company: 'My little Dahae made this. People love the things my daughter makes. Dahae is so talented. She's such an important part of society.' Indeed, everyone always thought I made Choco Chestnuts when I told them I worked at Maron Confectionaries. When my mother said this, I was overwhelmed with the desire to tell her what I really did at my company.

*Mom, I don't have anything to do with Choco Chestnuts. The product I'm working on right now is called Bana-tato Chip... A banana-flavoured potato chip. I'm sure you've heard of it. That's what I make, Mom. You probably don't sell it at your store. Not many places do. I'm sure they would sell a bit better if we changed the name to Ponana Chip. But they told me that wasn't possible because it's a banana-flavoured potato chip, not a potato-flavoured banana chip. Who eats such a thing, you ask? It might be polarising, but every flavour has its enthusiasts. Thanks to people like that, I can earn a living. It might sound odd, but it doesn't taste as bad as it sounds.*

These words stayed on the tip of my tongue. Eventually, I just smiled in silence and didn't contradict my mother's assumption that I contributed to the making of Choco Chestnuts.

I stopped writing for a moment and opened the lid to the jar of crème caramel Jisong had gifted me. I had intended on eating it with the plastic spoon from downstairs, but now I realised it was slightly too large for the opening of the jar. I tried forcing it in, but eventually gave up and instead stuck my tongue through the opening and licked as far as I could reach. The sweet taste of custard gently enveloped the tip of my tongue. I could only taste it for a little while though, because any longer was too exhausting. As I put the lid back on, the box of snacks under the table entered my vision. Inside it were Choco Chestnuts, Mini Choco Chestnuts and other Maron products. From these, I took a half-moon-shaped pie and stuck the whole thing in my mouth. The familiar taste of chocolate and flour filled my mouth like a giant banquet, followed by the sweet taste of moist, fluffy marshmallow. Before this mixture disappeared, I took a swig of iced coffee and thought to myself, 'You know what, this isn't half bad.'

Back when I was immersed in cryptocurrency, it was my dream to make a fortune and quit the company. But now that I had made my money, I wasn't as desperate as I was back then. Besides, what would I do if I did leave? I didn't have an idea for a business like Jisong, and I didn't have any passions. Of course, maybe it was time to find my passion. But I also doubted I would be able to. And perhaps most consequential was the fact that once I put down the several hundred million won to living in a place for jeonse, I wouldn't have much money left.

But I wanted to move as quickly as possible. I had already paid off all my loans, so once I found a place for jeonse, I wouldn't need to pay rent any more either. I was in my sixth year at the company. Finally, I could save the money I earned. It had always felt like I was pouring water into a leaky bucket. But now, my little baby of 320,000,000 won had finally plugged that hole for me.

To be honest, I didn't hate working at this company as much as I used to. I know I was being somewhat perplexing and vexingly indecisive. But for now... for now... As I repeated this one phrase over and over in my head, I wrote in my diary with the neatest handwriting I could manage:

For now, let's stay.

## *A Story Rolled in Sugar*

In my twenties I used to think — a bit too often for my own good — how nice it would be if only someone would give me one million won. Especially during that one- or two-week period before my next pay check, when I'd already burned through my last pay check, I'd think about money almost every moment of every day. And then in my thirties, when I married my long-time boyfriend and we were preparing to buy our first home, I started wishing that someone would give me just one hundred million won. That was all I needed. Until then, I could only check off one or two boxes of my ideal home before having to give up on the rest. It was around that time that I started to buy lottery tickets whenever I had an auspicious dream — you know, dreams about dragons, ancestors, celebrities, ex-presidents, blood, even faeces. And superstitiously, I would keep my dream a secret and only bought from places that had sold winning tickets. While waiting for the lottery to be drawn, I would daydream about the future. It's hard to believe that at the time of writing this book, just six years ago, all I needed to buy the home of my dreams was a mere three hundred million won. How times have changed.

I never won the lottery.

I did, however, become a novelist.

One perk of being a writer of fiction is that you can do your entire job with just a laptop. I'd always wanted to write a novel in which the main character was given three hundred million won, and so I decided to give Dahae and her friends three hundred million won each. It was such a simple desire, and now here I am. As with all novels, things got more complicated along the way. But I never gave up my wish to end the novel by rolling the story in sugar – the last step in the recipe that I'd decided on before starting the novel.


Maron Confectionaries is a made-up company. The ranking system and other humorous episodes were borrowed in part from conversations I had with colleagues while lamenting office life. The actual names for each ranking, of course, differ from reality. The seven-star hotel that Dahae and her friends visit, the suite room, the private staircase – all of those are also creations of my imagination. And Bus 09, which circles Asan all day, is also a fictional bus route. The stone towers held together by concrete *are* real, but they exist somewhere else in Korea, not on Jeju Island.

J, a managing director in the food industry and a close friend, reviewed the accuracy of corporate life in Maron Confectionaries. N, a doctor, helped me write the scene where Jisong hurts her foot and is taken to the emergency room. And W, a translator friend of mine, advised me on sections relating to the character Wei Lin. I want to thank these three people for taking time out of their busy schedules to read my manuscript.

The name 'Eun-sang Kang's Mini Mart' was inspired by K, my old co-worker who also ran a little shop in our office. But K's store was not-for-profit, a place to share and eat delicious snacks. Thank you, K, for allowing me to borrow the name. The phrase 'money goes to the people who like it' was something that my two friends and I studying sociology at my alma mater used to say in our group chat. I want to thank Y, who not only coined the phrase but also readily agreed when I asked if I could use it in my novel.

I also want to send my warmest thanks to the following three people: Chung Serang, who sent me firm yet dazzling text messages of encouragement; literary critic Han Young-in, whose analysis has been a source of great motivation; and my editor Kim Seon-young, without whom I wouldn't have been able to finish this novel.


This is my first full-length novel, so naturally I'm very nervous about how it will be received. When I was young, I remember sucking my fingers after finishing a bag of snacks and thinking to myself, 'Not bad.' I hope I'm not being too presumptuous in wishing that the reader who finishes the book will savour its last taste and think to themselves, 'Not a bad book.' It is this feeling that I hope remains with readers after closing the cover, even if they forget everything else.

Jang Ryujin
Spring 2021

## A NOTE ON THE AUTHOR

Jang Ryujin has a BA in Sociology from Yonsei University and later studied Korean Literature at Dongguk University. She worked in the IT industry for eight years before writing full-time. In 2018, she won the prestigious Changbi Prize for New Figures in Literature with her acclaimed short story 'The Pleasures and Sorrows of Work', and her 2019 debut collection went on to sell over 140,000 copies in Korea. *To the Moon* is her first novel.

## A NOTE ON THE TRANSLATOR

Sean Lin Halbert holds an MA in Korean literature from Seoul National University. He is the recipient of the LTI Korea Aspiring Translator Award, the Korea Times Korean Literature Translation Award and the GKL Translation Award. He lives in Seoul with his wife and daughter, and teaches at LTI Korea Translation Academy. *To the Moon* is his fifth novel in translation.

## A NOTE ON THE TYPE

The text of this book is set in Fournier. Fournier is derived from the *romain du roi*, which was created towards the end of the seventeenth century from designs made by a committee of the Académie of Sciences for the exclusive use of the Imprimerie Royale. The original Fournier types were cut by the famous Paris founder Pierre Simon Fournier in about 1742. These types were some of the most influential designs of the eight and are counted among the earliest examples of the 'transitional' style of typeface. This Monotype version dates from 1924. Fournier is a light, clear face whose distinctive features are capital letters that are quite tall and bold in relation to the lower-case letters, and *decorative italics, which show the influence of the calligraphy of Fournier's time.*